Falling For You

Heather Thurmeier

CRIMSON
ROMANCE

Avon, Massachusetts

This edition published by
Crimson Romance
an imprint of F+W Media, Inc.
10151 Carver Road, Suite 200
Blue Ash, Ohio 45242

www.crimsonromance.com

Dedication

TO MY GIRLS,

IF YOU WANT IT, NEVER STOP TRYING TO GET IT.

TO CASSIDY AND EVAN,

THANK YOU FOR SHOUTING YOUR STORY IN

MY HEAD AND DEMANDING I WRITE IT.

Acknowledgments

This novel will always hold a special place in my heart. Though it may not have been the first of mine to be published, it was the story that made me start writing romance novels. There's just something indescribable about this story and these characters that I love so much. I'm thrilled to finally get to share this story with readers. I hope you all love it as much as I do.

I also want to thank my family and friends for your encouragement and support when I decided to start my writing career. I'm blessed to have each of you in my life.

To my awesome agent Jill Marsal, thank you for taking a chance on me.

Chapter One

As Cassidy glanced around the formal living room, the ball of lead in her stomach grew. *What have I done?*

How on earth did she end up here in Denver, sitting in a mansion, surrounded by cameras and beautiful women—some of whom had obvious fake boobs and hair extensions? Of course, she knew how she'd ended up here and it had nothing to do with magic or any other Hollywood special effect.

Nope.

It had been her meddling little sister Keira who'd taken it upon herself to apply to be on a new reality dating show—using Cassidy's name. To Cassidy's horror, she'd actually been accepted. When she'd gotten the unexpected call from the show's producer, she'd wanted to kill her sister. Instead, she'd been convinced to go through with the rest of the audition process and screen tests. By the time it was all over and she was asked to be on the show, Cassidy had grown used to the idea of having an opportunity to fall in love with some mystery bachelor.

Her friends told her to forget the show and take a cruise instead, where she could soak in the sun while "Margaritaville" played over the pool speakers. But did she listen?

Not a chance.

Maybe he'll be the one. Cassidy searched the room for the bachelor of the show, her stomach twisting into a knot at the thought of being forced to date someone new. She hadn't been with anyone since Brad chose to leave her and New York behind to go back to California to start pro-surfing again. Maybe coming on the show would force her out of her six-month dating hibernation. Or maybe she'd throw up on the bachelor's shoes when she finally met him. Either was a definite possibility.

Coming on the show sounded like a good idea at the time. But now she was here—now it was real and not some *thing* she would do in the future someday. She casually wiped her palms across her thighs and prayed she wouldn't have to shake anyone's hand anytime soon.

Cassidy nervously scanned the room, checking out the other single girls who had also come on the show in the hopes of finding Mr. Right—or, at least, Mr. Right Now. They all appeared more confident than she felt, chatting and mingling with ease while she sat alone on the couch twisting a napkin between trembling fingers. Every hair color, eye color, height, and personal style was reflected.

She wondered how she would ever stand out in this crowd of glamorous women with her mousy brown hair and eyes the color of pistachio ice cream. No one even likes pistachio ice cream, nor wants to have any part of their body resemble it. She tugged at the hem of her plain white shirt, wishing she'd decided to wear something bright and bold instead. Maybe she should have taken a few more minutes in front of the mirror to touch up her makeup while she'd had the chance.

The production crew worked around the room checking lights, adjusting cameras, and hanging microphones—the tiny additions becoming almost instantly invisible. *No wonder people forget the cameras exist and end up acting idiotic on national television.*

In fact, no one else in the room even seemed to take notice of the production crew working around them. But the crew certainly noticed the room full of women. Cassidy had already caught a few of the men stealing glances.

Her nervous energy finally sent her body into motion and she sprang from the sofa. These kinds of social situations made her uncomfortable. She preferred orchestrating events from behind the scenes, like she did as a banquet manager in Manhattan. Staging the room was always her favorite part. She loved setting the scene for the party, making it perfect for whoever was in the spotlight that day. Now she was the one in the spotlight.

She stopped in front of a grand piano, its black finish shining under the extra lights hanging from the ceiling. Although the piano sat silent, she could imagine its beautiful music filling the large room during parties. She gingerly touched the cold ivory keys.

"Don't move," a deep voice said from behind her. "Stay still for one more second."

Cassidy froze, intrigued by the unexpected demand. Was the piano off limits? Was it only a prop? She peeked over her shoulder, trying to keep her body in the exact same position while pinpointing the owner of the voice.

"That's not exactly the definition of staying still," the man said. From her angle, she glimpsed the deepest blue eyes she'd ever seen. He peered into a handheld monitor while adjusting the small wall-mounted camera nearest him then hopped down off the ladder, landing in front of her with a soft thud.

"I...uh...sorry." Cassidy's pulse pounded in her ears at the sight of him. His slightly messy, light brown hair screamed for her to run her fingers through it. *Hot damn. If this is the crew, how hot will the bachelor be?* "I'll just...get out of your way."

"Actually, if you could stand there for another minute I can adjust the other camera, too," he said without even a glance toward her.

He shifted the bulky ladder over a few feet into the corner with the ease of someone lifting a week-old kitten. She was pretty sure she'd struggled more lifting a bag of groceries than he had with the heavy ladder. Of course, she didn't have biceps the size of his, either.

"That ought to do it." He climbed down the ladder to stand in front of her. "Thanks for—" he paused, clearing his throat and gazing at her as if seeing her for the first time, "—your help."

Cassidy worried she might melt into a puddle of goo under the heat of his gaze. She licked her lips and swallowed before finding her voice. "I only stood here. You did all the work."

"Well, thanks." His eyes stayed firmly focused on hers, causing goose bumps to prickle her skin. "I should go. I'm not supposed to be fraternizing with the contestants."

"Is that what we're doing? Fraternizing?" Wasn't fraternizing something a little more dangerous than this simple conversation between strangers?

"I think it might be and I'd hate to break the rules my first day on the job. I usually save that for later in to production."

Cassidy watched as he hoisted the ladder onto his shoulder and sauntered out of the room. He glanced back to where she stood rooted to the ground and gave her a quick smile before disappearing down the hall.

"I need a drink," she mumbled. She forced herself away from the piano and over to the bar. Maybe a drink would calm the butterflies tap dancing in her stomach.

Tall glass flutes filled with pink champagne sparkled on the silver serving trays. Reaching for a glass, Cassidy bumped the arm of the person next to her.

"Oh, sorry." Cassidy turned to see whom she'd bumped into.

"No problem," a petite brunette replied. "It always gets so crowded around the food and drinks. Hi, I'm Paige."

"I'm Cassidy. You know, people everywhere are the same. If they don't know anyone in the room, they migrate to the food." Cassidy chose a selection of little sandwiches, vegetables, and a slice of sinful-looking chocolate cake. She bypassed the naked strawberries and banana chunks—both fruits that should never be eaten without first being bathed in rich, warm chocolate. Cassidy's preference for chocolate-covered fruit was a quirk that annoyed her über-healthy sister—and which gave Cassidy a little thrill of rebellion every time Keira tried to scold her for it.

Paige grabbed a couple sticks of celery and a few strawberries and turned away from the food. "Wanna go sit down?"

Cassidy followed Paige and sat beside her on the sofa in the middle of the room, balancing the plate of food on her knees. She glanced at Paige's plate wondering how a person could choose strawberries and celery when you had fancy sandwiches, tortes, pies, and salads to pick from.

"Not hungry?" Cassidy asked.

"Oh no, I'm starved. But there's no way I'm eating all those calories when I have to go on television tomorrow. I've heard the camera adds ten pounds and I really don't need any extra. Well, unless they could add it to my boobs."

Cassidy evaluated her own plate. It wasn't overflowing, but it wasn't celery, either. "Hmm, you're probably right." She took a bite of chocolate cake. "But if I starved myself, I'd be cranky and trust me, no one would want to see that on TV." She savored the taste of the creamy chocolate as it melted in her mouth.

"Maybe you should follow her lead and put your fork down," a voice said, dripping with disdain.

Cassidy swallowed her bite. Of course, the voice belonged to the prettiest girl in the room. She had long blonde hair, vibrant blue eyes, and legs that could walk across the pages of the *Sports Illustrated* swimsuit issue.

"Why, exactly?" Cassidy paused, her fork poised above the cake.

"She's right about the camera." The girl eyed Cassidy up and down as she stirred a tall glass of iced tea. "But I guess you're not much competition anyway, are you? You may as well enjoy your cake while you're still here." The girl snickered and sauntered away.

"Wow. Who was that bitch?" Cassidy stabbed the cake and took another bite just to spite the bitchy blonde's jiggle-free, size two ass as it walked away.

"That's Zoe Oliver. She's some big-shot singer or something. I bet she's going to win this whole thing."

"Well she can't be that big if we've never heard of her." Cassidy watched Zoe laughing with another girl and tried to decide if she'd ever heard of her before. "Although there is something sort of familiar about her—like I've seen her picture on a magazine in the checkout counter at the grocery store or something. But that can't be right, can it?"

"No. It wouldn't be fair to put someone famous on here with the rest of us."

"You're probably right," Cassidy said, deciding she really didn't recognize the girl.

Zoe glanced up and caught Cassidy staring at her. A smile slowly spread across Zoe's face as she turned to whisper to the girl next to her who laughed in response.

"We better watch out for her," Cassidy said, setting down her plate on the cocktail table.

Susan, the production assistant, hurried into the room after a man who walked surprisingly fast for his short stature. He had a head full of dark brown messy spikes, which probably took mountains of hair product and plenty of attention to detail to perfect. It was not the kind of hairstyle Cassidy liked. She preferred hair she could actually run her hands through.

"If I could have your attention please," the man yelled above the noise of the chatting women.

The room quickly quieted. He paused a moment before continuing.

"I'm Chip Cormack, the show's producer," he began. "I believe I've spoken to all of you on the phone recently, but I must say it's a pleasure to meet you in person. And might I add, you are all even more beautiful than your screen tests led me to believe."

The women in the room glanced at each other and gave a collective giggle at his comments. Chip's flattery felt superficial to Cassidy, but it seemed the other women were already getting caught up in the moment.

"As you know, you're here to participate in what will be one of the hottest new reality shows on TV, *The One*. You'll be competing against each other in a series of challenges designed to help our bachelor find his perfect match." He swept his hands to the sides. "Look around you ladies, this is your competition."

He chuckled as the women glanced at each other. "After each competition, our bachelor will select the ladies to make up our bottom three. Then America will choose which two of them go home each week.

"Now, not to worry. You won't have to wait much longer to meet your bachelor. Tomorrow, you'll each complete your first private interview, then the following afternoon you'll compete in your first challenge."

Chip reached into a bag that Susan had set onto the table beside him. Fumbling around for a moment, he finally pulled out a small black box with wires dangling beneath it.

"These should be wrapped so they don't tangle. Don't you know that yet?" he said to Susan, not bothering to lower his voice so the others wouldn't hear him. Shaking his head, he continued.

"Tonight when you return to your rooms, you'll each find a package waiting for you. In it will be a few legal forms to fill out, some additional production information, and a personal mic pack you'll wear at all times, except while sleeping, of course. When you're in the bathroom, you may switch the mic off." He held up one of the black boxes. "If you have any trouble with your mic, don't hesitate to ask Susan or one of the other production staff to help you. If you don't wear your mic, we can't hear you on camera."

He set down the mic pack before continuing. "The rules of the house are simple. No speaking to outside friends or family. No physical violence between contestants or with crewmembers. Lastly, please use proper professional conduct during all interactions between contestants and crew. So, no getting cozy with the staff when you get lonely. Got it?"

Huh? Cassidy thought. *Crew and contestants fooling around?*

"The crew is here to film you. They're not here to be your friend or buddy or to keep you company when you're bored—that's what your fellow contestants are for. There are to be limited interactions between you and your cameramen, so please don't talk to them while they're filming. It distracts them and, more importantly, it ruins the footage."

Cassidy wasn't surprised by any of the house rules. She'd known coming on a reality show would involve a bunch of legalities.

Chip cleared his throat and got everyone's attention again.

"That's everything I have for you right now. I know it's been a long day for most of you. You may retire to your rooms to relax and unpack if you like. Remember, we get started filming first thing tomorrow morning. Enjoy your last mic-free night and I'll see you all at the first challenge in a couple of days." With one last glance around the room, Chip left the girls to themselves.

"I'm going to call it a night," Cassidy said to Paige, standing from the couch. "I'll see you tomorrow."

Cassidy said quick goodbyes to a few of the other girls before walking back to her room. She could already feel the jetlag setting in, her bones aching and her head throbbing. She hoped a long soak in the tub would help her recharge after the long day. She sighed, thinking about how good it was going to feel to relax in the quiet and privacy of a bath before she became just another reality show contestant.

Chapter Two

Evan walked into a small room off the main entranceway. It had probably once been a den but now was where they'd film the private interviews. A small formal loveseat, a coffee table, and a few decorative props in the background filled the small space. The arrangement appeared awkward and out of place in real life, but would look sophisticated on camera. Packed into the room were ten cameramen, some of whom Evan knew from other projects.

"Hey, Jake," Evan said. He shook his friend's hand and grinned at having an unexpected friendly face in the bunch. Evan glanced around the room trying to find Chip. As usual, he was missing, running on his own time with little concern for the rest of the world. "How are Erin and the girls?"

"They're good. They'd be happier if I wasn't spending the summer filming, but I can't exactly choose when the projects run." Jake shook his head.

Evan nodded, understanding as best he could. "I don't have kids, but I'm certainly going to have an angry dog on my hands when I pick her up. I dropped her at my brother's house while I'm doing the show."

Aspen, Evan's chocolate brown Labrador, officially held his heart in her front paw. He loved that dog more than he cared to admit. At least he knew his niece Annie would take good care of her while he was away.

"How's your brother doing?" Jake asked, concern on his face.

Evan shrugged. How good can you be when you've lost your wife and are now a single dad? "He's okay. Getting a little better each day."

Even after a year, losing his sister-in-law Melissa still made Evan's chest burn. He couldn't even imagine how Carter and

Annie functioned daily without her. If the sadness in their eyes was any indication, it still hurt. A lot. Evan wasn't willing to risk that for himself, so stayed away from getting involved with anyone as seriously as Carter had.

"Hey, guys." Chip sauntered into the room with a pile of file folders in his arms. He walked through the group, handing one to each of the cameramen. "Inside you'll find information about the contestant you're assigned to."

Opening the file, Evan's breath caught in his chest as he peered at the picture inside. Dark brown, almost mahogany, wavy hair and tranquil jade green eyes. His heartbeat quickened—the girl from the piano.

"Damn. She's smokin' hot," Jake said from over Evan's shoulder.

Evan cleared his throat, trying to cut through the fog suddenly filling his head and flipped to the next page in the file. "Um, yeah, she's a looker alright."

"Inside your file," Chip said, "you'll find your room number, taping schedule, list of responsibilities, et cetera. There's the first set of interview questions, too. Each of you will conduct your first interview tomorrow, so make sure you read those tonight. You'll still be behind the camera asking them, but it's better if you're familiar with the questions beforehand.

"Two PAs will be here at the house at all times. Feel free to ask them any questions. Remember, filming is ongoing. So, if your contestant is walking, you're walking. If your contestant is partying in the pool, you are at the pool's edge getting it all on tape. Some, of the best moments of reality TV happen when the contestants forget the cameras are rolling, and you better be there to capture it."

Chip paused, eyeing the men before continuing. "Now, I can't stress enough the importance of remaining neutral to your contestant. You're not here to be her girlfriend or to let her cry on your shoulder. However, you can prompt her into talking with a few questions. Most of your interactions will be during the interview segments. Otherwise, you're expected to film and not interact. Any questions?"

The room was silent. Chip grabbed his coat from the back of a nearby chair. "I'm out. You guys get some rest. This is your last night of freedom, so if you feel the need to stretch your legs, do it now. I'll see you at the first challenge."

Chip paused at the door. "Oh, and I shouldn't have to tell you this but I will just to make sure we're all on the same page. I know these girls are all babes, but keep it in your pants, okay? There's no fooling around allowed. Later." He disappeared through the doorway.

Evan and Jake walked out of the interview room and toward the grand staircases that led up the second floor, pausing by the front door to grab their suitcases. "What room are you in, Jake?"

Jake glanced at the folder in his hand. "Room three. You?"

"Seventeen." Evan hauled his suitcase up the stairs and started down the hall. Pausing in front of room three, he stuck out his hand to shake Jake's. "Good seeing you here. Give me a shout if you wanna grab a beer in the kitchen."

Evan wandered down the hall and into room seventeen. He hoisted his suitcase on to the bed. A comfortable bed and a TV were about all he needed to get by for the next few weeks. This place was a hell of a lot better than most of the places he'd been forced to stay for some of his other projects, so he really couldn't complain. It wasn't every day he got to live in a mansion filled with beautiful women.

Unzipping his suitcase, he began putting clothes into the closet and dresser drawers. He hated living out of a suitcase. If he didn't unpack now before filming started, he'd still be fishing wrinkled clothes out of the suitcase the day he packed to go home.

Evan grabbed his book from the front pocket of his suitcase and tossed it onto the bed, then noticed a door to an adjoining bedroom.

"I wonder which cameraman has that room?" He hoped it wasn't one of the new guys who'd have a ton of questions. He didn't have anything against the new guys; he just hoped he wouldn't have to spend all his free time helping someone figure out the job. The hours were going to be long enough without any extracurricular activities. He knocked on the door.

Evan looked at the carpet, trying to stretch out his neck as he waited. A moment later, the lock slipped and the handle turned.

The door opened slowly revealing hot-pink painted toenails.

Evan stared at the pink toes in front of him. This was not what he expected to see on the other side of the door. Generally speaking, cameramen don't wear polish on their toes.

His gaze traveled up from the toes. Calves with ivory skin that looked as smooth as satin disappeared under a pale blue robe, tied tight, accentuating a small waist. The edges crisscrossed in the front creating a plunging V between two enticing mounds securely hidden beneath the cloth. Long, dark waves of hair cascaded across her shoulders. Warm, soft lips—with just a hint of shine—glistened gently in the low light.

"Hi," the lips said.

Evan pulled his gaze from the inviting pink lips to peer into the eyes of the person who'd spoken. He opened his mouth to respond, but the words caught in his throat as he peered into the jade green eyes he'd seen in the photo earlier. The same eyes that had been burning a hole in his thoughts since he'd first gazed into them by the piano in the great room—eyes that reminded him of the little sculptures and pendants he'd admired in the street markets of Beijing when he was there filming the Olympics.

"Hi...I...um," he cleared his throat, "expected someone else."

"Sorry to disappoint you," she said with a smile. "If I'd known I was going to have a visitor, I would have dressed up for the occasion." She pulled the edges of her robe closed across her chest with her left hand and held out her right. "I don't think we were properly introduced earlier. I'm Cassidy Quinn."

"I know. I recognize you from your application picture." He shook her hand, holding it longer than he should have. It was more delicate than he'd guessed. His thumb traced a circle across the back of her hand before letting go. "Although, the picture wasn't nearly as good as the real thing."

He cleared his throat again, trying to gather his thoughts into something that didn't reflect the sudden urge he had to tear open her robe as if it was a brand new big screen TV that had just been delivered on Super Bowl Sunday.

It wasn't working.

"You've seen my picture why?" Her question interrupted his thoughts.

"I'm Evan Burke, your cameraman for the show." He smiled, relaxing a little. "I promise I'm not some random creep wandering around the house trolling for beautiful women."

"Well, that's a relief. I hate to think how disappointed you'd be at my door if that were the case." She ran her hands through her hair, gathering it at the nap of her neck and twisting it until it hung across her shoulder like a silk cord.

Disappointment isn't even close to what I'm feeling.

He couldn't express how much he loved seeing her in a robe, without makeup, and *with* crazy hair. Nothing was sexier than a woman who could pull off the all-natural look. Something about the way she looked at him or the easy smile playing on her lips as she greeted him sparked a reaction in him unlike anything he'd felt before. He longed to feel the secrets hiding beneath her robe pressing against him.

Stop. She's off limits. Don't even think about having sex with this woman... Think about something not sexy... Naked fat dudes in a locker room. Naked fat dudes dancing in a locker room.

Better.

He needed to maintain a safe distance from Cassidy—to focus on his work and not get caught up with her. He'd have to ignore the fact that she was beautiful, engaging, and apparently had a sense of humor so often lacking in the girls he'd dated in the past. His body would have to learn to be in the same room as her without getting excited.

His body strongly disagreed with that plan.

Cassidy coughed, forcing him to realize he'd been staring at her like a lion stalking a gazelle. "So, how do you feel about everything?" he asked quickly. "Do you have any questions?"

"Honestly, I'm pretty overwhelmed and nervous about everything. I've never been in front of a camera this way before."

"Well, try not to think about the camera. Imagine it's you and me in the room, like it is right now, with no one else around. Let the camera be invisible."

Cassidy giggled. "I'm not making any promises that I won't say something stupid or act like an idiot but I'll try not to give you too many blooper reels."

"Don't worry. Everyone's nervous at first."

"Sure, but is everyone usually clumsy and accident prone, especially when they're nervous?"

He laughed. She couldn't be talking about herself. She appeared too graceful and elegant standing there, with legs like a dancer. He couldn't imagine her being clumsy. "Maybe it's a good thing I'll be right behind you—I'll be there to catch you when you fall."

"Hmm, knowing you're behind me will probably make me even more nervous."

"Nah. In a day or two you won't even remember I'm in the room."

"I doubt that," Cassidy mumbled, wrapping one of the robe ties around her hand. "I think I'll have trouble forgetting you." She glanced at Evan, her cheeks turning scarlet. "I mean—what I meant to say is, um, I'll still see you even if I imagine the camera is invisible."

Interesting. Nervous about more than the cameras?

"True. You will be seeing a lot of me." He winked, suddenly eager for filming to start. He motioned toward her enticing robe. "We have a big day tomorrow. I'll leave you to finish up whatever it was you were doing."

"Oh, yeah. I should finish unpacking. See you tomorrow." She smiled and raised her hand in a small wave.

"Goodnight." He stepped back, taking one last look at the blue robe that he wished would suddenly fall to the floor as she closed the door between them.

*

As the door closed with a click, Cassidy turned the deadbolt. She leaned back against the cold wood, taking a deep breath. Her head spun with the influx of oxygen to her brain like she'd been holding it the entire conversation.

Holy, hunky personal cameraman.

She'd closed the door leading directly into the bedroom of the hottest man she'd ever laid eyes on. He made Dr. McDreamy look like Elmer Fudd.

He could probably roll out of bed and still look like a *GQ* model. Cassidy closed her eyes. She could still see his light brown hair, so soft and natural—the kind of hair she wanted to run her fingers through.

Maybe even tug on a little...

He had the most incredible dark blue eyes the color of the Mediterranean Sea. When she'd first seen him by the piano earlier, she'd thought the color was a trick of the lighting. Her breath caught in her throat as the heat from those eyes smoldered deep inside her. No man had ever looked at her that way before.

Evan. That's a nice name to go with a very nice face.

It wasn't only his face that had been nice. Cassidy could do little to pull her gaze from his strong, sleek body as he'd leaned so casually against the doorframe. He had broad shoulders and a strong, defined chest filling out his T-shirt so perfectly it was as if the shirt had been tailored just for him. Those arms—they must have been made to build houses, not hold a camera.

And his hands... Wow.

She'd just experienced possibly the world's most intimate handshake. She'd assumed his hands would be rough, but one soft circle on the back of her hand and her skin tingled. She shivered at the memory. If that was a handshake, what else could those hands do?

Cassidy pulled away from the door and hung her clothes in the closet, careful to shake the wrinkles from them so they would be crisp and ready to wear the next day. She needed to stop thinking about Evan. He was her cameraman. They'd be working very closely together. The last thing she needed was to become a blushing idiot every time he spoke to her, like she'd done earlier.

If this was the kind of man they had behind the scenes, what would the guy in front of the camera be like? She wasn't prepared to enter heartthrob country, but it seemed like she was there, passport in hand.

Cassidy was sure of one thing—men like Evan were always off limits. Either they had wives or girlfriends waiting for them at home, or they had the maturity of a twelve-year-old. Guys who were that smooth and charming without even trying didn't come without strings.

She needed to remember she was here for the bachelor, not the cameraman. Evan might be easy on the eyes, but she was going to have to try harder not to get lost in his. Suddenly, she understood why they'd made her sign the no fraternizing clause—because of crewmembers like Evan.

Grabbing her makeup bag, she went into the bathroom to arrange everything on the vanity so it would be organized for the next day. An envelope sat waiting on the counter as she came in. Chip had told them to expect a packet of information, but she hadn't bothered opening it yet.

She sat on the edge of the bathtub and turned on the faucet. As the tub began to fill with hot water, she flipped open the envelope and pulled out a note.

Welcome to The One.

As you know, you have signed consent forms that allow us to film you for the show and promotional purposes. This filming will take place twenty-four hours a day. Please be aware that we have outfitted all rooms with wall-mounted cameras. We are aware of your privacy needs, so there are no cameras in any restrooms or in your walk-in closet/dressing area. In all other areas, you're under constant surveillance.

Also, you're required to have your mic pack on and a cameraman with you at all times when you are out of your personal room. Your door has been equipped with a chime to let your cameraman know if you enter or leave your room. However, it is always preferable to let your cameraman know in advance of leaving your room.

We hope you enjoy your experience on The One.

Chip Cormack, Producer

"Oh my God." Cassidy's head felt hazy. She surveyed the walls of the bathroom, but found no evidence of cameras or areas where a camera could be hidden. She poked her head out of the bathroom and scanned the room. Sure enough, small black cameras were in every corner. She counted four cameras pointing in toward the middle of the room, and another pointed toward the door. All of them had tiny microphones attached to the tops.

"Well, that's just great." She pulled her robe tighter around her naked body, suddenly grateful that she'd changed into her robe in the bathroom.

Note to self, always read production letters immediately.

At least she could take a bath in privacy. She chose one of the fancy purple bottles of bubble bath provided and poured a generous dollop into the running water. Cassidy took a deep breath, inhaling the delicious scent of chocolate and strawberries filling the steamy air. Climbing into the deep tub, her worries and nervousness washed away.

Tomorrow she would be on TV, and who knew what chaos that would bring. For now, she would enjoy the quiet and calm of the bath.

Cassidy forced the show from her mind and instead pictured herself floating on a raft gently drifting with the current of a calm sea. She imagined the heat of the sun on her face and body, melting away her anxiety about the show, the dark blue water lapping beneath her.

Her skin grew hot, almost feeling feverish. Suddenly, she wasn't peering into the deep blue sea anymore. She stared directly into the smoldering heat of Evan's blue eyes.

She splashed water on her face trying to erase Evan from her mind, but every time she closed her eyes, Evan stared back at her with those piercing eyes.

Oh crap. This is bad. Very, very bad.

Chapter Three

Evan glanced up from the clipboard on the table in the interview room when he heard a gentle knock. Cassidy poked her head inside the door, offering him a quick smile.

"Am I early?"

"Nope, right on time. Have a seat," Evan said, motioning toward the small couch set along one wall. "I need another minute to finish setting up, then I'll be ready to roll."

He watched out of the corner of his eye as she settled herself on the couch, crossing her legs then uncrossing them again. She glanced up at him as she folded her hands in her lap for a moment before apparently changing her mind and placing them at her side.

"Try to relax. It's really not as scary as it seems." Evan tried to lighten the anxiety he could feel radiating from her.

"It's that obvious, huh?"

"A little, but don't worry. Everyone feels naked their first time in front of the camera. It's completely normal and expected."

"Naked, huh?" Cassidy giggled and smoothed her hands over her blouse, tugging on the material between the buttons as if to make sure there was no gaping—not that he would mind a little peek. "I'm not sure I'm ready to be naked around you just yet."

"It's a figure of speech not to be taken literally, of course." That sounded natural, right? The fact that she was nearly naked in front of him last night should be of little concern to him...

He fought the vision invading his brain of her standing in her robe again. *Naked would be good.*

"Here, use this to get yourself more comfortable." He placed a decorative pillow beside her, swallowing hard as the back of his hand brushed against her thigh. His eyes flickered to hers to see if she'd noticed.

If the pink hue of her cheeks was any indication, she had. He would need to be more careful of his appendages if he was going to get through this interview without acting like a teenager crushing on the cute new girl at school.

He settled himself behind his camera, and placed the clipboard of interview questions to his side. "Ready?"

"As I'm gonna be."

"Okay, these are all pretty straightforward, so they shouldn't be too hard to answer," he said, referring to the clipboard again. "Chip was pretty adamant that we don't interact too much during the interview process. I'm simply supposed to ask the questions he provided, and you're supposed to answer them in a compelling but honest way. Don't forget to rephrase the question in your answer so the editor can use your snippet."

"Got it." Cassidy's eyes jumped between the camera, the questions, and the door.

"Take a deep breath, Cassidy. You'll do great. Let's get started." He ran his finger along the camera and clicked the record button on, then scanned the page for his first question. "Can you tell me your name, age, and where you're from?" he asked.

"My name is Cassidy. I'm twenty-eight and I'm a New Yorker. I mean, I'm from New York City." Her answer sounded stiff.

Loosen up.

"What do you do?" He cleared his throat. "I guess I should say, what's your career?" Maybe he was nervous and needed to relax, too.

"I'm the banquet manager at an upscale boutique hotel in New York City. I help people plan all their special events. Weddings, retirements, sweet sixteen birthdays—I've done them all."

"Has anything interesting ever happened at one of your banquets?"

"We've had a few interesting moments." Cassidy smiled at the camera as though she was finished answering the question.

Did she really think that counted as compelling? He stuck his head out from behind the camera, and mouthed "more" to her while pulling his hands apart like he was pulling saltwater taffy in a shop window on an ocean-side boardwalk.

"Ah, my—my favorite moment was a fiftieth anniversary party. At one point, the husband sang one of those beautiful old love songs to his wife. He wasn't the world's greatest singer, I don't even think he was good by karaoke standards, but at that moment he sounded like Sinatra. I think the whole place was in tears by the time he finished. I can only hope to have a love like that someday."

There was a time when Evan had wished for a love like that, too. Those days were long gone.

"Why did you decide to be a part of *The One*?"

"I decided to come on *The One* because I wanted a little adventure. I needed to do something different and unexpected, and I really didn't want to go on a cruise, although *everyone* told me I should. Why does everyone always tell me to go on a cruise? Is there a pyramid scheme people are getting rich with by recommending cruises to other people, like some Amway of cruise lines or something?"

He laughed at her reference to the cruise industry. He had always wondered about the appeal of "cruising," too.

"Anyway, my sister is actually to blame for my being here. She thought it would be funny to apply for the show on my behalf, and then I got accepted. So, here I am."

"Are you expecting to find love while you're here?" He refocused on the questions, trying his best not to get distracted by her.

"Oh, um, well. I don't know if I'm *expecting* to find love." She stammered over her words, wringing her hands together in her lap. "But I suppose there's always a *chance* someone will find real true love on a reality show. Why not me, right?"

"Aside from possibly finding love, what do you hope to get out of this experience?"

"I'm hoping to meet some new friends, to try some new things I normally wouldn't do, and to have fun. And I pray I don't make a complete fool out of myself on TV."

Her laughter filled the small room. The sound of it made him want to start laughing, too. "What's your idea of the perfect man?"

Interesting question.

"The perfect man? Hmm, that's a really hard question. I guess it's someone who treats me well, someone who's fun and easy-going, and someone who's sure of who they are and what they want in life."

"I don't think that's quite what they were getting at." Evan studied the questions for a moment to make sure he understood what they were asking. "It says here 'characteristics' in parentheses. I think they want physical stuff...like, blue eyes—just as an example."

"Hmm, well I don't usually base my future with a man on looks. But if I had to pick a few things, I guess maybe lighter colored hair, strong build, but not like a body builder, and blue eyes are—" she paused, her gaze finding his through the camera as though it was invisible, "—nice. Certainly, I would be, um, okay with that."

Sounds a lot like me...

"Are you currently dating anyone?" he asked, reading the next question.

"No, of course not. Why would I be here if I had a boyfriend?"

"How long ago was your last relationship?"

"About six months ago."

"Why didn't it work out?"

Cassidy looked down and shrugged. "Not all relationships are meant to be. Everyone has priorities in life. For some people, a relationship isn't one of them." Cassidy raised her chin and squared her shoulders as though she were challenging him to ask her more about her previous relationship.

Relax. I'm just happy that dude's out of the picture.

"If you could only use one word to describe yourself, what would it be?" he asked, getting back on track.

"In one word, I guess—average." Cassidy sighed, looking dissatisfied with her answer.

Average? No way. "Explain that, please."

"I'm not like the other girls here. I'm not an up-and-coming singer, or a beauty pageant winner, or even a runner-up for that matter. I'm a girl from New York who organizes parties. I have a small, sixth floor walk-up apartment, not a stately plantation home in the South. That doesn't mean I think I'm boring or anything. I love my life. But it's not the kind of life people usually find memorable or exciting."

Sounds okay to me. "What's your best physical trait?"

"I don't know." She rolled her shoulders and adjusted herself on the couch. "I guess my best physical trait would have to be maybe my legs? They're not the longest legs in the world, but they get me where I need to go."

"What's your best personality trait?"

"I hate these kinds of questions. Personality trait? I don't know. My sense of humor maybe? But, I guess that depends who you ask. I think I'm funny, but I'm not sure if anyone else does."

"Lastly, as a lead-in to the first challenge, if there was one food you couldn't live without, what would it be?"

"Finally, an easy question. Pizza. New York-style, thin crust pizza. It's definitely the one thing I'd wish for on a deserted island."

Huh, a greasy pizza kind of girl. Refreshing.

He was more of a steak and potatoes kind of guy, but he'd happily share a pizza with a girl like Cassidy. He'd share a lot more than pizza.

"Okay, that's all of them." Evan clicked the camera off again. "I need a few minutes in here, but you're free to leave if you want. I can meet you out in the great room with the others as soon as I'm done."

"Did I do okay?"

"You did great." He smiled reassuringly. "You're a natural on camera."

"Thanks. You, um, made it easy to talk to the camera and not be nervous."

Evan was silent as she slipped out the door. What could he say to that? Was she simply complimenting his professionalism, or was there something more?

Chapter Four

Cassidy was supposed to wait for Evan in the great room with the other women while he finished logging the footage in the interview room. Everywhere she looked, cameramen followed contestants. They probably figured nine other cameramen would be able to cover her if she started doing anything worth filming, which she wasn't planning on doing.

Cassidy was glad to have the remainder of the day free to relax before the competition got started the next day. She planned to go for a walk later to see the grounds and gardens behind the house.

She scanned the room for Evan again, but still didn't see him anywhere.

Where is he? How long am I supposed to wait?

What she did see was a room full of beautiful women who the bachelor and America were sure to fall in love with. *How did I end up in the same mix as these girls? America is totally going to vote me out in the first round.*

Cassidy sighed, feeling the need to clear her head after that uncomfortable interview. She would go for a quick walk. They wouldn't care if they got that on film or not. How interesting could it be?

Cassidy wandered out into the backyard. The glare of the bright sunlight made her squint as she glanced up at the dozens of tiny cotton ball clouds in the sky. The grass was a lush, vibrant green, squishing softly under her feet. She wished she could take off her heels and run barefoot, but she didn't want to appear on TV running like a schoolgirl across the yard.

She still couldn't believe a cameraman followed her around at all times now. Well, not *now* exactly. Not since she'd been rebellious and impatient and ditched her cameraman.

She hadn't expected to be so uncomfortable during filming. Although, she never envisioned she'd have such a good-looking cameraman to deal with, either. Part of her nervousness in front of the camera was because Evan stood behind it.

She really needed to stop thinking about the hotness of Cameraman McCutie. Instead, she should focus on tomorrow's challenge if she wanted any hope of completing it. Whatever *it* was.

But he's hot. Cassidy shook her head. *No, I need more than looks this time.*

"You *will* stop thinking about him," she said out loud, then remembered her mic pack was recording every word. *Damn it*, she cursed inside her head. Hopefully the sound people would think the "him" she'd referred to was the bachelor.

I need to focus on why I'm here, she thought, careful not to speak out loud again. *Play the game. Enjoy the experience. Hang by the pool. I will not get caught up with the super hunky cameraman. I'll enjoy window shopping, but I will not swipe my credit card.*

She walked to the edge of a grassy area near the pond. Ducks squawked to each other as they nibbled the grass. "I can't believe I said my legs are my best physical feature. Seriously? Legs? I couldn't have said my eyes, or my lips, or even my hair?"

Her legs weren't even long. She considered herself far from being tall at only five and a half feet. Her legs were only good for getting her from point A to point B.

Cassidy startled at the sound of a loud snap behind her. She cried out in surprise and lost her balance. Her left ankle rolled to the side and a sharp pain shot up her calf. Before she could catch herself, she was on the ground, her leg bent under her with pain raging inside her ankle.

"Ouch! Crap." Cassidy grabbed her ankle. "Stupid, impractical heels." Tears filled her eyes as she rubbed her ankle. It was already starting to swell. She needed to get back to the house and see the production medic.

"Are you okay?" Evan appeared in front of her like her personal superhero—just missing the tights. And thank goodness for small miracles. Tights aren't sexy on guys. Any guys. Ever.

She eyed Evan, confused. "Where did you come from? I thought you were still in the interview room."

"I finished up with the interview stuff, but then I couldn't find you. I poked my head out the backdoor and saw you out here."

"Oh good, you have that on film." Cassidy's cheeks burned. "That's great. Peachy. Now all of America gets to see firsthand what a total klutz I am."

"Not a klutz so much as easily startled. Besides, you don't know what they'll decide to use and what they won't, so don't worry about it."

Evan gave Cassidy a little wink, set down his camera, and scooped her into his arms before she could protest. She hesitated before slipping her arms around his neck. The desire to protest disappeared instantly.

I could get used to this.

"Let's get you up to your room and I'll find some ice for your ankle." Evan readjusted her in his arms.

Oh crap. I weigh a ton. "I'm too heavy for you. Put me down." She wiggled to get out of his arms before they gave out and she dropped to the ground.

"You're not." He adjusted her again. "Stop wiggling."

"Look, your muscles are straining. I'm too heavy. It's okay. I know I'm not like some of the other waifs here. I'll walk."

"You're not heavy. My muscles are not straining, but thank you very much for that vote of confidence."

"That's not what I meant. Your muscles are obviously strong—I, oh brother, never mind. Just put me down so I can walk with dignity." She pressed her hand to Evan's chest, trying to free herself from his grip, but it was no use. His hold on her was strong and solid—oh boy, was it solid. There was no way those pectorals would let her fall.

Under her palm, Cassidy felt the contours of Evan's muscles and his steady heartbeat beneath them. Her hand lingered a moment longer than needed, but she couldn't force herself to move it. If anything, she wanted to trace the lines to see where they led.

"You're not walking. You don't want to risk hurting it more, do you? So I'm going to carry you with my dignity... and my wee, weak muscles." Evan smirked, his eyes getting a new twinkle in them.

"Oh, shut it. That's not what I meant and you know it."

"That was a pretty good fall you took." Evan's smile widened.

"Do *not* laugh at me." Cassidy wiggled her finger at Evan's face. "I wouldn't have fallen in the first place if someone had been a little quieter while they snuck around following me."

"I wasn't sneaking around. You make it sound like I'm some pervert. I followed you because it's my job. It would've been easier to do that job if you'd waited for me in the great room like you were supposed to. Instead, you decided to wander around alone in the backyard."

"It's not like I went into the jungle on my own—it's a backyard." Cassidy shook her head. "And for the record, I *did* wait for you. You just took your sweet-assed time getting your camera and finding me. It's not my fault you took so long."

Cassidy stuck out her chin, determined to be right. "Maybe next time you'll hurry up and stay a little closer to the person you're supposed to be working with instead of screwing around in the interview room doing God knows what wasting time."

Cassidy watched as the corner of Evan's lips pulled up into a smile. His eyes sparked.

"Sweet ass, huh?" He cocked one eyebrow at her.

"It's a figure of speech not to be taken literally, of course," she said, copying his very words from earlier.

Evan started walking toward the house. "Let me and my sweet ass get you back to your room. I don't want that ankle to swell up more before it gets some ice."

Cassidy cheeks flushed again for about the fourth time since meeting Evan.

*

"Just hang on and we'll be inside in a minute." He tightened his grip on her slightly, enjoying the feel of her body so close to his. Evan wanted to get Cassidy back to her room and have the medic check her ankle, if only she'd stop squirming and let him.

"Oh, this is so humiliating. Do we have to go through the great room? Isn't there a secret back way or something?"

"We're not staying in the bat cave, Cassidy. There are no secret entrances here. This is the most direct way to your room, so this is the way we're going."

Evan banged on the sliding glass door with his foot. Suddenly, everyone inside became a blur of motion, swirling around, trying to find out what happened to Cassidy.

"Everyone, she's fine. She needs to get ice on her ankle and she'll be as good as new." Evan spotted Paige in the corner of the room.

"Paige, go get the medic and bring him up to Cassidy's room, okay?"

"Of course," Paige said. "I'll go find him."

"Jake, I left my camera out by the pond. Would you mind running out to get it for me? I'm sure Chip wouldn't be too happy it's out there with the ducks." His friend simply nodded.

"Can we, um, go now, please?" Cassidy whispered against Evan's chest. She'd turned her face against him as though she was trying to hide. Her warm breath penetrated through his shirt. He liked being able to protect her.

Don't go there. You can't protect her.

Evan pushed the thoughts from his head and walked through the crowd, easily maneuvering around anyone who was too busy staring to get out of the way. When they'd reached the stairs he peered down at her again. "Better now?"

"I'd be better if you'd let me walk up the stairs on my own so I can maintain at least a small shred of dignity."

"What kind of gentleman would I be if I did that? Besides, my sweet ass needs the workout. Asses like mine don't just happen on their own."

Cassidy narrowed her eyes at him. "You're not going to let that go, are you?"

"Not a chance." Evan stopped in front of her bedroom door and waited as she fished the key out of her pocket. She fumbled with it before finally unlocking the door.

He crossed the room, placed her on the bed, and sat down by her feet. Slipping off her heels, he tossed them onto the floor near the nightstand then placed a pillow under her ankle, elevating it. "This should help with the swelling."

In slow, small circles, he gently rubbed the tender, swollen skin around her ankle. "Does it hurt when I do that?"

"Maybe a little, but it—um—also feels good."

Evan glanced up from her swollen ankle and found Cassidy staring at him. She appeared to be in much less pain, but still uncomfortable.

"Can I come in?" Paige called from the hallway.

"Yep," Cassidy called back without breaking his gaze.

Paige walked into the room followed closely by her cameraman and the staff medic. "I brought you a glass of water and an ibuprofen to help with the pain," she said, handing the things to Evan. "I mean, if the medic says it's okay to take one."

Evan shifted out of the medic's way to give him room to evaluate Cassidy's ankle.

"How does it feel when I do this?" The medic carefully nudged her ankle one way, then the other.

"Not good, but not too terrible."

He manipulated her ankle for a few more minutes then reached for an ice pack and placed it on her ankle before wrapping it with a towel. "You should be good as new in a few days. It doesn't appear to be broken, just a bad sprain."

"Can I still compete tomorrow?"

"I think so, but I'll need to evaluate it again before the competition starts." He rose from the bed and crossed the room to leave. "Go ahead and take the ibuprofen. It'll help with the inflammation."

Paige came to the side of the bed. "You're still going to compete?"

"I'm planning on it. I'm sure it'll be better tomorrow." Cassidy squeezed Paige's hand. "Thanks for worrying about me, but I'm worried for you. You're going to have to face Zoe alone at dinner tonight."

Paige rolled her eyes and started for the door. "So that's why you got yourself injured. It's all a big plan to let me get eaten alive by Zoe. Trying to thin out the competition, huh?"

"I want details later," Cassidy said as the door closed behind Paige.

"Not a fan of Zoe Oliver, huh?" Evan asked.

"She's not exactly on my list of favorite people." Cassidy adjusted herself on the pillows.

Evan got off the bed and walked into the large closet in the corner of the room to grab an extra pillow and blanket. "Is it because of that other reality show she was on?"

"She's been on a show before?"

"Yeah. What, you girls didn't know that?" He chuckled. "She was on another show a few months ago. But it wasn't a dating thing—some kind of reality game show or something. I can't believe you didn't recognize her. She almost won."

"Well I sort of did, but then I didn't know why I recognized her."

"So, why don't you like Zoe?"

"I don't know. She wasn't very friendly the first time I met her. Actually, she's downright bitchy every time I speak to her."

"On the other show she seemed a little high maintenance. Maybe she's one of those people you have to know for a while before you get to like them, or maybe she doesn't come off well on camera."

"She doesn't come off well in person, either," Cassidy grumbled.

Her annoyance for Zoe was sort of cute. And funny. Damn. Why did she have to have so many qualities he'd usually fall for when he didn't want to fall for her or any other girl right now?

Reaching up to the top shelf in the closet, he grabbed the extra blanket and pillow. As he left the walk-in closet he spotted Cassidy's robe. The whole night, he'd dreamed about her in that robe—out of that robe—*on* that robe. It was maddening.

"The ice will make you feel cold so I grabbed an extra blanket to keep you warm." He unfolded the blanket and spread it out across her legs.

Evan slid the pillow in behind her back. He held it in place as she leaned back into it again, getting herself into a more comfortable position. Her hair brushed against his wrists as she sank into the pillows, a few loose strands falling across her face.

Without thinking, Evan gently tucked the hair behind her ear. *Wow.* Her hair was even softer than he expected.

"I must be a mess."

"No. You're beautiful." He swept the loose strands off her shoulder, lazily running his hand down her arm to her wrist. Her skin felt every bit as soft and sexy as satin.

"How do you feel? Are you cold?" Evan sat beside her on the edge of the bed, his hand still lingering on her wrist.

"Not cold. Warm actually. Very warm...hot, even."

Evan brought his gaze up to meet her eyes. She definitely looked hot, a small fire smoldering behind her beautiful green eyes. Maybe it was the same fire that ignited inside him every time he looked at her. A fire he wished he could ignore.

"Good. Hot is good."

He knew he should move away. He knew he should take his hand back from her arm, but he couldn't. He could feel her pulse beneath his fingers, and it excited him to know her heart was beating as fast as his.

He stroked her wrist for a moment longer before willing himself to let go. Grabbing the edge of the blanket from her waist, he brought it up to her shoulders. As he did, his eyes never left hers, taking in the darker flecks of emerald green he hadn't noticed before.

The scent of tea lingered on her breath, making him wonder if she tasted like sweet tea, too. He was a coffee guy all the way, but right now, tea was very tempting.

Go now, before you do something stupid, Evan told himself.

"I should go." He hoped saying it aloud would solidify his choice. "You need rest."

"Okay," Cassidy whispered, "that's probably a good idea."

He got up from the bed, breaking his gaze with hers. "Yeah, I'm going now. I'll see you tomorrow, but call me if you need anything."

Or if you just need me...

His hand hesitated on the handle of the door to the adjacent room, not wanting to leave, but knowing he shouldn't stay.

More than anything else, he wanted to stay with her, but he knew it was a bad idea. The emotions swirling around inside him were something different than he'd felt before, and staying would probably lead to finding out exactly why. Then, there would be nothing to stop him from acting on those feelings. He couldn't do that. He couldn't cross that line with work.

He couldn't cross that line with his heart either, knowing where it had gotten his brother.

But he sure as hell wanted to.

"I'll leave this unlocked in case you need me to come in, okay?" He referred to the adjoining door between their rooms. The one little piece of wood keeping them separated.

"Okay," she whispered again.

Evan glanced at Cassidy lying on the bed one last time. He longed to join her there, to take care of her through the night. Instead he walked into his room, shutting the door behind him, leaving Cassidy and her bed safely on the other side.

Chapter Five

Cassidy sat on the edge of the bed and slipped on a pair of black ballet flats. She wasn't crazy about wearing heels, especially after yesterday's mishap with her ankle. She'd actually be happy if she never wore them again. Today, she would play it safe and wear something a little less lethal. She didn't need to make her ankle worse by twisting it again. And she certainly didn't want to make a fool of herself by tripping in front of the hot mystery bachelor.

She dressed semi-formally for her first competition since she didn't know what they were doing. She hoped the cranberry colored knee-length dress would be appropriate for anything they might throw at her, pairing it with a silver necklace with small teardrop diamonds floating around her neck on a nearly invisible chain. They weren't real diamonds of course—she couldn't afford rent and diamonds on her salary—but they were pretty, simple, and they complemented her dress perfectly.

Cassidy glanced at the clock again as she fastened the necklace— almost time to leave. She grabbed her little black clutch, tucking her room key safely inside, and opened the door. Evan leaned casually against the wall, his camera held by one strong arm at his side.

Oh my. He could give James Dean a run for his money. Yum.

"Ouff!" she yelped. The heavy door hit her in the rear as it closed, pushing her into the hall. She stumbled toward Evan, catching herself just as her hand landed on his chest.

Against her better judgment, her hand traced the lines of muscle beneath his shirt, her mind going back to the dreams that had made her so restless all night. Dreams of them together, of her touching him just like this...only naked and sweaty.

Remove your hand.

She tried, but it didn't listen. Apparently her hand had developed a mind of its own and right now it was content exploring Evan's chest. As her hand swept over one of his sculpted pecs, his heartbeat picked up its pace, pounding against his ribs beneath her hand. The thought of having an effect on him made her feel powerful and desired.

He raised his free hand to touch her, but before he could, she stood up straight and tried to give off an air of confidence and composure instead of the clumsy idiot she was. She swallowed hard, suddenly feeling like a hormonal teenager caught sneaking in late at night.

"Evan." She tried to speak with her most dignified voice.

"You certainly know how to make an entrance." He grinned. "Or an exit, as the case may be."

Cassidy watched as his eyes traveled the length of her body.

"You look...amazing," he said.

Cassidy's cheeks burned again. "Thank you."

Evan picked up his camera and began filming. "Should we go?"

*

Cassidy stood awkwardly with the other girls facing a very large kitchen. They'd been bused together to the Grande Palace Hotel and quickly escorted into the kitchen of Rouge, the hotel's five star restaurant.

Rows of gleaming stainless steel appliances and polished countertops filled the impressive room. Ten chefs faced them, each with an eager, friendly smile. Scattered around the room were a dozen cameramen, each capturing a different angle of the scene.

A tall, dark haired man walked to the center of the room. He was dressed in a formal deep blue suit that looked like it cost more than some small cars. Cassidy could see the perfectly applied makeup on his face, making him appear airbrushed and unnatural.

"Good afternoon, ladies," the heavily made-up man said. "I'm Spencer Daley, your host for *The One*. I'd like to welcome you to the show. You've each come here with the hope of finding true love and being chosen as The One by our bachelor. Are you ready to get started?"

A cheer went up beside Cassidy. She was a little stunned at their excitement. She cheered with the crowd, trying to appear excited.

Am I the only one who feels like throwing up instead of cheering?

"Let's get right to it then, shall we?" Spencer carried on without waiting for an answer. "Today is the first challenge. You and America have been waiting patiently to meet our mystery bachelor and we won't keep you from him too much longer."

He raised his hands and stared pointedly at the group of women before continuing. "But I'm afraid you'll have to wait a little longer. We have work to do before we meet our bachelor. This challenge is our way of getting to know a little bit more about you, and a fun way to break the ice with our bachelor. Would you like to find out what you'll be doing here in the amazing kitchen of the Grande Palace Hotel?"

"Yeah." A chorus of agreement echoed around the room.

"Earlier in your private interviews, we asked what one food you couldn't imagine living without. Do you remember your answer?"

The women in the room glanced around at each other with wary expressions, nodding.

"Great! You'll each choose one of the amazing chefs who work here at the hotel." He swept his arm out to showcase the chefs behind him like he was one of Barker's Beauties on *The Price is Right*. "With their help, you'll prepare the food you chose. Then, you'll each present your meal, and finally meet the bachelor."

Thank God my favorite food is pizza.

New York was a city of a million restaurants. A person didn't really need to know how to cook to survive there. Cassidy had the Chinese take-out place on speed dial, and a drawer full of delivery menus instead of cooking utensils. But pizza should be possible even for a very occasional cook like herself.

"All right, ladies. Go pick a chef. Remember, they're here for support only. We'll notice if they cook your meal for you."

Spencer made a forced noise Cassidy assumed was supposed

to be a laugh, although it sounded more like a creepy electronic clown. She'd never liked clowns. Did anyone? As she watched him, Spencer's whole demeanor changed, like his batteries had run out, as he wandered over to the PAs. "How was that?" he asked. "Did I sound enthusiastic enough?"

Cassidy didn't wait for a response. The other girls were already selecting their chefs. She walked to the first one available, not taking the time to deliberate over which chef she wanted as some of the girls seemed to be doing. Anyone would be able to help her make a pizza, right?

"Hi, I'm Cassidy." She shook the chef's hand.

"I'm Rachel, nice to meet you. So what are we cooking today?"

"New York-style, thin crust pizza"

Cassidy followed Rachel through the kitchen to an empty counter space in the back. A pristine white apron, towels, and utensils waited for her. She unfolded the apron, put it over her head, and tied it in the back, grateful to have something to cover her dress. The probability of spilling something on herself before the pizza was served was high. Basically a sure bet.

"Follow me," Rachel said.

They walked to a huge pantry and collected dry ingredients to make pizza dough. There were bags and boxes of food staples everywhere. A sense of comfort came over Cassidy from being submersed in the massive pantry. She was used to working in the kitchen at her hotel in the city, coordinating food and service for banquets. The familiarity of it made her feel as if she had a slight advantage… over some of the others. Good thing the other girls had chefs there to help navigate the pantry or it would take them all day to find the right ingredients.

"Can you grab the flour from the bottom shelf?" Rachel pointed to a large bag.

Cassidy bent to reach the flour. Suddenly, an acute feeling of being watched nagged at her senses. She peeked back over her shoulder, and of course, Evan stood there with the camera pointed directly at her.

She gasped and grabbed the heavy bag, quickly standing up. She tried to glare at Evan around his bulky camera.

Thanks, Evan. That's just what America needs to see—my giant ass bending over on a fifty-inch plasma.

Cassidy stared at Evan, fuming while the corner of his mouth curled upward slightly. Her eyes narrowed in response. Sure, it was funny on his side of the camera, but this side was riddled with humiliation and diet motivation.

"Seriously?" she whisper yelled at him. "You don't have to film every single second."

He shook his head slightly as if to tell her not to speak to him. He was lucky. She could suggest a few places for him to point his camera rather than at her ass.

"That should be everything." Rachel inadvertently broke Cassidy's focused anger at the camera when she spoke.

Cassidy measured, mixed, and kneaded the dough, stretching it into a circle then used a container of fresh tomatoes and spices to make sauce from scratch. Finally topping it all with pepperoni, pineapple, and cheese. She carefully placed her creation into the wood-burning stove.

As expected, by the time she finished, she could have walked off the set of a horror movie. Her clean white apron was splattered with bright red sauce, but by some miracle, she'd managed to keep her dress clean.

Cassidy tried unsuccessfully to wipe her apron clean. Sighing, she tossed the red-stained towel back on the counter, admitting defeat against the mess she'd made. A snicker sounded from behind the camera. She forced herself to ignore it. Ignore him.

Cassidy scanned the room. The other girls were all very involved in their dishes. She spied Paige putting the finishing touches on what appeared to a massive cheeseburger.

Huh? She won't even try a bite of my cake at dinner, but she'll eat that massive thing?

Cassidy gaze moved away from Paige to Zoe who carefully constructed a dish of lasagna with tongs. *Ha*, she giggled. *Heaven forbid you should actually get your fingers dirty.*

What was it about Zoe that bothered her so much? It wasn't like she'd never been around bitchy girls before—hell, New York was full of them. Maybe it was that Zoe had been on a show before and therefore had an advantage over everyone else. Or maybe it was because no one but Cassidy seemed to care.

I'm going to get laughed at on TV with a lame pizza.

Evan stood silently filming her every move. Would she ever forget Evan and the camera were watching her? *Not likely.* She eyed his flexed biceps as he held the camera steady. *Nice.*

Now why would a guy like Evan, someone who had the body to climb mountains, be hanging around filming a boring reality show? Why wasn't he out filming something exciting?

Evan's head peeked out from behind the camera. He raised an eyebrow at her, silently questioning her.

Don't stare directly at his muscles, dummy!

"Um, do you think pizza is okay?" She hoped to distract him from the fact she was caught ogling his body. Again. "It doesn't seem like much compared to everyone else's."

Evan grinned, giving her a slight nod.

Cassidy sighed as he tucked back behind the camera—almost invisible. If she could get her mind and body to forget he existed, she might actually be able to concentrate on her task instead of his bulging biceps.

Spencer strode into the kitchen. "Lauren, you're the first to meet our bachelor."

"Oh my gosh." Lauren screeched and turned pale. "I'm so nervous."

The room buzzed as Lauren left carrying a tray covered by a silver dome. Cassidy could feel the tension in the room increase as the girls whispered to each other. She wondered who would be called next, praying that it wouldn't be her.

After ten minutes, Lauren strolled back into the kitchen with her tray of picked-over food. She seemed dazed as she flopped into a chair.

Spencer reappeared again. "Courtney, we're ready for you now." Courtney bounced out of her seat with a squeal of delight, grabbed her silver tray, and disappeared out the door. As it swished shut behind her, the girls turned on Lauren, swarming her like a pack of piranhas.

"What's he like?"

"Was he nice?"

"Is he as cute as we imagined?"

"He's...amazing," Lauren started, sounding slightly bemused. "He's gorgeous, and funny, and nice, and so hot."

The girls continued to fire questions barely giving Lauren a chance to breathe. Before long, Courtney bounced back into the kitchen and another girl was called. The swarm of girls turned to question Courtney, leaving Lauren in peace.

Cassidy went to the stove. The cheese on the pizza melted and bubbled. She used the long wooden peel to slide the pizza out of the oven and placed it carefully on the tray Rachel had put on the counter.

Well pizza, let's hope the bachelor likes the simple things in life.

"Cassidy, it's your turn," Spencer called from the door.

Cassidy slipped out of the dirty apron and grabbed her pizza. She walked carefully to the door, paying close attention to putting one foot in front of the other.

Evan followed a few feet behind her. She seemed to have developed an unnatural ability to sense his presence, but she didn't have time to think about that now. She had to concentrate on walking without falling. This was not the moment for her clumsiness to strike again.

She followed Spencer into the next room. It was a large dining room adorned with red linen table clothes, gleaming silver utensils, and sparkling crystal wine glasses. In the center of the room sat a small, intimate table bathed in candlelight and surrounded by cameras.

Oh no, no, no. No way.

Behind the table sat a very tanned, bleach-blond man who could have washed up on the beaches of Hawaii. Make that the beaches of California. *Brad?*

Her ex? No way. This couldn't be happening.

Cassidy stumbled to a stop, unable to make her brain believe what she saw. There was no way the world was cruel enough to make her ex-boyfriend Brad become the mystery bachelor she had unknowingly agreed to date. This had to be a joke.

Oh, Universe, you have a vicious sense of humor.

Chapter Six

"Cassidy?" Brad laughed, shaking his head as she walked across the room and placed the tray on the table.

At least I made it without falling on my face.

"This is an interesting twist." He smiled, showing off a perfect set of white teeth. His voice dripped with self-confidence as though he wasn't flustered in the least at seeing her here so unexpectedly. He'd always been cool, even under pressure. "It's been a long time. Sit, join me for dinner."

Cassidy pulled out a chair and sat perched on the front edge of the seat. She closed her eyes and forced a deep breath into her lungs. *He's not here. He's a figment of my evil imagination. Why is my head spinning?* She opened her eyes again. Brad sat there, still smiling at her, waiting for her to say something. *Damn it.*

"How are you, Brad?" she asked, keeping her tone even. The last thing she wanted was to let him know how uncomfortable she was seeing him here.

She'd forgotten how cute Brad was—the perfect image of every girl's surfer fantasy come to life. Yet she couldn't bring herself to get excited. Sure, he had a hot body, but she also knew he cared more about himself and surfing than he ever would about anyone else. Memories of Brad telling her she wasn't enough for him and that he was moving back to California infiltrated her mind.

A familiar ache blossomed in her chest as the pain she'd worked so hard to push aside threatened to surface again. She clenched her hands together in her lap under the table, willing the sting of his rejection to dissipate. Brad wouldn't hurt her again.

"I'm fine," he said. "How's everything with you?"

"Fine. Great. Awesome." She didn't want to talk about her

life...the life he left for California.

Just behind Brad, Cassidy spotted Evan. She was surprised to see him there. She assumed he would always be following her. It made sense for him to be there to capture her reactions, but she hadn't expected it.

Cassidy wondered if Evan had placed himself in that exact spot with more than good filming angles in mind. It seemed too convenient. Every time she looked at Brad, she was also inadvertently looking at him. Or maybe she was reading into things too much—wishful thinking.

Now Evan I could stare at all night. He's completely drool-worthy.

"So," Brad said, getting her attention again. "What did you make today?"

Cassidy removed the silver dome. "Pepperoni and pineapple pizza."

"Oh, Cassidy. I can't believe you still eat that crap. Pepperoni and pineapple should never go together, especially on a pizza." His eyes crinkled slightly in the corners, giving the distinct impression of distaste.

"Maybe if you actually tried it for once, you'd see it isn't crap." She tried to tease instead of get annoyed at his all too familiar stubbornness. "It's sort of amusing that after months of refusing to try it with me, now you're being forced to." Cassidy slid a slice onto a plate and placed it in front of Brad with smile.

He carefully used a knife and fork to cut off a piece, hesitating briefly before taking a bite. "Not as bad as I feared. I'm not sure I'd wish for it if I was on a deserted island, but to each their own."

"Well, you're eating it wrong. You have to pick it up and fold it." Cassidy took a slice, folding it so the two sides of the crust squished together and held it like a paper airplane. Taking a bite, she closed her eyes, savoring the taste as the sweet and spicy mixed in her mouth. "Tastes great to me."

"I'm not sure if I like the pizza, but I certainly like watching you eat it." He raised an eyebrow at her, a crooked grin on his face. "I used to love watching you eat pizza like that. Why do you think I always suggested stopping to pick up a slice when I don't even like pizza?"

Cassidy glared at him. She finished chewing, and barely managed to swallow. She tossed the remainder of her pizza back onto the plate. Out of the corner of her eye, she noticed Evan's jaw tighten as though he was gritting he teeth together.

"Silly me. I assumed you knew it was my favorite. Sorry to make you suffer through the pizza."

"It was worth it to see you eat it like that again." Brad winked at Cassidy, flashing her a smile that could make a heart skip a beat—any heart but hers.

"Aren't you going to finish?"

Not with your pizza-fetish eyes watching me.

"I'm full."

"Pizza was an interesting food to pick. It wasn't like the rest of the girls—not your typical girl food."

"What exactly is a typical *girl* food?"

"Like the stuff the other girls made—vegetarian lasagna, veggie burgers, big salads. You know, healthy stuff. Rabbit food. I'm all for eating vegetables, but can I get them alongside a nice juicy steak and a loaded baked potato?"

Cassidy wasn't sure if she should feel flattered that her food wasn't "rabbit food" or annoyed that her food wasn't "typical girl food."

Brad sat forward, reaching for Cassidy's hand. She moved it into her lap and leaned back, putting as much distance between herself and Brad as she could.

The last thing she wanted to do was get all warm and cozy with her ex-boyfriend. That achy feeling in her chest she'd had earlier was gone and replaced by annoyance. She'd hoped to forget about her real life problems while on the show. Instead, she was having dinner with one of them.

Not cool, Universe. Not cool.

Brad leaned back to mirror Cassidy. "Not in the mood to talk?"

"I'm not in the mood for anything if you're involved."

"That's my girl. Feisty as I remember."

"I'm not your girl. I stopped being *your girl* when you dumped me and decided to move across the country."

"I'm sorry to interrupt, but your time is up, Cassidy," Spencer said, reappearing beside the table as if a magician had abracadabrahed him there.

"Great." She sprang up from the table. "Lead the way."

Brad came around the side of the table, pulling her into a tight hug. Cassidy stiffened. She wasn't ready to share a meal with him, let alone share her personal space, regardless of the past.

Cassidy peeked over Brad's shoulder to Evan, his camera focused on her in Brad's embrace. She shifted uncomfortably in Brad's arms as Evan watched her in the arms of another man. She didn't enjoy the embrace with Brad, but Evan didn't know that, and she didn't want him to think she had.

Cassidy watched as Evan's jaw tightened for the second time. He seemed a little flushed, too, but she couldn't be sure if that was an effect of the weird lighting and all the red linens in the room.

"It was good seeing you again."

Was that regret in his eyes?

Couldn't be. In all the time she'd known Brad, she'd never known him to regret a decision. Not even when they'd gone to Mexico for a long weekend and he'd insisted they could drink the water in town while they were away from the resort. Not even when she'd been confined to the bathroom for the rest of their trip. Nope. He stood by his decisions.

He tucked a loose strand of hair behind her ear. "I didn't realize how much I've missed you."

"Mmm," was all she could muster. Any form of agreement would have been a lie. She remembered all too clearly the pain he'd branded on her heart when he'd left and how hard she'd worked to get over him. Those feelings were in the past and she wasn't prepared to revisit them. Her love for Brad was gone and one meal together wasn't going to bring them back together.

And if that ache in her chest decided to return, she'd chew a few antacids and be done with it.

Cassidy walked back into the kitchen and was attacked by the waiting girls. While she answered questions, the last two girls presented their food to Brad.

"Isn't he everything you hoped for and more?" Julia had a dreamy quality in her eyes.

"Um, yeah, he's great." Cassidy hoped it sounded convincing since she wasn't fooling herself. Actually she hoped he would suddenly come down with a contagious disease and have to leave the show immediately. Then they could get a new bachelor—*that* would be awesome. It also wasn't likely.

She hadn't expected to see her ex-boyfriend and she had absolutely no idea what to say to the other girls. Should she tell them that Brad was actually her ex? Many sharp objects waited in the kitchen. Perhaps a confession about her and Brad's previous relationship could wait.

Her eyes flickered to Evan. Nervousness crept up her throat at the thought of answering more questions about Brad in front of him. Thankfully, Spencer walked into the room and called the women back to where they'd originally started so she didn't have to talk about Brad anymore—at least not yet.

"Great job, ladies," Spencer said. "You should be very pleased with your meals. They smelled fantastic." He rubbed his stomach like he was starving.

"Tonight Brad has a very difficult decision ahead of him. He'll have to choose girls to make up the bottom three. Those women will be up for possible elimination this week. Back at the house, you'll find out who he's chosen for the bottom three. Then, America will get their chance to vote for their favorite girl. Sadly, the other two women will be sent home."

Spencer looked sympathetically around the room. "All right, ladies, that's all for now. We'll see you again shortly."

As Spencer walked away the girls whispered to each other. The murmurs continued as they wandered back through the hotel to the buses.

"Who do you think he's going to choose?" Paige asked. "I hope it's not me. Maybe I should've cooked something else. Guys like veggie burgers, right?"

"Sure, veggie burgers are great."

So it wasn't a giant cheeseburger after all. Paige's meal must have been one of the "typical girl foods" Brad had criticized.

They followed the others on to the buses. She lowered her voice so only Paige could hear. "You're so pretty and you're the sweetest one here. You'll be fine, don't worry."

Would Brad keep Paige? Cassidy had no idea what his type of woman was except that she wasn't it. She hoped she hadn't just lied to her only friend in the house.

"Thanks, Cassidy. I think you'll be safe, too. What guy doesn't like a girl who makes him pizza?"

"I'm not so sure Brad liked it, but it's over now so I'm not going to worry about the challenge anymore."

Or Brad.

Cassidy slid into the seat on the bus and peered out the window as they pulled away from the hotel. She tried to ignore Evan as he continued to stare at her through the camera from the seat in front of her. Instead she worried about what the rest of the night would bring.

She wasn't sure what she wanted to happen tonight with the show. Part of her knew Brad might put her into the bottom three. Their relationship hadn't worked out so well the first time, so why would he bother with her a second time? And honestly, the other girls would probably be upset when they learned they had a history together. Going home now would most likely save both of them from a giant headache.

However, if she did go home, she wouldn't see Evan anymore.

She stole a quick glance at him. She found something so intriguing about him. Maybe it was the way he seemed to film her with more interest than a cameraman should? Or maybe it was the way her heart seemed to pick up its pace whenever he was near, like a sonar warning of an object's imminent approach.

*

Evan followed Cassidy into the house and toward the great room where production staff had set up an impromptu touch-up room. While the girls had their hair and makeup retouched, the camera crew had a few minutes to set down their cameras and relax.

Evan joined the rest of the crew—and Brad—in the kitchen. He grabbed a bottle of water from the ice bucket on the counter and pulled up a chair at the large solid oak table.

The guys laughed about the contestants' cooking skills. It seemed Cassidy wasn't the only girl to make a mess of herself in the process of cooking her meal.

A picture of Cassidy covered in pizza sauce came to his mind. He'd wanted to wipe the sauce from her neck. With his tongue preferably. Unfortunately, he'd been trapped behind the camera.

"Who wants to help me make my decision tonight?" Brad asked, wearing a smug expression like a king choosing his consort. A sudden urge to wipe the smile off his face almost clouded Evan's better judgment. Instead, he put on a very nonchalant smile.

"You haven't made your big decision yet?" Evan asked in a teasing voice. "Is it really that hard to choose?"

"Dude. It's totally harder than I expected." Brad leaned back against the counter and rubbed his forehead dramatically. "How can I pick between all these babes?"

"Well, you must have a couple you liked less than the others. So pick those ones," another cameramen said.

"I guess I didn't really hit it off too well with Julia or Courtney."

Brad raked his fingertips across his forehead.

"That's only two girls, Brad," Jake said. "You need to pick one more for the vote."

"Okay, I guess it's between Lauren and Cassidy then," Brad said. "Lauren seemed kinda ditzy. That's cool for a one-nighter on the beach, but I'm not sure I want to date that. Cassidy and I've actually dated before and I'm not sure I want her again. Although, she does have a great rack."

Evan's blood pressure shot up a couple of notches. He couldn't believe Cassidy would ever go out with this douche bag. What had she seen in him?

"I think you don't like Cassidy as much because she didn't drool all over you like the other girls did," Evan said, shrugging. "Maybe she's too smart for your tricks now. You might want to consider keeping the one girl who's actually a challenge for you. You don't want America to think you only like the easy girls, do you?"

"Dude. Harsh." Brad gave him a hurt expression. "I didn't say I didn't like her. I've just sort of 'been there, done that' with her already. But she was a tiger in the bedroom. Maybe I want to 'be there, do that again.'"

Not cool, douche bag.

"It's your choice, but I know who I'd keep around." *Cassidy, that's who.* Evan tried to act casual, but inside, his mind raced. If she stayed, he'd have to watch her date loser Brad. But at least he'd still get to see her, learn more about her.

If America voted her out she'd have to go back home. Evan might never see her again.

Brad crossed his arms in front of his chest. "Why are you so interested in keeping Cassidy around? You enjoying her rack, too? Hey, do you guys zoom in on the goods? I would totally sneak a closer peek if I could."

"I'm thinking about my paycheck, that's all. I'm not checking out her rack."

And he better stop checking out her rack, too, or I'm going to smack him upside the head with his surfboard. If he tries to touch her, I'm gonna break his fingers.

"I don't know, dudes. I guess I'll just wing it during the ceremony." Brad walked out of the room, leaving Evan with a pit in his stomach.

*

The women stood facing Brad and Spencer. This was it. The ceremony where Brad would decide who he was putting in the bottom three for America's vote.

Evan's palms turned clammy as he waited for the news. He had no idea this process would bother him so much, but he felt almost as nervous as the women looked.

He focused his camera tighter on Cassidy's face. He couldn't gage her expression, but she seemed nervous and uncomfortable.

Is she hoping to go home or stay?

She shifted her weight and straightened her dress. Her eyes glanced toward his camera. If she made it through this week, he would have to tell her not to look at the camera so much. Throughout her dinner with Brad, Cassidy had glanced up at the camera—a big no-no in reality TV. Contestants were supposed to pretend the cameras didn't exist, not talk to them and scold them.

If looks could kill, he'd definitely be dead after Cassidy caught him filming her bending over to get the bag of flour at the challenge. The scenery had definitely been pleasing, as was her reaction. He couldn't help but smile at the memory of her embarrassment when she realized he stood behind her, filming her every move. He liked seeing her flustered. It was cute and sort of sweet.

"Welcome to the first bottom three ceremony, ladies," Spencer started, pulling Evan out of his thoughts. "So what did you think about Brad?" He patted Brad on the back.

The women cheered.

"Excellent. We had a feeling you'd like him." Spencer turned to Brad, addressing the next questions directly to him. "So, Brad, how did you enjoy meeting these beautiful women?"

"What's not to like? These women are extremely beautiful. I loved getting a chance to have a little one-on-one time with them. I'm looking forward to getting to know them better."

"I'm sure you are." Spencer laughed again, although it sounded forced and unnatural.

Ugh. Can they make this any cheesier? Does America really fall for this fake crap?

"It's time to get on with the ceremony." Spencer said, a serious expression creasing his brow. "It's time to hear who you've chosen to put in the bottom three."

Brad put on a grave expression to match Spencer's.

Oh, come on already.

"Dude, this decision is so hard." Brad shook his head. "I hate to put any of them in a position to go home."

I bet you have other positions you'd like to see these women in, don't you?

"I know this can't be easy for you, but in the end you can only date one woman," Spencer said. "Now, who's the first unlucky woman in the bottom three?"

"I'm really sorry, but it's Julia."

Julia's face fell and she was ushered to the side, away from the other girls.

"Why Julia?" Spencer asked.

"I just didn't feel like we connected as well as I did with some of the other girls. It's nothing personal. She's a beautiful girl."

"Okay, who's next?"

Tension floated in the air as the other women waited to hear their fate.

"I'm sorry to say that Courtney and I didn't seem to have much in common so I've chosen her for the bottom three as well."

"Courtney," Spencer said with sympathy, "if you could please join Julia. Your final choice tonight?"

"Oh man, this is the worst." Brad threw his head back dramatically.

"What's going on? Talk to me." Spencer stared at Brad with concern.

"It's so hard to choose another girl. Two girls are bad enough, but to make me pick three feels impossible. I've been wrestling with this last choice in my head all night and I still don't know."

"Take another minute and look at these women across from you." Spencer held his hands out toward the women. "Think back to your dinner with them and about how you felt spending time with each one. Then, trust your instincts."

Evan held his breath as he watched Brad stare at the women. What he was thinking? Had he really not made a decision, or was he being overly dramatic for the viewing audience?

All of the girls looked nervous. Even cool Zoe looked as if she'd had better moments. She stood there rubbing the pendent on her necklace between her fingers, almost like it brought her some kind of comfort.

Brad seemed to stop at Cassidy.

Evan's heartbeat stuttered. *Move on, dude. Don't do it.*

"Okay, I think I'm ready." Brad kept his eyes on Cassidy as he spoke.

"Go ahead."

Evan's heart sank. *Oh no.*

"I have to send…Lauren to the bottom three," Brad said, finally shifting his gaze from Cassidy to Lauren. "I'm really sorry."

Evan exhaled, relief washing over him. He focused his camera on Cassidy's face only to find her staring at him. Was it his imagination, or did it seem like she suddenly had a weight lifted off her shoulders?

Cassidy smiled at him—different than the other times she'd smiled into the camera. This time, it seemed like she gazed past the camera to him personally, almost as if she were trying to send him a message.

Evan couldn't help but smile back. Message received—she's happy to stay.

"Okay, Lauren, please join Julia and Courtney." Spencer motioned for the three girls to move in closer. "I'm sorry, ladies, but you've been chosen for the bottom three. Only one of you will continue on with the hopes of being chosen as The One."

Spencer turned away from the women to speak directly into a camera near the edge of the gathering. "America, now it's your turn to have your say. That's right. You get to vote for who you'd like to stay. Dial the number you see on your screen. Press one for Julia. Press two for Courtney. Press three for Lauren. You can also log onto our website to cast your vote or text your vote to the number you see now. The lucky lady with the most votes will continue on this journey to find out if she is...The One."

Spencer paused, smiling into the camera for what seemed like an abnormally long pause. "How was that?" he asked Chip who was standing beside the camera. "Are we good for tonight?"

Chip nodded and gave a thumbs-up sign. "Can you take Brad back to makeup for a touch-up before we film his challenge and ceremony recap segment?"

"Sure thing. This way, Brad." Spencer led him back to the makeup area.

Chip turned to the women. "Ladies, if I can have your attention." He waited for them to quiet down again. "We've learned some interesting news today and we think it's important to fill you in.

"Today, at the first challenge, it came to light that our bachelor Brad and our contestant Cassidy were previously in a relationship together."

Chapter Seven

Chip held up his hands to calm the women. "Now, I know you're thinking this puts you at a disadvantage because they have a history together. However after much consideration, we think it won't affect the competition and we're allowing Cassidy to continue as a contestant. Brad still has to decide if he likes her and wants her to stay as much as he has to with anyone else. Before anyone asks—no, they are not still an item, right, Cassidy?"

"No," she replied softly, uncomfortable talking about her former relationship with Brad. "We broke up six months ago."

Cassidy chanced a peek at Evan. The expression he'd worn during the dinner challenge had returned and seeing it again made her feel sick. And knowing she was the one who caused that expression—that her relationship with Brad had caused it—made her feel even worse. She didn't want Evan looking at her like that. There were plenty of ways he'd looked at her already that were great...desire, amusement, even concern. This—whatever this expression was—wasn't one of them.

"And for the record," Chip continued, stealing Cassidy's attention back, "we had no prior knowledge of this either. We're just as surprised by this as you are. I assure you this was not a stunt set up by us. Now, does anyone have any questions?"

"Why did they break up?" Savanna asked.

"I don't think we need to discuss that right now. If you have questions you'd like to ask about their relationship, I suggested you ask Cassidy or Brad directly. However, I sincerely hope we can simply put this behind us."

"I think it's fine Cassidy's still here," Zoe said. "I mean, Brad didn't want her the first time around, so I doubt he'll want her a second time. She wasn't a threat, anyway."

"Thanks, Zoe. Why don't you tell us how you really feel?" Cassidy asked. "Hey, while we're getting things out in the open, maybe we should also talk about how Zoe's a reality TV celebrity already."

"We know," Lauren said. The other girls nodded, unconcerned.

Cassidy stared at them, shocked. And annoyed. Had she been living in a hole for the last six months? How was she the only one who didn't know about Zoe until now? "And we're okay with this? We don't think this is a huge advantage to her?"

"I have a lot of advantages over you. Being on TV before is only one of them. So really, why worry about it?" Zoe asked, looking at her as if Cassidy was a sad, lost puppy. "Feeling a little jealous, honey?"

Great. Now I'm the jealous, bitter girl.

"Nope." Cassidy laughed weakly. "Have any tips for us?" She didn't want tips, but she didn't want to be seen as jealous either.

"We're done for tonight," Susan the PA said, stepping in to finish for Chip who'd already walked away. "The show airs tomorrow evening, then America gets a few hours to call in their votes. The next day we find out who stays and who goes home. Any questions?"

The girls remained silent.

"Get some sleep and enjoy your day off tomorrow." Susan eyed Evan, almost glaring at him before turning and wandering away, leaving the girls on their own to deal with the aftermath of Brad's decision and the news of his previous relationship with Cassidy.

Odd. What the heck did Evan do to piss off the PA?

Cassidy's gaze flickered from Susan to Evan. Funny, he didn't seem surprised by her attitude. What was going on between them?

*

Evan leaned back against the half wall separating the pool from the rest of the grounds. He panned his camera around the pool and chairs, taking in a general overview of the area.

The girls were enjoying their day off sunbathing by the pool. Everywhere he turned, women in bikinis lounged, sipping fruity drinks and cooling off in the pool.

Life is good.

He had followed Cassidy downstairs about an hour earlier. She'd eaten lunch with the other girls, chatting casually about Brad and the experience as everyone else speculated about which girl they believed America would choose to stay.

"Seriously, I don't know why his decision was so difficult," Zoe had said, her usual tone of superiority and disinterest hanging in the air. She poured two packets of sugar into her iced tea and stirred.

Cassidy whispered into Paige's ear so quietly Evan could barely hear her through the mic. "How is she so skinny with so much sugar? I'm gonna gain a pound watching her drink that. Stupid Zoe and her stupid high metabolism."

Zoe sipped her drink and leaned back in her chair. "Only one girl can win in the end—me. So really, the sooner he gets rid of the rest of you, the better."

"I like the girls here," Savanna said. "None of y'all really deserve to go home. It's the worst part of the show."

"That's a Miss America answer if I ever heard one." Zoe rolled her eyes at Savanna. "Leave the pageant days behind and grow a personality already."

"Once a pageant queen, always a pageant queen." Savanna smiled a huge bright white, perfect-teeth smile at Zoe.

"I think all of the girls are sweet and pretty, but not every girl is going to be a match for every guy," Cassidy said. "If Brad isn't interested in them for some reason, then I guess it's better they go home before their hearts get broken."

"Really, Cassidy? You're so sweet." Zoe smirked. "Is your heart going to break when you get sent home? Oh wait, your heart's already been broken by Brad, hasn't it?"

"Who said I'm going home?" Evan heard the annoyance filling Cassidy's voice. "It's a little early to tell who'll be the final two, don't you think?"

"Maybe for you, but I already know I'll be there. The only question is which poor girl will make it to the end only to leave in tears during the live finale." Zoe examined her perfectly polished nails.

Cassidy crossed her arms. "We'll have to wait and see what kind of girl Brad decides he wants."

"Poor Cassidy. It must be killing you to wonder if Brad wants you back or not."

"I'm still here, aren't I? Isn't that answer enough for you?"

"True, but how long until he tires of you and dumps you again...like last time?" Zoe smiled wickedly. "He did dump you last time, didn't he?"

Cassidy glared at Zoe before leaving the table. Evan would have liked to know the answer to that question, too, but he'd have to wait until she decided to share that information with someone.

After the lunch drama, he'd followed Cassidy out to the pool to join the rest of the group. She'd worn a simple pink sundress all morning and he'd been intrigued all morning about what hid under that dress. Now it appeared he would finally find out.

Evan focused his camera as Cassidy and Paige walked around to the far side of the pool to a couple of empty lounge chairs. Cassidy set down the bag she carried with her and pulled out a trashy celebrity magazine and a pair of sunglasses. With her back turned to him, she pulled up the hem of her dress, slipped it over her head in one smooth motion, and let it fall into the bag beside the chair.

Evan had never been one for bold bright colors, but today, hot pink was his new favorite. He could stare at hot pink all day.

As Cassidy got comfortable on the lounge chair, Evan couldn't help but stare. Her hot pink bikini wasn't skimpy like some of the other suits the girls were wearing. It covered more than enough of her ample breasts, maybe even too much, and the bottoms tied at the curve of her hips.

I love my job.

Evan leaned against the wall thankful he didn't have to move again immediately. Seeing Cassidy in her swimsuit caused all the blood to rush away from his brain, invading other regions of his body instead. A few minutes against the wall should be all he needed to let things settle down.

Leaning is good. Focus on something else. Ah, lovely day today. So sunny and bright. Birds, flowers, pink flowers, pink bikinis covering soft ivory skin glistening in the sun. Damn it.

Evan remembered the feel of her skin beneath his hand a few nights ago. He longed to feel it again, but he couldn't. That wouldn't be good for his job.

Watching from a distance and suffering in silence was his only option. He worried tonight's dreams would be filled with hot pink bikinis falling to the floor—and tomorrow morning would start with a cold shower.

Evan shook his head and tried to clear his thoughts of Cassidy. She was off limits, and nothing he could do or say would change that. He needed to be smart and not let himself get carried away by his thoughts of her.

We work together. No more touching her hair or arms or anywhere else. No more getting too close in the moment. And hopefully it'll rain for the next month so there'll be no more bikinis.

Movement near Cassidy caught his attention. Paige sat on the edge of her chair and grabbed a bottle of sunscreen as Cassidy rolled over onto her stomach. Cassidy swept her hair off her back and shoulders, and turned her face toward Evan. She shrieked as

Paige squirted cold lotion onto her sun-warmed skin, and laughed as Paige rubbed it on her back.

You've got to be kidding me. And there's another shower. Tonight. Before bed. Good thing cold-water showers were plentiful in a mansion full of women.

I'm going to get frostbite.

Evan held his camera still and closed his eyes. Maybe if he held them closed long enough, the sun would fade away and they'd be able to go back into the house and get her out of that bikini. Well, she'd get out of the bikini.

He'd be in the hall thinking about her getting out of that bikini.

*

The day had been longer than feared, followed by a restless night of dreams. He had no idea his mind could be so creative with ways to remove a little pink bikini. Who needs hands when you have teeth? In his dreams, he would sweep her into his arms, kissing her, tasting her...touching her. Every dream ended with him startling awake. He either woke fearing they'd been caught by Chip and his career was over, or worse—remembering the pain on his brother's face the day he lost Melissa.

Evan couldn't risk the same fate. He wouldn't.

He couldn't think of Cassidy that way. She was his assignment. She was a risk too big to take. And she could still have feelings for her ex, douche bag Brad. Or was Chip right when he said the past was in the past?

He took a big gulp of steaming coffee. He didn't have time to let it cool, but he also couldn't function without it. Coffee was the one thing that he could always find anywhere in the world and the one thing he couldn't go without. He took another gulp and peeked out the window to see clouds filling the sky.

Thank God for perfectly overcast, no-bikini-wearing days.

Grabbing his camera, he opened his door to find Cassidy leaning back against the opposite wall, sexy as all hell in a white see-through blouse and capris. He could see the silhouette of her shape through the thin material and her tight tank top left little to his imagination.

Damn, she's hot.

"Hey, Cassidy." He held his gaze at her eyes, refusing to glimpse anywhere that might lead to more dreams. "We're getting a bit of a late start today, huh?" He checked his watch and saw it was after noon already.

How long was I in the shower this morning?

"Well, I didn't want to sit around speculating on which poor girl is going home in tears today. I know that's the only thing everyone will be able to talk about," Cassidy said.

"Ready to join the others?" Evan asked.

"As ready as I'm going to be."

*

Evan stood opposite Cassidy so he could get a good shot of her reaction as the ceremony began.

"Welcome back to *The One*. I'm Spencer Daley and we're about to find out which lucky girl will get another chance at becoming The One. America, over 2 million of you voted last night."

Spencer motioned for the bottom three girls to come up to the front. "Julia, Lauren, and Courtney, if you'll please join me. Brad, before we find out who's leaving us tonight, is there anything you'd like to say to these ladies?"

Brad sighed. "I just want to say it's nothing personal. I think you are awesome girls. I wish you could stay longer. To the girl who stays, I'm looking forward to a second chance at getting to know you."

Spencer held up two small white envelopes in his hand. "I have here the names of the two girls with the lowest votes. Brad, please pick an envelope and tell us the name of the first girl going home."

Brad hesitated before choosing an envelope. "The first girl going home tonight is," Brad paused momentarily while opening the envelope, "Courtney."

Courtney covered her face in her hands when tears sprang to her eyes. Brad gave her a quick hug.

Cassidy's expression changed from concern to sympathy. It was clear on her face that she was sorry to watch one of the girls getting so upset about leaving.

"Please take a moment to say goodbye," Spencer said to Courtney. She walked around the small group hugging the women goodbye.

"Don't worry about him, I'm sure someone else will want you," Zoe whispered as they hugged for the camera. As Courtney moved on to the next girl, Zoe rolled her eyes at Savanna.

She really is a bitch. I'll have to thank Chip for not sentencing me to weeks of following Zoe around. Her cameraman must have a never-ending headache.

Evan refocused on Cassidy as she hugged Courtney goodbye. "You're better off without him," Cassidy said quietly, but not too quietly for her mic to hear. "He doesn't know what he's missing. I bet you'll have guys knocking down your door when you get home."

"Thanks, Cassidy. Good luck." Courtney finished her goodbyes and walked into the house to gather her things with her cameraman following closely behind.

Brad took the last envelope from Spencer and turned to face the two remaining girls. He slowly slid the card out and read it to himself. "Julia, I'm sorry, but you're not The One."

Lauren sighed with relief before giving Julia a hug goodbye and rejoining her fellow contestants.

Julia made the rounds as the girls hugged her. She gave one final wave before turning away from the group and walking back into the house.

"Congratulations, Lauren. Your journey continues."

"That's all for tonight. Please join us next time when we'll see our ladies participate in their next challenge on *The One*." Spencer smiled at the camera and waved.

"We're clear," Chip called from beside the camera. "Great job tonight, Spencer."

"Excellent work these last few days, ladies," Chip said. "Take tonight to rest and enjoy your evening. Tomorrow we're filming your next interview, which you'll do after every elimination ceremony. Then it's right into the second challenge. I can't tell you what you'll be doing, but please dress casually for the event. Jeans or other long pants would be best." Chip smiled and walked away with no further instructions or clues.

Evan wondered what surprise Chip had in store for them next. There was no doubt in his mind Chip wanted to get the girls into as many interesting situations as he could. But long pants could mean any number of things. He was just going to have to wait until tomorrow like everyone else.

Chapter Eight

"Is it okay if I sit like this? Or do I have to sit with both legs down?" Cassidy asked from the interview couch where she sat with one leg tucked under the other. She leaned against one of the throw pillows and adjusted her shirt to make sure it wasn't bunching up around her.

Evan stopped shuffling papers on the desk, tilting his head as he looked at her. He twisted one of the lights slightly. Cassidy squinted when she accidentally glanced directly at it. She could already feel the heat from the lights warming her skin, making her more flushed than she usually was around Evan.

"You're perfect right there." He finished with the light and turned back to the papers, stacking them. He stepped behind the camera and sat casually on a high stool. She couldn't help but notice his jeans stretched tight across his lap. "I'm ready when you are."

Oh, I'm ready...

She took a deep breath, forcing away the intruding thoughts of Evan and his tight jeans. "Me too."

"When you finally met the bachelor, were you surprised to see your ex-boyfriend Brad?"

"Jumping right to the hot topic, huh?" Cassidy shook her head. She really didn't want to talk about this with Evan even if he was her cameraman. "Surprised is an understatement. I had no idea I'd have to see my ex-boyfriend. I certainly didn't expect to date him again. But I'm here now and the show must go on, as they say."

"Did seeing Brad again bring back old feelings?"

"I don't know yet. I only spoke to him once for a few minutes. I think our first meeting was spent in shock at seeing each other again and it seemed to go by so fast. Maybe once the surprise has worn off,

I'll be able to think about it and decide if there are any old feelings there or not. Meeting someone for a few minutes on one 'date' isn't usually enough time to decide if I feel something for them or not."

Evan peeked out from the camera enough so she could see his blue eyes peering at her. "But sometimes a few minutes is enough?"

"Sometimes," she said, staring back at him instead of the camera. "There's an exception to prove every rule, right?" Evan was certainly an exception. A few minutes with him at the piano on her first day was all she'd needed to feel captivated by him.

"Right." He cleared his throat and disappeared behind the camera. "So you cooked him pizza. How did he like it?"

"I'm pretty sure he hated it. It's kind of funny that this is how we would meet again—over a slice of pizza. When we were dating, I used to love to stop in to the pizza place around the corner from my apartment, and Brad always hated it. And he hated my pepperoni and pineapple indulgence even more. I can't even count the number of times I must've asked him to try one bite before deciding if he liked it or not. But in all the time we dated, he never did. It made me laugh a little that *finally* he was forced to try it and he couldn't tell me no."

"If you could do it over again, would you have picked a different favorite meal?"

"That's tough. They asked me for the meal I couldn't live without, and that would be pizza, because really, it's the perfect food. Meat, carbs, sauce, cheese. That's seriously all you need in a meal. But, if they'd asked me what meal I'd serve on a first date, it definitely *wouldn't* be pizza. I think the perfect meal really depends on the situation and the person you're with. Sometimes you need a nice juicy steak, other times all you need is a PB&J sandwich."

"How do you feel about not being in the bottom three this week?"

"I feel—confused. I'm not sure I understand why Brad is keeping me here since we've already been through this whole dating thing and it wasn't even that long ago."

She shrugged. "I'm also a little sad for the girls who had to go home. I think they were developing feelings for Brad already."

"Are you developing feelings for Brad already?" The edge of Evan's cheek bulged like he was clenching his jaw.

"I already said I don't know how I feel about Brad."

"Do you think he's attractive?"

Do we have to talk about this, now—ever?

"Of course he is. They don't put unattractive people on these shows. And I did date him, which I wouldn't have if I didn't feel some attraction to him. But, I also believe there's a lot more to a person than what I see on the outside."

Evan drummed his fingers on his thigh. "So you like that sexy surfer dude look?"

What? That's not what I said.

"I guess—I don't know," she stammered. "I just said he's good looking. That's all. He's not the hottest guy I've ever laid eyes on, but he's definitely not an eyesore either. I don't know. He's just—Brad."

"A simple yes or no would have been sufficient." Evan folded his arms across his chest.

"Then ask a simple yes or no question." Cassidy crossed her arms to reflect his. He could be so damn infuriating. Why couldn't he take her initial answer for what it was without all the extra questioning? What the hell was his problem?

Relax, Cassidy. There's no reason to be grouchy.

She forced herself to uncross her arms and relax her shoulders. Why was she getting so defensive all of a sudden? Evan was simply asking the questions he was given, right?

"Are you looking forward to the next challenge?"

"Yes. I think they'll have something fun for us to do again. Part of the reason I'm here is for the experience—the adventures, whatever they are—so I'm excited to see what will happen next."

"Do you have any guesses about what the next challenge will be?"

"No, not a clue. Do you know what we're doing?" she asked, a spark of hope filling her. Surely the production crew knew the schedule.

"No, and even if I did, I couldn't tell you. Besides, I'm the one asking the questions here." Evan shuffled the papers on the desk again as though he was trying to prove his point. "Lastly, I have a couple of questions about your housemates. How are you enjoying living with a bunch of women in one house?"

Cassidy sighed. Would it kill him to give her a little hint since she was at a disadvantage with her ankle already? He'd been so sweet when he'd rescued her the other day, but since the first challenge ended, he'd seemed less sweet and a lot more sour about anything having to do with her and the competitions. So basically everything.

"It's okay." She shifted in her seat. How was she going to answer this tactfully? "It's nice to have people around to talk to, and some of the girls are really fun and sweet."

Paige is really sweet at least.

"Anyone you'd like to see go home sooner rather than later?"

"Well, there are definitely some girls I don't care for as much as some of the others, but everyone's here for their own reasons. I hope every girl gets what they want out of this experience before they have to leave."

Good job, C. You could totally be a pageant queen with answers like that.

"Are you getting what you hoped for out of this experience?"

"So far, yes." Her eyes fluttered across Evan's chest. If she closed her eyes, she could imagine how sculpted it must be under his shirt. She swallowed hard around the lump in her throat. "Actually, I think I'm getting even more than I expected or hoped for."

"Care to elaborate on that?" Evan asked, giving her the hand signal to stretch her response to a more elaborate answer.

"I think it's pretty self-explanatory, don't you? My ex-boyfriend is the bachelor I'm supposed to date." *My cameraman is super-hot.*

"That's not exactly something I planned on."

"Any girls you're becoming friends with?"

"Sure, Paige is a great friend. She's the one person I feel I can really talk to. I think we'll stay friends long after this is over."

"How will you feel if Paige is chosen as The One?"

"If Paige and Brad are meant for each other, I'll be happy for her. I know the person meant for me is out there somewhere. Who knows, maybe I've already found him and don't realize it yet."

Cassidy stared at her hands, which were currently twisting the bottom hem of her blouse into a tiny corkscrew. Was Evan that someone?

Chapter Nine

Cassidy knelt on the floor of her walk-in closet, trying to determine which pair of shoes would be right for today's competition. Since she still didn't know what it was, she had to guess and hope for the best.

"Casual-but-sort-of-dressy boots or plain-old-boring sneakers?" she debated out loud. She seen the house medic again earlier and he'd given her the all clear to compete on the condition she'd refrain from wearing heels to give her ankle time to rest. That was fine with her.

Why can't they be easy and tell us what we're doing so we can dress appropriately? Why does everything have to be a surprise in this place?

Speaking of surprises, Cassidy had been taken aback by Evan's apparent concern that she thought Brad was attractive. Of course Brad was cute. He was the star on a reality dating show.

In fact, Evan seemed jealous. But that couldn't be right. Evan didn't have anything to be jealous about.

Brad was her ex and just because they were now on a dating show together didn't mean all of the other stuff between them was suddenly forgotten. Cassidy wished she could say that in the interview, but that's not what the producers wanted to hear. She was supposed to be here for Brad, even if he was her ex, which meant giving him a fair chance—and she knew one meal together wasn't fair enough. Maybe now that the shock of seeing him again had started to wear off, they'd be able to have a normal conversation the next time they were together.

Jealous. Evan's definitely jealous.

Cassidy laughed at the idea of Evan being jealous of Brad. Brad had nothing on Evan as far as Cassidy was concerned. Sure Brad was cute, but Evan was on a different level of hotness completely. Evan was Edward Cullen hot. Brad...well, Brad was great, but he would never make a girl want to become a vampire so she could be with him for all eternity. A regular lifetime would be plenty with Brad.

Cassidy was constantly amazed at how gorgeous Evan was. Every part of his body was defined and sexy and caused her to have dirty dreams about tearing his clothes off with her teeth.

Brad could keep his clothes on then wrap himself in a parka.

Besides his appearance, Evan always treated her with respect, which was more than she could say for Brad. Cassidy loved the way she and Evan joked with each other and seemed to feed off of each other's energy. He might be a bit of a smart ass sometimes, but she was too, and it was nice to finally meet someone who didn't cower away from a girl with a personality.

Cassidy grabbed her black boots and sat on the edge of the bed, pushing her feet into the supple leather. She zipped the boots up to the knee over her skinny jeans, glancing in the mirror to give herself a final once over before she left for the competition.

There's no reason casual can't be cute and sexy, too.

She gathered her hair into a simple ponytail at the nape of her neck and tied it loosely with a small silk scarf.

A knock on the door startled Cassidy. She pulled it open to find Susan the PA standing in the hall.

"Hey, what's up?" Cassidy asked. It wasn't like production people to stop by unless something was wrong. "Wanna come in?"

"I thought you deserved a heads up." She glanced both ways down the hall before speaking again. "I can't legally tell you anything, but you would be best off at today's challenge if you relaxed with a Corona instead of picking something a little wilder and harder to handle."

"Um, what?" Was Susan speaking in code?

"I've already said more than I should. I'm sure you'll figure it out when the time comes." Susan walked away without another word.

Cassidy closed the door annoyed at the cryptic message she

didn't understand. How did this give her a heads up? And why was Susan trying to help her when she was clearly breaking the rules by giving her a tip about the challenge?

*

Evan didn't know how Cassidy made it happen, but he couldn't believe how great she looked every single day. Today's choice was relaxed and casual, and she looked more fantastic than ever. She could wear a garbage bag and her ass would still look fantastic.

Speaking of asses, although not the fantastic kind...

"Chip. How's it going?" Evan asked as Chip Cormack sauntered up beside him.

"It's great." Chip smiled one of his token asshole smiles and put his hand on Evan's shoulder. "So, what happened in the interview this morning?"

Ah, shit.

"Not much. Why?"

"You took a few liberties with the interview questions, huh?"

"Sorry. I got caught up with her answers and I asked a couple of extra questions without thinking. It won't happen again."

"Don't be silly, Evan. Those questions were perfect. Of course, we never thought you guys would pay enough attention to ask questions of your own, but now that you have, it's great. Those questions you added really made the interview come alive and gave Cassidy so much more personality on camera."

Chip patted him on the back. "Keep up the good work. I can't wait to hear what you ask in the next interview." Evan watched dumbfounded as Chip walked off to talk to the contestants.

Evan relaxed, realizing Chip mustn't have noticed those extra questions were sparked from Evan's interest in Cassidy on a more personal level. If Chip could hear Evan's thoughts about Cassidy, there was no doubt in his mind he'd be fired in a heartbeat.

Next time, he needed to be more careful with the kinds of extra questions he asked. They'd have to be specifically about the show and not about the girl he found so interesting. He couldn't let his guard down when the cameras were rolling. He couldn't risk Chip finding out he had feelings for Cassidy. Feelings he still didn't understand or want.

Evan walked around the side of the gathering where he could get a better shot of Cassidy. Centered in the frame, Cassidy stood with the rustic red barn behind her. Beyond that, the ruggedness of the Rockies contrasted with the polished, sophisticated women, adorned with pristine painted nails, teased hair and dripping with beautiful jewelry. They looked ridiculous in the most put-together impression of casual Evan had ever seen. Each one stood out like a ballerina at a rodeo.

Everyone except Cassidy.

For being a city girl, Cassidy didn't appear out of place at all in a setting like this. All she needed was a cowboy hat and she'd blend right in. To someone who didn't know any better, you might think she'd lived here her whole life. Dressed like that, Evan could almost picture Cassidy on the front porch swing beside him and Aspen.

Whoa, easy now. Let's not get ahead of ourselves. Looking is one thing but porch swings are a little much right now.

"Welcome back to *The One*." Spencer Daley addressed the girls. "Today you will again be competing and spending time with our bachelor Brad while enjoying some exciting horseback riding here at beautiful Mountainside Ranch.

"Brad's waiting inside the barn. He'll help each of you select a horse. Then you'll saddle it and lead it out to the field behind the barn where you'll leave for an amazing scenic trail ride."

Evan followed as the girls walked into the barn. As his eyes adjusted to the low light, he spotted Brad perched on a pile of hay bales in the middle of the room, grinning like the Cheshire Cat as the women approached.

The barn had a center walkway with what had to be at least fifteen stalls on each side. A string of lanterns ran down the center of the aisle, casting a warm glow into the stalls. Off to the side of the entrance, a room bigger than Evan's living room was devoted entirely to tack and feed.

"Hello again, ladies." Brad laid on the charm so thick Evan could barely keep down his lunch. "You look gorgeous today."

The girls swooned as though no one had ever paid them a compliment before.

Brad sure did know how to work his angles with the girls. He played the perfect boyfriend—caring, sweet and complimentary. It wasn't until he was hanging around with only the guys that Brad became just another dick in the crowd. If the girls got to see the truth, this would be a completely different show.

"First thing we need to do is find each of you a horse." Brad raised his eyebrows and smirked. "Who's ready to find something to ride?"

"I'm ready for a ride." Zoe stepped out of line. She put her hand on Brad's knee. "But I'm not sure I need a horse for that."

Wow. There's no misinterpreting that.

"You know," Zoe started, batting her eyes at Brad—and the camera, "I used to be an equestrian jumper."

"Did you ever place?"

Zoe tossed her hair over her shoulder with a perfected head-flip. "Of course. I won them all."

"So you still ride now?"

"Oh, no. I got rid of that horse right after my championship ride. I took up gymnastics instead. It made me very flexible."

Brad grinned. He hopped off the pile of hay and wrapped his arm around Zoe's waist, leading her down the pathway. "Let's walk and talk."

"She's disgusting," Paige whispered in Cassidy's ear. "I can't believe she said that to him with all these cameras watching."

"That's probably the main reason she did say it. I think she's hoping for a little more screen time. She certainly knows what sells on TV—sex."

"She's such a tramp."

"Agreed. But he's not much better for falling for it."

"I heard she had a breakdown when she lost that other show," said Savanna.

"I guess if you're used to winning everything, losing would be a shock," Lauren said.

Rich, good at everything, and a poor loser? Lethal combination.

At the other end of the barn, Brad had Zoe leaning back against a wall as he hovered over her intimately. They separated long enough to select a horse then as Zoe stood at the stall door, Brad kissed her.

"Oh my God, he's kissing her," Cassidy whispered to Paige.

What, is Cassidy hoping she'll be next? Not wanting to share him?

Brad sauntered back up the aisle, a smug expression on his face like he was exceptionally proud of himself. "So, who's next?"

None of the girls stepped forward.

"Everyone's shy all of a sudden?" Brad smiled and wiped the corner of his mouth with his hand. His eyes drifted across the women, sizing up his next target. "How about you, Cassidy?"

"Um, sure. I'll pick a horse next." She smiled at Brad, took his hand, and walked beside him while peering into the stalls.

Evan tried to concentrate on not tripping over his feet as he walked backward in front of Cassidy and Brad. But it was hard for him to concentrate on anything when he watched Brad's hand wrapped around Cassidy's. He wondered what it would feel like if it were him instead of Brad.

Cassidy stopped in front of a stall with the name Corona written on the door. A golden face with deep brown eyes peered out of the stall.

"Corona, huh?" Cassidy reached out and stroked her hand up and down the horse's forehead. "You seem like a nice girl."

"You've chosen your horse already? We haven't even had a chance to talk yet."

Cassidy shrugged and smiled. "Sorry. She seems like a nice horse. It's not that I don't want to talk."

"Good, then let's sit for a few minutes and talk." Brad led Cassidy to a wooden bench across the aisle from Corona's stall and pulled her gently down beside him, never letting go of her hand. "How've you been?"

"I've been fine. The usual, just working, hanging out with Keira. How about you? Happy to be back in California?"

"Oh man, being back with the old crew, surfing the waves... it's awesome."

"I'm happy for you. That's great."

"I have a question." Brad paused like he was thinking very hard to phrase the question in just the right way. "How do you feel about me?"

A rose hue suddenly colored the apples of her cheeks and she shifted on the bench.

"That's a very direct question I didn't expect to have to answer yet."

Brad dropped Cassidy's hand and tucked a hair that had come loose from her ponytail behind her ear.

Evan's grip on the camera tightened involuntarily. *Focus.*

"Well, we get such a short time together here I thought we should get things out in the open quickly rather than letting them simmer on low." Brad put a hand on her knee and ran his fingers up and down her thigh. "You were never shy with your feelings before."

What's this joker doing? He can't touch Cassy like that. Great, now I'm thinking of her in nicknames. Shit. What part of not getting involved don't I understand, exactly?

"I'm not sure what to tell you. Honestly, I've only recently adjusted to the fact that you're actually here and I'm supposed to date you again. You have to admit this whole situation is a little weird."

"Sure it is, but that doesn't mean we can't enjoy this second chance. I think it's okay to explore our feeling for each other again, don't you? You don't have to worry about hiding your feelings from the other girls. They know we have history together."

"I'm not hiding my feelings. I'd have to know what they are to hide them."

"Maybe you need a little sugar from me to refresh your memory." Brad leaned in, shortening the gap between them. "Come on, Cassidy. It's been a long time since I've tasted your lips."

I will make sure you eat horse shit if you put your lips on her.

"It's a little too soon, Brad."

"That didn't stop Zoe from showing me how she felt."

Cassidy shifted back further along the bench. "What Zoe does is her business. I'm not about to follow in her footsteps and I'm certainly not going to make out with you in some random barn."

That's my feisty girl.

"I can wait a bit for you. But don't make me wait too long, or I might fall in love with one of these other beautiful women." Brad jumped up, striding toward the remaining girls.

"I'll take my chances," Cassidy mumbled, her eyes flickering toward Evan.

He grinned and let out a long slow breath. *Dude, get a grip. She's not your girlfriend so stop getting all, "I'm going to beat the shit out of you," every time the pansy-ass surfer boy is around.*

He lingered near the door as Cassidy went into the stall to meet Corona. He wasn't looking for a girlfriend, so why was he so bent out of shape about Cassidy? He didn't want to get involved with anyone—he wouldn't *let* himself get involved.

A man brushed past him with a large saddle in his arms. "My name is Roberto and I'll be helping you." He set down the saddle in a clean patch of hay. "Have you ridden before?" Roberto asked, as if he could read the questions in Evan's mind.

"No." Cassidy shook her head. "There aren't too many opportunities to ride in the city. But I've always wanted to. It looks like so much fun."

Cassidy appeared surprisingly comfortable and at ease in the small space, given the large size of the horse and the fact that she had no experience being around them.

"Well then, let's get you on this horse." Roberto handed her a rectangular wool blanket. "This goes on first. Up there by the shoulders."

Cassidy flung the blanket onto the back of the horse and smoothed it out.

"Hmph," snorted Corona, sneezing at Cassidy, then sniffing her face.

"Hey." Cassidy wiped her face with her hand. "That wasn't nice."

Evan suppressed a laugh and tried to hold the camera still. Only Cassidy would get sneezed on, in the face, by a horse.

"Easy, girl." Roberto patted Corona on the side. "Now the saddle. Put it right up on the blanket."

Cassidy squat down in front of the saddle and lifted it. She peeked over her shoulder at Evan.

No bending over on camera today, huh, Cassidy?

She hauled the bulky saddle to the horse's side and lifted it onto Corona's back. As she adjusted it, Corona shifted her weight, bumping into Cassidy. She lost her balance and fell against the wall.

Roberto reached out to steady Cassidy on her feet. "Are you okay?"

"I'm fine." She stood tall and straightened her clothes. "Just a bruised ego."

"You need to pay more attention around the horses. They move when they want to, not when we want them to."

"I'm beginning to see that."

Evan smiled in spite of his best efforts not to. He couldn't believe how accident-prone she was. If anything could happen in a situation, it *would* happen to Cassidy. She was the living definition of Murphy's Law.

He pictured what it would be like to take her to his brother's ranch. He could teach her to ride slowly, without all these cameras around to spook the horses. Carter had gentle horses that were easy for new riders. Even his niece Annie could ride them—and she was only five. Cassidy would be safe on a horse like that and less likely to find herself in a compromising position—unless of course it was Evan who put her in that position.

No, he couldn't take her there. Too much emotion still lingered to bring a girl over. Melissa had only been gone a year, Carter and Annie were still hurting...that was exactly what he needed to remember when he started thinking about Cassidy as anything more than an assignment—the reason he couldn't be with her.

He knew Cassidy had come here for the adventure, but surely putting a city girl on the back of a huge horse and going out on rough Colorado trails was more than she expected. The trails could be dangerous for a new, inexperienced rider and he didn't want to see Cassidy get hurt. Why did they have to go out on the trails? It would be so much safer if the girls stayed in the riding ring.

Roberto finished adjusting the saddle on the horse. "Okay, now you need to grab the cinch strap from that side and feed it through the loops on this side."

Cassidy bent down and peered under the horse's belly. "I have to grab that strap over there, from here?" She scooted forward in a crouched position and leaned under Corona. The strap was a fraction of an inch beyond her reach.

Evan zoomed in as she stepped a little closer and stretched, extending herself under the horse. Her hand circled the strap and she stood quickly, getting out from under the horse. "I got it!" She cheered and smiled directly at Evan. Not the camera—Evan.

He couldn't resist smiling back. Sweat from the heat and humidity in the barn made her skin glisten, but in that moment, she'd never looked more radiant to him. He gave her a nod before she turned back to the horse.

"All right, now loop it through here and we're done."

Cassidy fed the strap through the set of loops as Roberto directed her, yanked down hard on the cinch. "Done. That's good, right—oh my God!"

Cassidy froze and peered down at her foot. Evan followed her gaze to find a large hoof covering the end of her boot.

"Ouch. Help. Now. Please."

Evan moved quickly, his camera still perched on his shoulder. He wrapped his free arm around her waist and pressed her body to his, then shoved his shoulder into the side of the horse until she shifted her weight and picked up her hoof. Evan twisted his body away from the horse taking Cassidy with him and freeing her foot.

He gazed down at Cassidy and found her staring back up at him, realizing then how tightly he held her. Her body molded against the length of his and he could feel her body heat radiating through his clothes, warming every inch of him.

"Are you hurt?" He managed to choke out the words through the familiar fog that seemed to constantly clog his brain whenever she was around.

Cassidy blinked and shook her head. She opened her mouth as if she wanted to say something, but instead closed it again, remaining silent.

"You need to stop hurting yourself, or I'll have to carry you to the challenges."

Cassidy mumbled a reply he couldn't make out.

Evan held her close for another few seconds, reluctant to let her go. It felt so good to hold her against him. It felt right, almost as if her body had been made to fit with his and his arms were made to hold her—to protect her. He could protect her, couldn't he?

Like Carter thought he could protect Melissa?

Her breath tickled his face, gentle and warm as her lips parted to speak. He wanted to cover those lips with his. Would they fit as well with him as the rest of her seemed to?

Stop. Not here. Not now. It's not worth the pain later.

But what if she was worth the risk of losing it all later?

"Thanks for saving me. Again." Cassidy sounded breathless. "You always seem to be right here when I need you."

"I'm the camera guy. It's my job to be one step away at all times."

"Is that all it is?"

"No." Evan leaned forward and whispered in her ear. "You're too damn cute when you're being clumsy. I can't resist saving you."

Evan released his hold on Cassidy and stepped back before he had the chance to say anything else he shouldn't. He righted the camera on his shoulder and refocused it on Cassidy.

"Roberto, can you help Cassidy to the bench while I call for the medic?"

Roberto moved toward Cassidy but she limped away from him, her eyes never leaving Evan's. "No, I'm fine."

"You're limping," Evan reminded her.

"I got stepped on by a horse."

Evan ignored Cassidy's next protest and waved to Susan, giving her the signal to send the medic. A moment later a man arrived with a first aid bag in hand.

Cassidy sat on the bench outside the stable as the medic slid off her boot and evaluated her foot. "I'm fine. Really," she protested. "I can walk on it and everything."

"I think we should get this checked to be sure it isn't broken. I don't think it is, but when in doubt, check it out. Let's go."

"No. I don't want to. I've lived through worse before. I'm fine."

"Are you refusing treatment to stay in the challenge?" Evan couldn't believe she'd do that. Besides, a fieldtrip to the hospital would mean her spending less time with Brad on dangerous trails and more time alone with him.

That's a win-win situation.

"Yep. I'm good to go."

The medic stared at Cassidy for a moment before shaking his

head and reaching into the front pocket of the bag he'd brought. He pulled out a yellow form and a pen. "If you're sure you don't want further medical treatment, you're within your right to do so, but you need to sign this waiver."

Evan sighed as Cassidy signed her name and hobbled back to Corona's stall. "Roberto, can you help me finish with Corona?"

A few moments later, Roberto handed her the reins. "Here you go, Cassidy. She's all yours."

Evan stepped aside so Cassidy could lead the horse past him. So much had happened in the barn. Evan wondered what could possibly happen once she actually mounted her horse. He had a feeling this wasn't going to be the easy trail ride Cassidy expected.

Chapter Ten

Cassidy leaned against the rough wooden posts fencing in the corral trying not to put any weight on the foot currently throbbing like it had a heartbeat of its own. Her foot wasn't broken—she knew what that felt like—but it was probably badly bruised. Unfortunately, she couldn't do much about it right now, so she pushed the pain from her mind.

Pushing thoughts of Evan from her mind didn't come nearly as easily. She could still feel his body press firmly against her own. Hard, sculpted muscles holding her tight as he rescued her from Corona's heavy hoof. Heat transferring exponentially through their clothes.

His mouth had been so close—kissably close—a fraction of a breath from hers and so tempting. It took all her willpower not to give into temptation and bridge the gap between them with her tongue, taking the tiniest taste of his lips. The same lips that whispered he found her cute when she was clumsy.

Good thing falling came naturally for her.

Erica and Savanna emerged from the barn with their horses in tow. Spencer stood in the middle of the corral and motioned for the women to join him there. Cassidy had been so preoccupied she hadn't noticed him walk out of the production trailer beside the barn.

She stepped forward, pulling gently on Corona's reins. The horse pulled back against her, hooves firmly planted in the mud. She tugged harder trying to coax the horse from her place by the fence.

"Come on," she said quietly to the horse. "Just a couple of steps and we'll be there."

The horse twitched her head and snorted in disagreement. She stomped her hoof into the soft ground as if daring Cassidy to pull on her reins again.

What happened to Corona being a nice, calm horse like Susan claimed?

"Fine." Cassidy slid her hand to the very end of the reins and walked forward as far as she could with her arm outstretched behind her. It wasn't pretty, but it was the best she could manage with the stubborn horse and still be able to hear what Spencer had to say.

"Now that everyone is ready, you'll be heading out on that trail with a couple of ranch guides. Along the way, you'll find two special picnic areas. At these stops, Brad will choose four girls to join him for a short picnic."

Spencer paused before putting emphasis on his next statement. "I can't stress enough how important these picnic dates are. Make sure you focus on getting to know Brad and letting him get to know you. He won't get many chances to learn more about you before the next eliminations. Enough talking. Everyone mount your horses." Spencer wandered back into the trailer, leaving them to figure out how to actually do that.

One of the guides helped Erica onto her horse. It didn't look too hard. Evan swung his leg over his horse and seated himself into the saddle, putting his camera up on his shoulder. Another guide walked in front of his horse with the reins in his hand, leaving Evan's hands free to film.

Doesn't look too hard. You can do this.

Cassidy pulled her knee up to her chest, slipping her sore foot into the hanging stirrup and bounced a few times trying to gain a little momentum to help propel herself up and onto the horse. She counted to three, then jumped, putting all her weight into the stirrup and using her arms to pull herself toward the saddle. She hit the side of the horse with her chest and fell back to the ground, landing hard on her good foot.

Okay. Not as easy as I thought.

Cassidy bounced again, pulling with her arms a little each time, trying to get a feel for how high she needed to jump to pull herself onto the horse. All at once, she pulled with her arms, jumped and tried to stand in the stirrup. The muscle in her bent leg strained against her body weight. She gripped the saddle harder, struggling to raise her chest above the horse's back.

How tall is this frickin' horse?

Finally standing in the stirrup, she swung her leg in the direction of the horse's rear, cringing when her knee connected with its side. Corona stumbled, nickered, and shook her body as if it was covered in flies. *Maybe that's how she views me. Just another fly on her ass.*

The saddle slipped from her hands. She hit the ground with a thud, landing hard enough on her ass that her teeth chattered together. She sat stunned and unmoving for a moment before strong hands pulled her to her feet.

"You okay?" Evan's eyes twinkled as he bit his lip, a smile tugging the corner of his mouth. Somehow in the time it had taken her to attempt to mount her horse, Evan had already mounted *and* dismounted his horse. Now he stood near her, waiting for her to make another pathetic attempt.

"Fine, thanks." She wiped the back of her pants clean as best as she could, blushing at the chorus of giggles echoing around the corral.

"Would you like a hand? Corona's pretty tall."

Cassidy eyed Evan cautiously. He seemed genuine. And she did have to get on her horse somehow since she appeared to be the only girl remaining with her feet on the ground. "Sure," she agreed with reservation.

She assumed the position again with her hands on the saddle and her foot in the stirrup. Evan placed his hands on her hips. His fingers pressed against her flesh as his grip on her tightened.

"You okay, Cassidy?" Brad asked, strolling up beside Evan.

"I'm fine. Just trying to get on my horse."

"I can give you a boost," offered Brad, moving toward her.

Evan motioned to Cassidy who was currently in his hands and

smiled at Brad. "I've already got this covered, but thanks." Evan turned back to Cassidy, essentially dismissing Brad.

Brad turned and stalked away with heavy steps. *He doesn't look happy about not being needed, but I stopped needing him the day he left.*

"Just pull yourself up as much as you can and throw your leg over the saddle when you get to the top. I'll give you a lift and make sure your horse doesn't move again."

She pulled herself up and Evan's grip tightened as she became weightless in his hands. When she neared the top, his hand left her hip and slid onto her butt, making it easier for her to balance and throw her leg over the horse. The feel of his warm hand through her tight jeans made her flushed like she'd been in the sun all day.

Now this I need. Again.

As quick as it was there, his hand disappeared and she sat into the cold hard saddle. She hooked her other foot into the stirrup while Evan grabbed her reins.

"Thanks," she managed as he peered up at her.

Cowboys are hot. I need to start watching westerns.

"My pleasure." He patted Corona on the side of the neck. "You be good for Cassidy, okay?" The horse nickered and closed her eyes while he scratched behind her ear.

I get sneezes, he gets nuzzles. Nice.

Cassidy followed the group down the trail, gawking at the view while the other girls chatted. The mountains were stunning. She'd never realized how beautiful the world outside the city could be. She'd gotten complacent seeing the same cold gray cement buildings and sidewalks and had almost forgotten places where she could be surrounded by nature for miles existed. Unlike Central Park where there were always buildings in background as a lingering reminder of work waiting to be done. She could get used to this.

She saw Evan on his horse, his tight jeans covering what appeared to be a nicely sculpted butt. *I could get used to that, too.*

His hips rocked gently in the saddle with the movement of the horse. The sight of it made her mouth go dryer than if she'd been riding through the Sahara Desert.

They walked up to a small clearing on the side of the trail. A picnic table sat in the middle of the clearing with wine and a small assortment of food laid out.

"This is our first stop. I'd like Zoe, Paige, Holly, and Cassidy to join me," Brad stated. "If the rest of you wouldn't mind following the trail a little further, there's a beautiful spot to stop and see the view. We'll meet you there in a little bit."

Brad stopped his horse near Cassidy and threw his leg back over the horse in reverse of how he'd done it earlier, then landed on the ground with both feet. Paige and Zoe followed his lead and were also off their horses and safely on the ground.

This isn't going to be as easy as it looks, is it?

Brad came up beside Cassidy and stroked her leg. "Do you want help getting down?"

"Sure. You made it seem so easy."

"Just put your weight into the stirrup and swing your other leg back around."

Cassidy did as he suggested and ended up slumped over the saddle on her stomach. "Uh, Brad, I'm not so sure this is the right way to get down."

"Don't worry, babe. I've got you." Brad put his hands on her waist. "Now slip your foot out of the stirrup and jump down."

His grip was strong. Not as sturdy as Evan's had been, but enough to help her off the horse safely. Her foot wiggled out of the stirrup and her arms gave way under her awkward position in the saddle. Brad's hands tightened on her but gravity took over and she fell. He stumbled trying to guide her to her feet, but she was too off balance and he didn't have the arm strength to support her coming down off of such a tall horse.

Cassidy yelped as they fell backward and the ground rushed up to meet them. She landed hard, ass first on top of Brad.

Not again. I should sign a stack of those stupid medical treatment forms.

Brad groaned from beneath her before starting to laugh. "I don't think we did that right after all."

"Ya think?" Cassidy rolled off Brad and onto her knees beside him. "You okay?"

"Yeah, I'm fine." Brad climbed to his feet then helped her up. "That's not exactly how you used to sit on my lap, but it was still nice."

She dusted off her jeans and said a little prayer that it would be the last time she'd have to. She could already feel the bruises blooming on her ass, her muscles yelling at her lack of balance and coordination. You'd think her body would be used to this kind of abuse after twenty-eight years.

Evan peered at Cassidy from behind the camera with that now familiar expression on his face. The one he seemed to get every time she was near Brad. But this time, it seemed like there was more to it, a nervousness or concern she hadn't seen before. Was he worried about her fall or her time with Brad? Perhaps he worried about both.

"Be careful," Evan whispered almost too quietly for her to hear.

"I'm fine," Cassidy said as if telling America instead of Evan. "It was only a tiny fall. No harm done."

He cocked his head and scowled at her.

Well, if he was worried about her, he could get over it. It was a teeny, tiny fall and she didn't need him to protect her from the big, bad horse. She'd already had one boyfriend who treated her with kid gloves, she wasn't signing up for that again. Not that Evan was going to be her boyfriend, but still.

Cassidy became aware of the smirking faces around her, her cheeks growing hot. She hated being laughed at. There was only one way to handle this embarrassment—face it with a smile.

"Thank you." Cassidy forced a smile to her lips and pretended to curtsey. "I'll be here all day."

Brad put his arm around her shoulders. "I forgot how clumsy you are. I miss saving you from disaster."

"Well, don't get too nostalgic because I'm really trying to be more careful. I'm hoping to make it a few days at a time without needing to be saved."

"Come on. Let's go eat and relax before we have to risk your life getting you back on that horse. You couldn't have picked a smaller one, huh? Maybe a Shetland pony so you'd be closer to the ground?"

"Very funny." She laughed and pushed him away, walking off to join the others while pretending to be offended. She'd forgotten how smart-assed he could be. She'd forgotten how much she liked that about him.

He was right—about the horse at least. She should have picked a smaller horse, and maybe one who listened to her. She'd been foolish to pick one based on Susan's recommendation. Now she was stuck with a monstrosity of a horse who listened about as well as a two-year-old.

Perhaps instead of picking a horse named Corona, I should have drank a Corona. Of course, I probably still would have ended up on my ass at some point. I don't get along with beer, either. That should have been my first sign of impending doom.

She settled onto the picnic bench beside Paige and gulped a big mouthful of water out of a cold bottle. Cassidy sat quietly, nibbling on a sandwich as the others chatted easily with Brad. She was happy to be invisible for a few minutes since it seemed like there'd been a lot of focus on her already. Focus she wished would be on someone else for a change.

Cassidy glanced across the table and found Zoe glaring at her. She whispered something to Holly, who giggled and tried to hide a smile behind her hand.

Awesome. It's like high school all over again.

"How're you feeling?" Brad asked.

"I'm good. Nothing to worry about. Or, um, talk about even." She tried to put on an easygoing expression, but inside she wanted to crawl under the table and hide.

"Maybe if Cassidy's not feeling well, one of the guides should take her back to the barn," offered Zoe, twisting her necklace. "Maybe you should have a doctor examine you. With all those falls, it's amazing you're even able to sit here with us on this hard bench. Good thing you had enough padding to cushion the fall."

Take a deep breath. Don't fall into her trap.

Cassidy pouted her lips slightly and put her hand on her chest. "That's so sweet of you to be worried about me. But I'm fine. Really. I wouldn't want to miss all the fun here."

"We'd miss you if you weren't here," Brad added. "I'm glad you're well enough to stay with us."

Anger and hurt flashed across Zoe's face before she turned to Brad and started asking him questions about being a surfer. Cassidy didn't need to listen to his answers. She'd heard them all before. "Surfing's a rush of exhilaration and a feeling of complete freedom..." Blah, blah, blah. Surfing also made you break hearts.

"Paige," Cassidy whispered. "What's with Zoe and that stupid necklace she always wears?"

Paige shrugged. "Apparently it's her grandmother's. She inherited it and hasn't taken it off since."

Cassidy eyed the tiny cluster of pendants hanging from it. A cross, an anchor, and a heart. Seemed uncharacteristic of Zoe to be so sentimental. Now if it were a two-carat diamond pendant, then it would perfectly fit Zoe's shining personality.

Cassidy zoned out for the rest of the picnic. She nodded her head and laughed along with everyone else when it was appropriate, but she couldn't actually recall a single thing they'd talked about. She could have agreed to go live on the moon for all she knew.

The rest of the trail ride passed in a blur. After what felt like only minutes, the second set of girls finished their picnic with

Brad. Together, everyone sauntered back to the barn. Cassidy glanced around quickly, nervous to get off the horse again and fall. Her body could only take so much.

"Stay still, Corona," she pleaded, patting the horse on the shoulder. She swung her leg over the horse, determined to successfully complete one dismount before the challenge ended.

Her arms shook as she lowered herself carefully from the saddle, finally giving up their fight part way down. Gravity took her the last few feet and she hit the ground with both feet, stumbling backward a step before bumping into something solid.

"How, Cassidy? How do you always end up in my arms?" Evan's voice rumbled in her ear, his warm breath on her earlobe making her girly bits tingle.

She found her footing and turned in his arms. She could see the dust and dirt clinging to his five o'clock shadow, his brow beaded with sweat. He desperately needed a shower and there was nothing she could have fantasized about more than being in one with him. Instead, she pushed herself back from him and swallowed her urge to climb him like a jungle gym.

"What can I say? I guess I just keep falling for you," she said, before her brain caught up to her mouth and she was able to censor herself.

Crap.

"I, uh—I'm going to go put my horse back before she finds another way to humiliate me today. Bye." Cassidy turned on her heel and pulled hard on Corona's reins, not allowing the horse to resist her. She didn't want to stand out in the corral for another second alone with Evan, or who knows what else she'd decide to blurt out. Nope. Corona was coming with her whether her huge horse ass liked it or not.

Cassidy passed by Susan at the barn entrance. "Thanks for the recommendation. Corona was a real peach." Cassidy laughed halfheartedly.

"Sorry. I was only trying to help." Susan smirked. "I can't help it if you don't know how to ride."

Ouch.

Cassidy sucked in a breath. Recommending Corona hadn't been an accident at all. "Just trying to help. That's why I ended up with the only horse that wouldn't listen, huh? What did I do that made you not like me?"

"I like you fine. But maybe some of the other girls are better suited to be here."

How dare Susan make the assumption that she wasn't cut out for these challenges? Cassidy could do anything the other girls could—she'd just do it with a few more bruises and a lot less grace.

"Keep your nose out of my business from now on. I don't need you looking out for me." Cassidy walked away from Susan before saying anything else she might regret. She'd prove to everyone she deserved to be here. And she wouldn't need anyone protecting her while she did it.

Not even super sexy Evan.

*

Spencer walked into the barn. "Can I have everyone's attention?"

Cassidy wandered into the main hallway to join the rest of the girls.

"Brad has decided who he wants to put in the bottom three this week, so without making you wait longer, we're going ahead with that ceremony now. Here."

Cassidy glanced around. All of the girls looked shaken by this sudden turn of events. Everyone except Zoe, of course. She always looked confident.

"I'm sorry to do this so quickly but sometimes you have to pull the bandage off all in one go, right?" Brad asked. "So, the first girl in the bottom three is Paige."

Paige bit her lip, her chin quivering. Cassidy hated seeing her upset, taking everything to heart.

"The second girl in the bottom this week is Nicole. This last one is really difficult, but I have to go with my gut." Brad looked down at his feet as if he couldn't bear to look the final girl in the eye. "Zoe, I'm sorry. I'm not sure we click."

Chapter Eleven

Cassidy eased into the outdoor Jacuzzi beside the pool, letting her body acclimate to the heat. It bordered on too hot, and she felt a little bit like a lobster going into a steaming pot, but she'd tolerate the heat if it meant she'd feel better afterwards. Her muscles ached after the long day on the trails.

She'd mistakenly believed horseback riding would be fun. Everyone on TV was always laughing and smiling while they galloped through fields or on the beach with the wind streaming through their hair all cool and sexy.

That was a total load of bullshit.

It wasn't fun. It wasn't exciting, and Cassidy never wanted to do it again.

She rested her head back against the side of the hot tub. As the water lapped over her shoulders, the heat finally penetrated deep into the muscles, dulling the aches she felt *everywhere*. She ached in places she didn't even know a person could ache. Not only was her ego badly bruised but it felt like her ass would probably be a brilliant shade of indigo by morning.

"Hey, Cassidy, great riding today," Zoe snickered. "You should, like, give lessons or something."

Even with her eyes closed, Cassidy could see the smiles, and there was absolutely no missing the laughter echoing around the tub.

Bitch. Deep breath...count to ten... One, two, bitch, three, four. I hate you. Five...

"That's funny, Zoe," Cassidy said, not bothering to open her eyes. "You should, like, be a comedian or something."

"Aw, what's wrong, Cassidy?" Zoe's voice dripped with artificial concern. "Not feeling well tonight?"

"I feel fine, Zoe."

"All right, honey. If you're floating down a river called denial, I'm not going to force you to swim to shore. Maybe the hot water will help your bruised ego as well as your ass."

Gee, thanks.

"Don't let her bother you," Paige whispered. "She's jealous because Brad paid you so much attention today."

"Yeah, negative attention."

"It's attention nonetheless." Paige sighed. "And she's pissed to be stuck in the bottom three with me."

"How are you doing?" They hadn't had much time to talk since the surprise announcement in the barn.

"Okay. It sucks, but somehow it makes me feel better knowing Zoe's in the bottom with me."

Cassidy grinned. "I couldn't be happier at the possibility she might actually go home this week."

"Don't get your hopes up. There's no way America will vote out the girl who causes the most drama. I'll be going home."

"Don't send yourself out the door yet."

"At least I'll only have to deal with Zoe for a few more days."

"I'm too damn sore to deal with her issues tonight."

"Are you all right?" Paige's voice was barely audible above the rumble of the Jacuzzi jets. "I know today was pretty rough on you"

"Yeah, I'm fine. Nothing a little hot water and a good night's sleep won't fix." Cassidy groaned and turned her head to whisper in Paige's ear. "Of course, I'm not so sure I can say the same for my ego, but if you tell anyone I said that, I'll kill you. Well, when I can move again, I'll kill you."

"Don't worry. Your secret is safe with me."

Cassidy sank deeper into the water. Any lower and she would need snorkeling gear. She let herself drift in the current created by the water jets while her mind and body relaxed. Around her, the murmur of voices blended together into an incoherent white noise.

Until she heard something she couldn't ignore.

"I don't know about you girls," Zoe said, "but I definitely think there are more hot men here than just the bachelor we're all fighting for."

"What are you talking about?" Holly asked. "Brad is super-hot. Like *hawt*."

"Yeah I know, but you can't honestly say you haven't noticed the guys following us around, right?" Zoe nodded her head in the general direction of the cameramen surrounding the pool a few feet back.

"Zoe, you know they can still hear us in here," Erica whispered.

Cassidy opened her eyes at the talk of cameramen. *What is Zoe up to now?*

"I know they can hear us, moron. That's the point." Zoe propped herself up on the edge of the hot tub on her forearms, forcing her breasts to jut out in front of her. "And I'm hoping one particular cameraman likes what he hears...and sees."

Cassidy's jaw dropped into the hot water as she realized Zoe was not only being overtly sexual, again, but this time it was projected directly at Evan. Her Evan.

Back off bi-otch. Six, seven, eight... Just relax. Keep your mouth shut. This is none of your business.

"You know we can't do anything with the crew," Erica said. "It said so on one of those forms we signed."

"I know that," Zoe huffed, "but that doesn't mean I can't have a little fun while I'm waiting around for the finale, does it? Besides, *someone* needs to give America something good to watch. You girls certainly aren't helping the ratings."

Holly rolled her eyes. "So you're going to screw around with the crew to help ratings?"

"Oh relax, girls. It's not like I'm going to sleep with him or anything." Zoe smirked. "Just a little harmless flirting, that's all. Unless of course, someone else already has her eyes on him?"

Cassidy locked eyes with Zoe.

Is she implying there's something going on with me and Evan? Why would she think that? Just because I want to jump him every time I'm near him doesn't mean I have a thing for him. I can't help it if my mind goes to dirty places when he's around. I've never acted on one of those thoughts, so what's she getting at? It's not like she can read my mind... Can she? No, idiot, she can't.

Say something, she's still staring at you.

"You can do whatever you want, right girls?" Cassidy said to the other women. "Maybe you'll even get yourself kicked off the show."

"They can't kick me out for saying hello and being polite."

I can kick you.

Cassidy tried to act unconcerned as Zoe hopped out of the hot tub and dried herself off with a towel like she was starring in a beer commercial. Then, she sauntered over to Evan using her towel to dry her hair instead of wrapping it around her body.

Cassidy couldn't hear what Zoe said to Evan over the noise of the Jacuzzi, but it didn't matter. She couldn't stand watching Zoe flirt with him. She shifted uncomfortably, suddenly feeling like she was overheating. She stood up quickly and perched on the edge of the Jacuzzi with her legs still in the water.

"You okay?" Paige asked.

"Yeah, just really hot. I think I've been in the Jacuzzi too long already. I'm not used to this kind of heat." Cassidy wiped a towel across her face, sneaking a glance in Evan and Zoe's direction. His camera was still directed at Cassidy, but his eyes were on Zoe.

Just then, Zoe laughed, throwing her head back dramatically and grabbing onto Evan's shoulder in an effort to control herself.

Nine, ten... Counting isn't helping.

"You know what, Paige," she said loud enough for the cameramen to hear. "I think this heat has gone straight to my head. I'm going to bed." Cassidy climbed out of the tub and wrapped a towel around herself, then walked toward the house without so much as a glance at Evan.

She didn't need to see if he followed her or not. A moment later, she heard his familiar footsteps fall into place behind her. Hell, she could be blind and deaf and she'd still know he was behind her—like she could sense him on the most primal level.

You might have your sights on Evan, Zoe, but as long as I'm here, his attention will always be on me.

Cassidy smiled at the image of Evan walking away from Zoe in mid-flirt. Evan was her cameraman, and nothing Zoe said or did could change that.

At the bottom of the stairs, Evan held her arm while she limped up them slowly. The strength in his hand sent a shiver of electricity down her spine. When they reached the top, he dropped his hand without a word, leaving a tingle on her skin. His touch did more to warm her than the twenty minutes she'd spent cooking in the Jacuzzi.

As she reached the door to her room, she turned to say a quick goodnight to Evan, only to find he'd put his camera down and now stared at her with his thumbs hooked in the front pockets of his jeans.

Hot. Damn. Seriously, he should be in front of the camera, not behind it.

"What was that cat fight about back there?"

"I don't know what you're talking about." Cassidy glanced away, not meeting his gaze.

"Really? 'Cause I was worried you and Zoe were about to start mud wrestling in the flower beds." He cocked an eyebrow at her. "Not that I would've minded seeing that."

"Zoe was just being Zoe, and I wasn't in the mood to deal with her tonight." Cassidy lounged against the door to her room, trying to act indifferent.

What was that all about? He's not my boyfriend so why was I staking my claim out there by the pool?

Because he's not Zoe's boyfriend, either, and he's not going to be if I have anything to say about it.

"So you were fine with all that stuff she said about hitting on the cameramen?"

"You heard that, huh?"

"Yep."

"Like I said earlier, she's free to do whatever she wants. It's her life." Cassidy held her head high and faced Evan straight on. She wouldn't let him see it bothered her when Zoe made it clear she had her eyes on Evan specifically.

Because of the show, Evan got to know every move Cassidy made and when she made it. He didn't need to know what she was thinking every moment, too.

"So it didn't bother you when she came over and flirted with me in what can barely be called a bikini?"

"Nope. Did you have a nice chat?"

"Well, we didn't really get to talk much since I had to follow you back up here."

Cassidy crossed her arms. Did he really *want* to talk to Zoe? Had forcing him to follow her into the house been a hardship for him?

"Sorry. I didn't realize I interrupted your good time. Next time, I'll cook in the Jacuzzi until I'm sure *you're* finished socializing."

Evan smirked. "I never said I wanted to talk to Zoe and you certainly didn't interrupt anything. You're jumping to conclusions." Evan leaned closer, causing Cassidy's heart to feel as if she'd just finished running a marathon.

"I wouldn't want you to cook too long. You're hot enough already." Evan reached past Cassidy and opened her door behind her. "You should get some rest. After the day you had, I'm sure you need it." He hovered over her, smiling.

Cassidy took a deep steadying breath. He was so close. She caught the slightest scent of his cologne mixed with sweat after the grueling day of filming. It smelled like a long night of fulfilled desires—wrapped in chocolate. His lips were right there—only inches from her. If she tilted her head slightly...

She ignored her own dirty thoughts. "Don't even start with me about what happened with that stupid horse. You might think it was hilarious, but I don't."

"Who said anything about the horse? I just thought you might be tired after a long day. Do you need anything for your foot before I go?"

Cassidy struggled with another deep breath.

Just you. You could rub it or something...

"No. I'm good. Fine. I'll see you tomorrow." She limped back a couple of paces into her room and closed the door, leaving Evan standing in the hall.

What was going on with her? She couldn't seem to breathe the same air as Evan without imagining what it would be like to feel his lips on hers. Those beautiful, soft-looking lips.

She needed to get a grip before her imagination ran away with her. The last thing she needed right now was to get involved with the hunky cameraman. She'd signed her life away with those contracts for the show and she didn't want to think about what would happen if she got caught making out with Evan. Not that she'd mind making out with him, but that was a whole other issue. Wanting was not the same as doing and she had to remember to keep it that way.

*

The night was still and quiet, a welcome change from the chaos of the day. Evan leaned back in his chair and took another gulp of his ice-cold beer. Cassidy was in her room sleeping while he sat out on the back patio, relishing the calm of the night.

If he closed his eyes, he could almost convince himself he was on the front porch of his cabin, away from the drama of a house full of girls. God, he missed the cabin. He ran through his mental list of things still needing fixing before winter. Hopefully he'd have the time and the money to complete them after filming was done.

"These hours are harder than I expected." Jake groaned, rubbing the back of his neck, interrupting Evan's reverie. "I think I might be getting too old for this."

"I hear you." Evan put his feet up on an empty chair. "These challenge days are brutal."

Evan and Jake had been friends for a long time. They'd met during a Miss America Pageant. Neither knew what the hell they were doing or how they'd gotten hired for such a high profile gig. In the end, they'd become good buddies.

Over the years they'd gotten into plenty of trouble together. Many mornings he'd woken up with a hangover after a late night with Jake. Those days were behind them now that they were older and Jake had a wife and kids.

Evan had been ready to settle down and start a family too, until Carter lost Melissa in a rock climbing accident and everything Evan thought he wanted changed. He often wondered if falling in love was worth it if it could be snatched away at any moment.

Then he met Cassidy. She complicated everything.

She was smart, feisty, funny, and everything he hoped for in a girl to settle down with.

But she was also here for the adventure.

That was a sore spot he wasn't sure he'd be able to get over even if there was a way for them to be together. Being adventurous had killed Melissa. And really, was an adrenaline rush worth risking your family's happiness?

Nope. Which is exactly why he'd given up flying around the world to film. His niece and brother needed him here and that was more important than any paycheck.

"How's your girl Cassidy working out for you?"

"She's fine. Who's your girl?"

"Erica," Jake said. "She's alright. But it seems like every time I turn around she's trying to talk to me. It doesn't matter how many times I explain she's not supposed to talk to me, she does anyway. Seriously,

Chip's gonna be up my ass soon about all the footage she's ruining."

"That's sucks, man. Cassidy was like that the first day or so, but she seems to have the hang of it now."

"Erica's also friends with that Zoe chick, so half the time I end up having to listen to her bitch, too." Jake rubbed his forehead like he had a headache.

"Luckily, Cassidy hates Zoe so I don't have to spend much time around her."

"I don't know about that. You haven't forgotten the whole Jacuzzi scene already, have you?"

"I wish I could." Evan shook his head. "Zoe's going to get my ass fired if she tries that shit again."

"That girl is trouble."

"I don't plan on getting mixed up with her," Evan said. "Maybe if I ignore her long enough, she'll go bug her cameraman and leave me the hell alone."

"What about Cassidy? You plan on messing around with her?"

"No. Where'd you get that idea?"

"I see the way you guys look at each other when you think no one else is watching. It seems like there might be something more there." Jake shrugged.

"Sure, I'll admit Cassidy's a cute girl, and if the situation was different I'd probably be interested in her. But I'm not about to lose my job over her."

Or follow in Carter's footsteps.

"Sorry, man. I wasn't trying to accuse you of anything with Cassidy. It's just that I've seen you with a bunch of girlfriends, many of them on-set, but I've never seen you look at any of them the way you look at her."

"It's all right. I just don't want rumors starting when there's nothing going on. Those other girls were always crew. This is different; Cassidy's on the show. Off limits." Evan brushed off Jake's accusations and peered into the perfectly clear sky. Stars twinkled and speckled the night like confetti.

Probably going to be sunny tomorrow. That means more bikinis... never thought I'd dread women in bikinis.

Evan took the last swig of beer and groaned as he rolled forward to rest his elbows on his knees. "I'm beat. I'm going to call it a night and hit the sack."

"All right, dude. See ya tomorrow."

Evan wandered back into the house, stopping in the kitchen to throw his bottle into the recycling. Susan was in the kitchen fixing what looked like a massive midnight craving.

"You're up pretty late. I don't usually see you wandering at this hour," she said over her shoulder as she stacked a few more layers onto an already huge plate of food.

"I needed to unwind with a beer. A rare taste of my old freedom before this crazy schedule started." Evan yawned and stretched his stiff muscles. "But now I'm beat so I'm off to get a few hours of shut-eye before I have to do this all over again tomorrow."

"Night, Evan. Tell Cassidy I say goodnight, too."

Evan froze. *What the hell?*

"It's almost one in the morning. Why would you think I'd see Cassidy again tonight?"

Susan continued with her food, not looking up at him. "No reason. Well, just that I have eyes and happened to notice how you looked at her in the stable when she was injured."

"I was concerned because I'm her cameraman. I don't know what you think you saw, but you're wrong...as usual," he muttered that last part. God, why did Susan have to be on *this* production team?

"Oh, really?" she laughed, pointing her fork at him. "Wrong like the last time we worked together and you ended up in bed with the model? Or wrong like the time before that when I caught you with the craft services girl? Or maybe the time before *that* when it was me you were with in the editing suite?"

Fuck.

"I know you're still bitter that what we had didn't last, but I'm not fooling around with Cassidy."

"Not yet," she scoffed.

"Drop it and mind your own damn business." Evan practically growled the words. Susan could piss him off like no one else—precisely the reason they hadn't dated long.

"No, you drop it with Cassidy. This is your one warning, then I get involved."

"If you're too jealous to do your job objectively, then quit, but leave me and Cassidy and our *working* relationship out of it."

Evan didn't wait for her reply before leaving the kitchen. What the hell was with people around here? Was he giving off some kind of "I'm screwing Cassidy" vibe? He did find her unbelievably attractive. Sure, they'd done a little harmless flirting with each other here and there. And yes, once or twice he'd had to restrain himself from doing something he shouldn't—like kiss her—but those things had always happened in private.

Regardless, he'd be more careful about how he acted around her from now on. He couldn't have people starting rumors about him and Cassidy being more than cameraman and contestant.

Especially if it wasn't true.

Tomorrow, he'd put his most professional foot forward and show everyone there wasn't anything going on between them, even if that meant turning a blind eye to Cassidy in her hot pink bikini.

*

Evan stood in his usual spot alongside the action as the girls waited to find out who would leave the show. Paige looked as if she was on the verge of tears the entire day, as did Cassidy. It would hurt her if Paige went home.

Zoe tried to hide her worry, but Evan could see it. She'd spent her time since being nominated laughing and joking with the girls as always, but Evan had seen her playing with her necklace more than ever. Obviously it was some kind of comfort to her in times of stress and she had certainly been stressed a lot in the last twenty-four hours.

"Welcome to another elimination ceremony. Tonight we'll find out who America has voted to send home." Evan tuned out as Spencer and Brad did their usual mindless and only-for-show cheesy banter.

"Here's the first envelope, Brad."

Brad opened the envelope, pulling out a white card. He paused for a moment before reading the name. "Nicole."

"Nicole, please say your goodbyes and head back into the house to collect your things." Spencer gave her a look of sympathy before shoving her off in the direction of the girls waiting to give her farewell hugs.

"Tell us the final girl going home tonight." Spencer handed Brad the last envelope as soon as Nicole disappeared into the house.

Brad took it, glancing at Zoe and Paige before opening it. Evan zoomed in on Cassidy to capture her reaction as the last name was read. Either her only real friend in the house was leaving or her only real enemy in the house would.

"The last girl going home is," Brad said, slipping the card out of the envelope, "I don't believe it. I—I really didn't think—"

"Who is it, Brad?" Spencer encouraged. "Who's the last girl going home?"

Brad looked up, obviously stricken with surprise. "Zoe."

Chapter Twelve

Cassidy eased onto the sofa as a soft groan escaped her lips. She gingerly adjusted the pillows before sighing and remaining still. Evan knew she'd been to makeup before the interview, but he could still see the darkness beneath her eyes peeking through the makeup foundation.

"Tired today?" He moved the light so it would bounce off her face at a slightly different angle. It wouldn't cure the darkness under her eyes, but it would minimize it to the best of his abilities.

"Very." She yawned. "I haven't been able to sleep well even with that huge comfy bed. I think my body is mad at me for abusing it." She chuckled and rubbed her hands along her thighs like she was trying to massage the aches out of them.

I could massage those.

"I'll try to make the interview as quick as possible today," he said, focusing on the details of the shot so he wouldn't get distracted with thoughts of Cassidy again.

"Thanks. I plan on soaking in the tub for the rest of the day. I don't know how I'm going to be able to do the next challenge feeling like this."

"I'm sure you'll be good as new by then." He tried to sound reassuring, but truthfully it seemed like the last challenge had really taken everything out of her. He grabbed his stool, the interview notes he'd made and sat behind the camera, clicking it on to record. "Okay, let's get going. What was the second challenge and how did you like it?"

"We went horseback riding at a beautiful ranch near the mountains. It was one of the most gorgeous places I've ever been, but I can't say as I loved the experience."

"Have you ever been horseback riding before?"

"No, but I've seen people riding in Central Park and I always thought it looked like fun."

"And was it fun?"

"Nope, not even a little."

"Why not?"

"Because horses don't speak English very well and I had some major communication issues with mine." Cassidy folded her arms across her chest.

"So you're saying that maybe if you had a different horse, one that listened, your experience would have been better?" he asked, unable to stop himself from smirking at her apparent hatred for her horse.

"I'm saying my experience would have been better if it hadn't involved a horse at all. Horses and I don't get along apparently."

"Can you explain a little more for me? What exactly went wrong?" He sat forward in his chair. He'd been there for the event, but she hadn't spoken about what had happened to anyone, not even Paige. He was eager to hear her thoughts.

Cassidy shifted on the sofa, grimacing a little as the movement undoubtedly made her muscles scream again. "First my stupid horse sneezed in my face, which was completely disgusting. Then she body checked me into the wall like an angry hockey player. And if that wasn't enough already, she tried to crush my foot with one of her giant hooves. Happy?"

He suppressed a laugh. "How's your foot now?"

"It's getting better. It wasn't broken, just badly bruised. The blue bruises go great with my pedicure."

"So, after you got out of the barn, and onto the horse, did your experience get any better?"

"No, I wish."

He made the hand signal for her to keep talking. Cassidy's short answers weren't enough.

"I don't want to elaborate on it." She spoke to him instead of the camera. "You elaborate on it, you were there. Why do I have to relive it when all I want to do is forget?"

"It's not as bad as you remember. Why don't you tell us what happened?"

"First of all, who's 'us'?" Cassidy asked, motioning around the room and peeking under a couple of throw pillows. "There's no one here but you and me. And secondly, I remember it perfectly well, and I don't want to talk about it."

Evan tried to remain calm even though he was on the verge of laughing out loud. She was even cuter when she was upset. "'Us' is the viewing audience who's going to watch this interview during the show. I'm supposed to ask these questions, and you're supposed to answer them. What happened during your trail ride, Cassidy?"

"You're not going to let this go, are you?" She glared at him around the camera. "Fine. After I left the barn with Corona, my stupid horse who should be sent out to pasture permanently, I waited for the other girls to get their horses ready. Then we went for a lovely trail ride."

"Did you have any trouble mounting Corona?"

"You know I—" She glared at him again. "If that stupid horse would have just stayed still. It's not my fault she moved right when I swung my leg over her back."

"Well, you did sort of kick her," he added quietly.

"Don't you dare laugh," she shouted, pointing at him. "It hurts to fall off a horse. You try it sometime and see if you're still laughing after that."

"You also had a picnic with Brad and some of the others. How was that?"

"It was fine."

"They're going to want more than that. Why don't you tell us what happened when you got to the picnic area?"

"Okay, fine. Let's just say I discovered getting off my horse wasn't any easier than getting on it so I fell. Again." Cassidy folded her arms defiantly across her chest. "And to make it even more embarrassing, I fell right into Brad and knocked him down, too. Can we please move on now?"

Evan motioned for Cassidy to take a deep breath. He didn't want her getting this worked up on camera since there was no telling what Chip would do with the footage. He had very good editors working for him and Chip used them to their full potential. He needed to make sure Cassidy didn't give Chip anything too juicy to pass up messing around with in editing.

"It sounds like there were some pretty intimate moments between you and Brad during this competition." Evan ground his teeth together as he waited for her to respond.

"Oh, Christ. I didn't get intimate with him. You make it sound like we were out doing the nasty in the bushes. It wasn't like that. I don't consider falling off a horse onto someone and knocking them and myself, asses first onto the ground, very romantic. So don't start with me about getting intimate with him when you know it wasn't like that."

"But you did end up lying on top of him, didn't you?" He smirked again at her irritation. It was sort of fun to watch her get all riled up and hotheaded.

Hotheaded and sexy.

"Technically, but not in any sexual way."

"You also shared a rather intense moment in the barn before the trail ride even started, correct? Why don't you tell us about that?"

I wish I didn't have to sit here and listen to it.

"Brad helped all of the girls pick a horse and I chose mine very quickly, so we had a few moments to sit and talk. He wanted to know how things were with me back home, and he also asked how I was feeling about him now that we've been thrown together into the show."

"And how do you feel about him?" Evan could feel the first bubbles of annoyance building in his blood.

"The same as I did before, only more embarrassed." She rang

her hands together in her lap. "Just because we had feelings for each other at one time doesn't mean they're going to come back or be the same this time around."

"But hasn't he already been kissing some of the other women? So he must be developing feelings quickly for some of them, right?"

"Yeah, he kissed Zoe in the barn. I honestly can't speak for how he's feeling about the other girls."

"So if he kissed Zoe, why didn't you kiss him?" He wanted to know the answer for his own personal reasons. "Didn't he ask for a kiss?"

"Because I'm not the kind of girl who goes around kissing every guy I meet, even if I've already known him for a while. Yes, he sort of suggested he wanted to kiss me, but I had just watched him make out with Zoe. I wasn't really feeling *in the mood* to kiss him after she'd just had her tongue down his throat."

"So you'd like to kiss him, but maybe in a more private setting, when he hasn't been kissing other girls moments before?" Another wave of annoyance flashed though him as he asked the question. He wanted to know what she planned on doing with surfer boy. Did she want to kiss him?

Cassidy rolled her eyes. "I didn't say that. I just said that was one of the reasons I wasn't into kissing him at that time. I don't know how I'll feel at another time in another place."

Wrong answer.

"So you might want to kiss him?" The tension boiling inside of him erupted to the surface as he imagined having to film Cassidy kissing that punk.

"I don't know." She rubbed her hand across her forehead as though she had a migraine starting. "Sheesh, how many times do I have to say it?"

Evan leaned forward to rest his elbows on his knees. "You seem awfully defensive about the whole thing."

"The only reason I'm being defensive is because you're twisting my words."

"I'm not twisting your words. I'm simply asking questions based on your answers. Moving on. Are you happy you've survived the vote again this week?"

"Of course. I may not be good at the challenges, and it's really weird to sort of re-date my ex, but for the most part, I'm having a good time being here and I'd like to see what happens next. I'm getting used to doing all these new adventurous things every few days. It's exciting."

And dangerous. Why can't she see that part of it, too? How many more times does she have to get hurt before realizing being adventurous isn't all it's cracked up to be?

"How do you feel about Zoe going home?"

Cassidy tried unsuccessfully to hide a grin. "I think it sucks for her but it's kind of nice for the rest of us. There's already a lot less drama around here." Cassidy laugh rang out in the room as he switched off the camera.

"Great job, Cassidy. We're all done here."

*

Cassidy glared at Evan as he turned his camera off and started shuffling through papers. How could he be so calm after all that?

Oh right, he laughed at me the whole time.

She fumed inside after barely keeping her cool during the interview. Now the cameras were off and she felt like a pot of steaming water on the verge of boiling over—and Evan risked a severe burn.

"So, you think everything that happened at the challenge was pretty funny, huh? Do I amuse you?"

"Actually, you do," Evan said, not turning around. "And it was pretty funny."

"You don't even try to hide laughing at me. Do you have any idea how embarrassed I am?"

"I have a pretty good idea, since I was there when it happened." Evan turned and smiled at her. "But honestly, Cassy, you need to calm down. I promise you it wasn't as bad as you think. You should try to laugh about it, too."

"I don't want to laugh about it. It happened on national TV. I'm going to go home eventually and I'll be teased forever about being the stupid girl who fell off her horse—twice!"

"It's not that bad." Evan laughed out loud this time.

Cassidy glared at the smirk on his face, the playful twinkle in his eyes. She grabbed a pillow and threw it as hard as she could at his cocky smile, hoping to wipe it off his face so she wouldn't have to see it anymore.

"Hey." Evan deflected the pillow with his arm. "What's that for?"

"It's for being such a cocky jerk and thinking my humiliation is hilarious."

"Cassy, I didn't mean to be a cocky jerk—ouch, name calling hurts, by the way. It's not very nice to call me names. I think you need to be a little less serious and laugh at yourself a little more. It's really not worth trying to destroy the props over."

"I'm not destroying the props. It's a throw pillow—I threw it. It's not my fault your annoying face got in the way."

Annoyingly cute. How is that possible?

Cassidy stormed passed Evan and out the door.

"Wait up. Where're you going?" Evan called, chasing after her.

She didn't glance back. "I'm going to my room, so you don't have to follow me with your camera."

Cassidy limped up the stairs as fast as her foot would let her, trying to escape Evan and his stupid smiling face. She fumbled with the lock to her door. Frustrated, she jammed the key in again but still the door wouldn't budge.

"Come on." She fiddled with the lock again. *Why won't you ever work, damn it?*

"Let me help you," Evan said quietly behind her. He took the key from her hand and slowly, purposefully slid it into the lock, twisting the handle and pushing it open.

Cassidy stared straight ahead at the door, refusing to acknowledge his help. When the door opened she pushed past it into the room.

Cassidy heard the door click closed behind her, followed by silence—glorious, laughter-free silence. If there was one thing she hated more than anything else, it was being laughed at—and horses. They were on her shit list now, too. Defeated, she sat on the edge of the bed and put her head in her hands, the tension from the day aching in her neck and shoulders.

"You know, I wasn't really laughing at you." Evan's quiet voice spoke from inside her room. "I thought I was laughing with you."

"Oh great, you're still here. I thought I made it clear your filming services weren't needed for the rest of the night."

"Good, because I left my camera in the interview room."

"Evan, please go. I can't deal with this anymore today. I'm exhausted and sore and I really need to get some sleep."

"I'll leave you alone, but not until you let me apologize."

"Apologize for what? I was under the distinct impression you didn't do anything wrong when you spent the entire interview laughing at my expense."

"I don't exactly feel like I was wrong, but you do and I'm sorry. It wasn't my intention to make you upset." He threw another cute smile her direction like he was trying to charm his way out of being in trouble.

No way, Cameraman McCutiepants. There's no way you can win me over that easily. You need more than a nice smile to get your ass out of this fire.

"Enough already, Evan." She sprang from the bed, charging at him. "If you were really sorry, you'd wipe that annoying smile off your face. You're still laughing at me even now when you claim to be apologizing."

"Cassy, come on. Let me talk for a minute."

My name is Cassidy.

"You think you're so cool, hiding behind your camera. But how would you like it if every little thing you did," she said, poking him in the chest with her finger, "was on film for everyone in the world to see?"

She poked him a few more times as she spoke. "Huh? How would you like that? Would you still think everything was so funny if you were the one people talked about and laughed at?"

"Cassy, stop poking me." Evan caught her hand and held it against his chest.

Evan's heart raced under her hand. Her heart picked up its pace to match. His hand was warm on top of hers. The heat spread quickly up her arm, dampening the angry fire inside her and replacing it with a different kind of flame, one burning even hotter. She stared into his eyes, almost forgetting her anger and annoyance.

"You're right. I shouldn't have been laughing at you. It's not as funny when you're the one in front of the camera."

Cassidy held his gaze. She could see in his eyes he meant every word.

"I couldn't help but laugh. Watching you just be *you*, almost like the camera wasn't even there, was great. You're a funny girl despite all that sarcasm and tough New Yorker attitude you try to conjure. I'm sorry if I find it amusing that you're a magnet for trouble, but you make it so damn easy."

Cassidy held her breath, not sure if she was still mad at him. He certainly didn't seem like a cocky jerk anymore. Not when he was holding her hand to his chest and staring at her with intensity she'd only seen in movies.

"I laughed because it was safer than my gut reaction."

"What do you mean? What's your gut reaction?" she whispered.

Evan's face hovered only a few inches away. He tilted her chin toward him with his free hand and held her there, his mouth nearly touching hers as he spoke.

"In the barn when you were pressed up against me, and on the trail when you were covered in dirt from falling, and in the interview room when you were throwing pillows at me, and here, now...my gut reaction has always been the overwhelming and undeniable urge to kiss you."

"It was only one pillow," she said breathless, barely able to respond. *He wants to kiss me? Ohmygod, ohmygod. Enough chitchat—do it.*

Evan squeezed her hand once then let it go. It fell to her side, limp and useless.

"But I can't let that happen, Cassy. I can't kiss you. I won't. I can't stay here—not alone with you like this."

Cassidy watched, too dumbfounded to respond, as he reached the door in two quick strides, disappearing into the hall. She stood frozen unable to do anything but stare. *Wait, why can't he kiss me?*

Chapter Thirteen

Cassidy hopped on her good foot from the bathroom trying to reach the phone before it stopped ringing. *Be Evan, be Evan.* She grabbed it on the fourth ring. "Hello," she said louder than she'd meant to.

"Hello to you, too," came Paige's chipper voice. "Why are you yelling at the phone?"

"I'm not, sorry. I was in the bathroom when it started ringing and then I had to hop to get it before you hung up. I didn't mean to yell."

"That's okay. Why were you hopping? Is your foot still bothering you?"

"It's not as bad as it was, but I'm trying to rest it before the next challenge tomorrow."

Cassidy flopped onto the bed and adjusted the towel wrapped around her. She eyed the cameras in the corners of the room. She didn't need them getting a peek at any of her girly bits while she talked to Paige.

"So what's with the late night phone call? I thought you'd be in bed getting your beauty rest by now."

"I couldn't sleep. I keep thinking about the elimination ceremony. I don't understand why he doesn't like me. Am I ugly or not funny enough or something? He can't possibly have wanted me to stay instead of Zoe. You know him better than anyone else, what do you think it is?"

She should've been there for Paige after the ceremony instead of going straight to her interview. It didn't matter that America voted for her to stay, Brad had still put her up for the vote.

"I'm so sorry, Paige. You know Brad is a big huge jerk if he doesn't like you," Cassidy continued. "There's absolutely nothing wrong with you. It's all him."

"If there's nothing wrong with me, then why did he choose me for the bottom three? There must be something I'm doing wrong."

"Honestly, I can't figure him out. He kissed Zoe in the barn then put her in the bottom two. I have no idea why he's keeping me around at all. I suck at everything. And he's already dumped me once. You've been great at everything, and you're funny and smart and so pretty."

"Thanks, but I don't think Brad feels that way." Paige's voice trembled.

"He doesn't deserve you, anyway. Besides, if it's not meant to be with you and Brad, then that means there's someone else who's totally awesome waiting for you."

"A lot of good that does me right now."

"Maybe seeing this show is how he finds you? You don't know how all of this will turn out. But you can still enjoy the process while you're here. It's not so terrible trying new things and hanging out by the pool on our off days. It's a hell of a lot better than working. And it's even better now that Zoe's gone. It's going to be like paradise around here."

"You're right. I guess I should try and enjoy it while I can. I'll probably be gone after the next elimination anyway."

"It could just as easily be me who goes home next time." Cassidy yawned. "I'm sorry, but I'm just so tired."

"I need to go, too. Thanks for the chat, I feel a little better now. I should probably try to get some sleep."

Cassidy laughed. "I need to rest up, since who the hell knows what I'll be falling off of in the morning."

Paige giggled. "Night, Cassidy."

Cassidy hung up the phone, climbed into bed and turned off the light, casting one last glance at the door to Evan's room. It had been a very interesting and intense day. She could only imagine what tomorrow would bring.

*

Evan woke to sunlight streaming in his windows. His tired eyes burned in the bright light.

All night he'd tried to sleep, but instead he'd tossed and turned. He'd been exhausted after the long day, but when it came to relaxing, he couldn't seem to stop thinking. Thinking about Cassidy and the kiss he almost hadn't been able to resist.

The urge to kiss her had been overwhelming, stronger than any desire he'd experienced before, and it'd been harder than he'd expected to walk out of her room when everything inside him yelled to stay.

How would he get through yet another competition with so little sleep and so much distraction? How would he possibly get through another day filming Cassidy without violating his work contract or his own personal vow to not get involved with anyone? At the maximum, he had another three weeks of filming left, and that was only if she made it to the finale. He could control himself for a few more weeks, couldn't he?

After last night's close call, and contemplating his every thought and feeling about her throughout the night, it was now completely obvious to him—he didn't know how, but she made him feel something different—something he needed to explore further. But was he ready for that? Was he ready to risk getting involved with her, knowing the future was anything but predictable? Knowing how klutzy this girl was?

Dating her would definitely mean dealing with his fears of her getting hurt on a daily basis. And if she really did start to like the adventurous things in life like on the show, how would he cope? How would Carter and Annie cope?

No reason to worry about that yet.

They'd both get in a heap of trouble if anything happened while on the show. Susan would make sure of that. Hell, Susan would hand him over to Chip wrapped in a giant bow if she suspected he'd fooled around with Cassidy.

After the show was over, all bets were off and he wouldn't have to worry about Susan or the production limitations. Hopefully by then Cassidy would have had her fill of adventuring, too. Then they might actually stand a chance together.

The clock on the bedside table said it was already half past nine. A few more minutes and Cassidy should be ready to head out to the competition.

He gathered up his gear and stood in the hall outside her door. He always liked this moment waiting to see Cassidy. He enjoyed letting himself imagine for a few moments what she might be wearing and how amazing she'd look in it.

Evan glanced at his watch. *Quarter to ten already? What're you doing in there?*

Evan paced as the laughter of the other girls leaving the house drifted upstairs. Cassidy should be with them. What was taking her so long this morning?

He rapped on the door quietly, not wanting to startle her. A few moments passed but the door didn't open. "Cassidy? You in there?" He knocked on it harder, then stopped for a minute and waited, listening for noise.

The lock on the door clicked and it opened a crack.

"What's up, Evan?" Cassidy yawned. "Why are you beating up my door? What did it ever do to you?"

Evan pushed the door open gently. Cassidy wore a tank top with matching lace-trimmed shorts. Her hair stuck up on one side of her head in a mess of tangles, and pillow creases decorated her cheek.

Damn, Cassy's hot. She even makes bed head sexy.

"Cassidy, why aren't you ready? We have to go."

Cassidy rubbed the sleep out of her eyes and glanced at the clock on the bedside table. She raked her hands through her hair as if trying to tame the craziness. "I can't believe I slept through my alarm. I need a shower."

"Make it a fast one. Everyone's already leaving for the competition." Evan paced around the room as Cassidy bolted into the bathroom, cursing loudly. "I'll run down and get you some breakfast while you're in the shower, okay?"

Evan ran down the stairs two at a time and went straight to the breads. The girl needed carbs to get going. He didn't have time to make anything fancy. Grabbing a couple of chocolate croissants and a bottle of water, he sprinted back to her room, hoping she'd be out of the shower and dressed by now. He could only imagine how long it would take for her to do her hair and makeup. It was already after ten and Chip would be seriously pissed if they arrived too late.

Evan stood in the hall outside Cassidy's room and dialed Chip. He picked up on the second ring.

"Evan, what can I do for you?"

"Hey, Chip. Cassidy's had a few rough competitions and I think they finally caught up with her. She sort of slept in."

Chip sighed. "We only have the facility for a few hours and we need her here before we can start filming."

"I know. She's getting ready now. We'll be there as soon as we can."

"We can't have one girl holding up production like this. Light a fire under that girl's ass and get here." Chip hung up the phone without waiting for a response from Evan.

Not good.

Evan cracked open Cassidy's door and called inside. "Can I come back in?"

"Yeah, I'm trying to finish my hair," she called from inside the bathroom.

Evan walked into the bathroom. "Here. Chocolate croissants."

Cassidy grabbed one and took a bite, chewed quickly, and took another. "Thanks," she said with her mouth full. "These are my favorite."

She looked great, as always. He was amazed she could look this good in fifteen minutes when it would take other women hours to accomplish the same effect. She had true natural beauty.

Cassidy pulled out a complicated, multi-strand necklace. She fumbled with it, trying to arrange the strands so they would hang perfectly around her neck. "Can you do this up for me?"

Evan tried to hold the two little clasps between his large fingers. He reached around Cassidy's shoulders as she leaned in toward him and draped the necklace across the front of her throat. She tilted her head to the side so he could see the clasp of the necklace behind her neck.

Cassidy's hair was still wet from the shower, but she'd pulled it back and rolled it up into a clip. The loose ends cascaded in waves to her shoulders.

As he leaned in to get a better angle on the necklace, the scent of strawberry shampoo greeted him. He hesitated with the clasps, taking a moment to inhale deeply, enjoying the intoxicating, damn it—arousing—smell.

Evan slid the clasp together then laid the necklace carefully on her neck. Her skin was silky beneath his fingers as he traced the slope of her neck. His hand lingered on her neck as his thumb kneaded the warm untouched skin behind her ear.

Cassidy pulled back slightly, her eyes questioning him. He held his hand on the back of her neck, staring into those green eyes. The same eyes that had visited his dreams night after night for weeks. The urge he'd become so familiar with nagged at him again, begged him to take action.

Just one little kiss. There are no cameras in the bathroom to catch us...

He pulled Cassidy's face to his, inching her lips closer. His breath grew heavy and deep as he paused, trying to fight the urge pounding deep in his chest. When he knew he couldn't resist any longer, he brought his lips to hers, barely touching them, like a whisper on a breath.

Her lips were warmer and softer than he'd imagined in his best dream. His mouth lingered on hers, savoring the moment, finally giving in to the longing burning inside.

Cassidy responded against him, her mouth moving eagerly. She slid her hands up his chest and gripped his shirt in a fist, pulling him closer. Her lips parted, inviting him in.

With that, his final wall of resistance crumbled. The raw emotions of the last few weeks rushed forward like floodwaters over a broken dam. Wrapping his free arm around her waist, he pulled her body tight to his. He pressed his hand against the small of her back trying to get her even closer. He panicked for a moment when he felt her mic pack. Thank God they hadn't started filming yet or else she'd have turned it on by now.

We're good. Pay attention to the hot girl.

A small groan escaped his lips as he explored her mouth with his tongue. Time became instantly irrelevant. All that mattered was the touch and taste of Cassidy.

Chocolate and mint...

Their breath grew ragged. His hand tangled in her hair as he tilted her head to the side. His mouth left hers and traveled down the side of her neck leaving a trail of kisses behind.

"Evan," she whispered. "Evan, we...we have to stop."

His lips pressed to hers again, silencing her protest. He didn't want to leave now, maybe not ever. This felt so right, so good.

Evan's pocket vibrated. Sighing, he pulled his mouth from hers and reached into his pocket with one hand while holding Cassidy close with the other, not ready to let her go. The caller display flashed onto the little screen.

Ah, shit.

"Hey, Chip," he said clearing his throat, trying to sound normal.

"Where are you guys? We're almost ready to get started."

"We're leaving the house now. We'll be there soon."

"Well, hurry the hell up." Chip hung up on Evan for the second time.

Evan tucked his phone back into his front pocket and hooked his arms together behind Cassidy's back. She peered up at him, her eyes heavy-lidded.

"That was Chip. We have to go." He raised his eyebrows and grinned at her. "I think we might be in trouble."

"In more ways than one, it seems." Cassidy motioned to his arms wrapped around her.

"This is trouble, but only if we tell him." Evan leaned forward, his lips hovering above hers. "I don't plan on telling him about this."

His lips claimed hers again. She mumbled something quietly. He ignored her and kissed her harder, deeper than before. After one final peck on the lips, he stepped back. The expression on her face was a reflection of his desire.

"Telling would be bad," Cassidy muttered.

"We have to go."

Evan walked out of the bathroom and grabbed his camera gear. Cassidy followed behind him with her purse and slipped into her shoes. He held the door open for her as she grabbed the last chocolate croissant. Watching her take a bite as she passed in front of him made the taste of Cassidy's mouth flood his mind again.

"I never knew chocolate could taste so damned good," he whispered in her ear as she passed through the doorway.

Closing the door behind him, he mentally tried to force the last few minutes out of his mind. He had to focus on work or Chip would know something had happened. No one could find out. *So much for not getting involved with Cassidy.*

Chapter Fourteen

As they walked into the crowded room, Cassidy stole a quick glance at Evan. He appeared calm and completely at ease—and sexy. So. Damned. Sexy.

She tried to mirror his expression, worried if she didn't the others would take one look at her and know what had happened between them. They hurried to join the group standing in front of a giant clear tube-like structure in the middle of the room. Everyone seemed to be eyeing it with trepidation.

What the hell is that thing?

Cassidy had no idea where they were. She'd been so focused on not thinking about Evan and that absolutely-mind-blowingly-amazing kiss, she hadn't paid a moment's attention to where they were actually driving. Now she wished she'd seen the sign on their way into the building.

She hadn't paid any attention to where they'd been *kissing*, either. Thank God they'd kissed in her bathroom, away from the spying cameras in her bedroom. A chill ran down her back at the thought of how close she'd come to making a serious mistake with Evan, like kissing him in full view of the cameras in her room where Chip would surely find out. Chip could not find out.

Chip rushed over to greet them with a scowl on his face. "What the hell took you guys so long?"

"Sorry, Chip," Evan apologized before Cassidy had a chance to respond. "I knew Cassidy was pretty tired because of her injuries. I should have checked on her earlier to make sure she was awake."

"Damn right you should have. She's your responsibility. Your mistake cost us forty-five minutes of filming time."

"I won't let it happen again."

"See that you don't, or I'll find Cassidy a new cameraman." Chip walked away, leaving them staring after him. Evan's jaw tightened in silent response.

"You didn't have to do that," Cassidy whispered. "It's my fault we're late, not yours."

"It's fine, Cassy. Don't worry about it," he whispered back. "I've worked for Chip before. He's not going to fire me. One time I showed up ready to film with the stomach flu so he can cut me a little slack for being late once. Join the other girls and blend in before we get in more trouble."

Cassidy's heart did a little flip at hearing Evan call her Cassy. It was funny how only yesterday she found it really annoying when he called her that, but now it made her feel sort of giddy. Normally she hated nicknames. But she liked the way a nickname sounded coming from Evan. She knew she would like it even more if he were groaning her nickname in bed, but she couldn't entertain that dream right now.

"Now that we're *finally* all here, let's get started." Chip stared at Cassidy to make his point crystal clear, as if any doubt lingered in anyone's mind who he referred to. "We're moving quicker than usual today since our time here is limited."

Chip motioned to a door on the left and everyone turned to stare. Brad strolled out in a dark blue jumpsuit accompanied by two other men in matching suits. They strode forward with an air of confidence and joined Spencer in front of the ladies.

"Welcome back to *The One*," Spencer said, addressing the group. "We're here today at Sky's The Limit Indoor Skydiving Training and Recreation Center. Today you're getting a special opportunity to do some exciting indoor skydiving."

Cassidy wasn't sure she liked the sound of that, but by the amount of "ohs" and "ahs" around her, she assumed the other women thought it was a great idea.

"You'll each have a turn in the vertical wind tunnel you see behind me. Together with Brad, you'll soar to new heights and maybe even to love." When the red light flickered off on the camera pointed at Spencer, he moved to the side of the room to have his makeup retouched.

Susan hustled over with a rainbow of colorful jumpsuits draped over her arms. "I need you to put these on over your clothes. Be sure to empty your pockets and remove any jewelry that isn't covered by the suit. Anyone with sandals, heels, or boots, please grab a pair of sneakers from that bin over there." She looked at the tags and started matching suits to girls. She called Cassidy's name, throwing a suit in her general direction where it landed on the floor in a bright red heap of fabric.

Nice. Why's she such a bitch to me?

Cassidy wiggled into the one-piece jumpsuit and zipped it up to her neck. It was more form-fitting than she'd expected, and left little to the imagination. She fiddled with the clasp on her necklace before finally getting it open and dropping it into one of the individual baskets provided. The feel of the necklace under her fingertips sent her thoughts back to her room and Evan's lips pressed hungrily against hers. Her body tingled at the memory of his touch—his kiss.

"Today we have Bill and Austin joining us," Spencer said, addressing the group again. "They're the two best flight instructors here at Sky's. They'll be helping you inside the tunnel while the rest of you watch from out here through the glass. Now, who would like to go first?"

"Maybe I should be the one to pick," Brad said, grinning.

"Absolutely. Who will it be?"

Brad walked up to Paige and held out his hand to her. "Care to go flying with me?"

Paige seemed nervous but nodded. After a few minutes getting ready, Paige and Brad held hands and leaned forward into the powerful upward draft. Instructor Bill guided them into the center of the tunnel where they floated on the air like skydivers in a free fall.

Suddenly, Paige flipped upside down in the tunnel. She clung to Brad's hands, accidentally forcing him to flip over with her. They both lay spread-eagled and suspended in the air on their backs like overturned turtles.

Bill used hand signals to tell them how to flip again, but Paige didn't seem to understand. Fortunately, Brad got the message and attempted to roll them both back over onto their stomachs, but struggled without Paige's help.

Paige looked frantic, her face turning red. She tried to shake Brad loose, but only managed to get one hand free and reached for her goggles.

With that, Bill grabbed her by the leg and pulled her to the side of the tunnel and into a standing position. The door to the tunnel opened and Paige jumped out onto solid ground. She gasped for air and pulled her goggles and helmet off, collapsing on the floor. Tears flooded her eyes as she struggled to get her breath.

Cassidy raced to her side. "Paige, are you okay? Are you hurt?"

"I'm...not...hurt." Paige stammered trying to catch her breath around her tears. "I felt like the wind took my breath."

The medic appeared to evaluate Paige. Cassidy recognized him as the same medic from the stable. "Hey, Cassidy. You didn't hurt yourself again already, did you?" He winked at her before helping Paige stand.

"Very funny, Mr. Funny Man. But it's not me this time." Cassidy turned away from the tunnel as Brad got ready to fly with Holly and focused on Paige, who looked like the lone survivor of a Vera Wang sample sale. Not good.

"Feeling better?" Cassidy squeezed Paige's shoulder.

Paige rubbed her forehead. "I feel so stupid for freaking out. I just couldn't breathe with the wind in my face. Then I flipped over and I didn't know how to get back the right way around. God, I'm such an idiot."

"Don't be so hard on yourself, you did the best you could." Cassidy shook her head at the wind tunnel and laughed. "You know

I'm going to suck at this worse than you, right? I've actually tripped up the stairs before and now I'm supposed to fly. Yeah. Right."

A tap on her shoulder made her turn to find Brad. He took her by the hand, pulling her toward the tunnel. "Hey, beautiful. It's your turn."

Cassidy called over her shoulder to Paige. "I'll check on you when I'm done with my flight, fall—whatever."

As they approached the entrance, one of the instructors stepped forward. "I'm Austin. I'll guide you through your flight today. I need you to put these on before you go into the tunnel." He gave her a pair of safety goggles and a helmet.

Cassidy unclipped her hair and let it fall past her shoulders. Her bulky hair clip wouldn't fit inside the helmet.

"Wow. You're so hot in that tight suit with your hair all loose and crazy." Brad cocked an eyebrow suggestively. "I always loved your hair down and sexy."

"I'll be sure to add this suit to my wardrobe," Cassidy said sarcastically, carefully ignoring his reference to the past. She peeked over Brad's shoulder at Evan. She wondered how that comment made him feel. His jaw had that familiar clenched look.

Cassidy secured her helmet and goggles. "Okay, Brad. Let's get this over with before I lose my nerve to try."

Brad took her hand again and climbed into the wind tunnel with her. The door behind them closed, leaving Evan on the other side peering in. By now, Brad had flown four times and looked like a pro. He told Cassidy to lean into the wind and the instructor helped guide them into the middle of the airflow.

Cassidy had forgotten how in control and confident Brad could be. Surfing huge waves had made him brave and fearless when it came to doing anything adrenaline inducing. His hand gripped hers and for a second, sparked a twinge in her heart.

The force of the air hitting her face took her breath away and she instantly understood why Paige had turned into a panicking, chaotic mess. Cassidy floated in the air like a kite in a tornado. She focused on taking small, shallow breaths.

And still she wasn't freaked out.

In fact, she'd never felt more exhilarated. The material of her suit whipped around her body in the force of the wind. Her arms and legs pushed up toward the roof as she glided on the strong current.

She was overwhelmed with excitement and assumed this must be what it felt like to fall out of a plane, only better—the ground was still safely located only a few feet below her. This had to be one of the most amazing feelings she'd ever experienced. Cassidy wished she could do tricks like the flight instructors. What would it feel like to do flips and spins in the air?

Before she could wonder more, Austin had grabbed her free hand, pulling her up to the side of the tunnel and onto her feet. A moment later Brad wrapped his arm around the small of her back, steadying himself. The door opened and they stumbled out of the tunnel. Cassidy laughed as adrenaline flooded her system.

"That was amazing." Cassidy said breathless from the wind and excitement.

Brad laughed and wrapped her into a hug. Cassidy hugged him back for a moment before pulling away, still smiling as she tried to remember every second of her two-minute flight, focused on committing the experience to permanent memory.

Then Brad kissed her and all other thoughts fell out of her head.

Cassidy froze as his lips pressed against hers. She tried to move away, but he held her tight. Finally, after what seemed like years, he let go. All she could do was stare at him disbelieving.

Brad smiled. "Now, *that* was amazing, and just as good as I remembered."

Cassidy didn't respond—she couldn't. How could she tell him that was without a doubt the worse kiss she'd ever had the misfortune of experiencing? Sloppy, wet, lukewarm. Possibly, it was similar to kissing a Basset hound, although she couldn't confirm that since she'd never actually kissed a Basset hound. But, if she ever wondered what it would be like, she thought she might draw back on this moment with Brad as reference. How had she kissed him for months and never realized he was so bad at it?

Because I'd never experienced a real kiss until Evan.

"We'll have to do that again. Alone," Brad whispered into her ear. Cassidy stood paralyzed by shock as Brad sauntered away, already sweet-talking the next girl. She wished she could erase that kiss from her thoughts, but unfortunately it was seared into her memory. She hoped she wouldn't suffer nightmares from the ordeal.

She sighed as her eyes naturally glanced to Evan, as they always did. Her cheeks flamed as she realized Evan had witnessed that kiss, too.

What's he thinking? It can't be good. He's doing that thing with his jaw again. He has to know I didn't want that kiss, right?

Evan had the camera pointed in her direction, but he wasn't looking at her. He focused on Brad, glaring at him across the room. She didn't like the pained expression playing on Evan's face. She liked even less being the person to cause it.

Cassidy coughed, clearing her throat, hoping to pull Evan's attention from Brad and back to her. She walked to the changing area and unzipped her jumpsuit, thankful to be in her normal clothes again.

Spencer called for the women to gather together beside the wind tunnel.

"Well ladies, you did a fabulous job flying today." Spencer clapped for the women, as if applauding their efforts. "Brad certainly has his work cut out for him this afternoon. In a little while, we'll meet again back at the house where we'll find out who Brad has chosen to be in the bottom three. Then it's up to America again to decide who goes home and who stays."

Concerned expressions crossed the faces of her fellow contestants. You didn't need to read minds to know they were worried about who Brad would choose, but even more worried about who America would vote for after the surprise at the last elimination. If Zoe wasn't safe here, no one was.

"Now Brad, there's one more very important thing you should consider while you make your decision. Up until now, it's been mostly group dates, and we know it's been difficult to really get to know these girls. For the next challenge you'll get to have another private romantic date with each of the remaining ladies."

"Oh, that does make my decision harder." Brad dramatically put his hand to his forehead like he was getting a headache thinking about having to make a choice.

"Yes it does, Brad." Spencer laughed and slapped him on the shoulder. "If only every man suffered your difficult decisions, right?"

Spencer held a huge smile on his face for the camera until given the all-clear signal then he turned and walked away without another word to the women. Cassidy was always amazed at his ability to turn his television personality on and off like he had a hidden power switch on his back.

Chip walked forward and addressed the group. "I want to see all of you out by the pool at seven, sharp. I expect everyone will be awake and on time for this evening's ceremony," he added directly at Evan and Cassidy. "You're free to head back to the house now."

Evan switched off his camera and brought it down to his side. He rolled his shoulders back and stretched his neck. "Ready to go?" he asked.

"Yeah," said Cassidy, following him out of the building and back toward the car.

The ride back to the house was silent. An awkward tension filled the tiny space between them. Earlier, they had to tear themselves away from each other, but now because of Brad's kiss, it was as if Evan couldn't get enough distance from her. Cassidy slouched in the seat. They'd had rare time alone, without any prying eyes or ears, and they hadn't even said two words to each other, let alone talked about what happened earlier in her room.

Cassidy reach for the door handle.

"Cassidy," Evan said quietly.

Oh good, he's still talking to me.

"Yeah?"

"Would you mind hanging out in your room for a few minutes so I can have a break? I need to clear my head and it would be easier if I weren't following you around. Maybe fifteen minutes?"

"Oh, okay."

"Thanks. I appreciate it."

Cassidy got out of the car and walked up to her room. Evan followed silently behind her. She got to her door and paused. Should she say something to him? But what? If this was about that kiss with Brad, she didn't know what to say. It's not like she could take it back or apologizing for something that had been out of her control.

As she turned to talk to him, the door to his room closed. Cassidy was left in the hall alone and she suddenly felt very lonely. Her chest ached. She hadn't felt this way since Brad had left her standing alone on the sidewalk, brokenhearted. Why did everyone leave her?

*

"We'll see you back here in a few days to find out who stays and who goes home." Spencer turned from the ladies to the camera. "America, it's up to you to decide which of these three young ladies still has a chance at becoming The One."

Paige stood beside Spencer in the bottom three again, already looking crushed. Cassidy knew all the girls had their own reasons for being here and that everyone deserved to stay, but she couldn't help wishing that this time it would be Holly and Lauren who went home instead of Paige.

"I'm sorry, Paige."

"Thanks," Paige said, wiping her eyes with the back of her hand. "I hope they send me home this time and put me out of my misery. I can't take hanging out for another week just to be in the bottom three again. I mean, it's obvious he doesn't like me."

"I don't know what he's thinking." Cassidy wrapped her arm around Paige. "Let's get you a drink and we'll drown your 'bottom three' sorrows until you've forgotten them."

"Sounds good. Anything to dull the humiliation of being in the bottom three—again."

Cassidy and Paige walked into the kitchen. As Paige got comfortable on the stools beside the kitchen island, Cassidy found a bottle of champagne in the fridge and a couple of glasses. She filled them and handed one to Paige.

"Champagne? Does my humiliation make you feel like celebrating?"

"Don't be silly, Paige. We're going to celebrate this experience and our friendship, which we wouldn't have had without coming here and sacrificing our dignity for the betterment of American television."

Cassidy and Paige clinked their glasses and polished off the champagne in one shot. "How 'bout another?"

"You certainly know how to put a positive spin on things."

"I know this is hard, Paige, but coming here was about more than just meeting Brad, right? It's about the experience, too. Just because Brad is too stupid to see what an awesome girl you are, doesn't mean the whole thing was a waste."

"I guess you're right. I just really wanted to fall in love, ya know?"

"I know. But you can't fall in love unless it's the right guy, and maybe Brad isn't him. I bet Mr. Right is out there now, shaking his head at the TV, wondering how Brad could be so stupid to let you go and thanking his lucky stars he'll get a chance with you."

"I hope you're right," Paige said, emptying her second glass in one last gulp of champagne. "Maybe I'll take a refill up to my room to help me pack."

"Who said anything about packing? You don't know you're going home."

"Call it a hunch or intuition or whatever. But I feel like I'm definitely going home." Paige sighed and put her head in her hands. "Honestly, I'm ready to go home. I don't think my ego can stand another round in the bottom three."

"You want help packing?"

"Sure, if you don't have anything better to do."

Spending quality time kissing Evan was out of the question since he was still acting pissy toward her. Hanging out with Paige sounded exactly like what she needed right now. Cassidy grabbed the bottle of champagne. "It could be a long night of packing. We might need refreshments."

"Good thinking." Paige grabbed it from her hand and took a drink right from the bottle before leaving the kitchen and heading up to her room.

*

Cassidy stumbled out of Paige's room, slamming the door behind her. "Shhh," she whisper-yelled at Evan. "You're being too loud."

Cassidy glared at Evan as she walked backward down the hall. "Did you just roll your eyes at me? You shouldn't do that. If you're not careful, they might get stuck that way."

"I'll take my chances."

Cameraman McCutiepants is very cute tonight. He's so yummy, I just want a little taste.

Cassidy smiled in what she hoped was a sultry way and wiggled her fingers at Evan to follow her. She leaned up against her door and fumbled with the key. "Can you help me, Evan?" She placed the key in his hand, letting her fingers linger on his.

He took the key and opened her door. "I think you might need lessons in how to open your door. It seems I help you with that key a lot."

Cassidy locked her eyes on Evan. "You can give me lessons in whatever you want tonight."

Chapter Fifteen

Evan shook his head. "I don't think so, Cassidy. What you need right now is bed."

"And here I thought you might want to pick up where things left off earlier." Cassidy attempted to make sexy eyes at him, hoping to entice him into her room for some fun.

"I think you're drunk, and you need to lower your voice before someone hears you." Evan put his hands on her arms and guided her into the room.

Cassidy gazed up at him through heavy lashes. "No one will hear us. Everyone's in bed."

"You should be in bed, too."

"Aren't you going to help me find it?"

"You're standing right beside it. I think you can find your own way under the sheets."

"Why are you being so cold? You weren't cold earlier." Cassidy walked her fingers up Evan's chest. "If I'm remembering correctly, you were very hot and very excited earlier. I'm ready for a little more excitement, aren't you?"

Evan took Cassidy's hand and gently pushed it away. "I think between myself, Brad, and a bottle of champagne, you've had more than enough excitement for one day."

Cassidy slumped to the bed feeling annoyed and confused as he turned away.

"Get some sleep. I'll see you tomorrow." Evan walked out of her room, closing the door behind him.

What the hell's his problem? One minute he wants me, and the next he can't get away from me fast enough.

Cassidy climbed under the sheets, not bothering to undress.

"How do I make my ceiling stop spinning?"

One stupid, unwanted kiss with Brad and Evan's all pissy? Doesn't he know I didn't ask to kiss the Basset hound?

Cassidy yawned and closed her eyes. Her head spun and danced like bubbles in a glass of champagne.

Best kiss and worst kiss all in a matter of hours. Weirdest day ever.

*

Evan panned the camera from Cassidy to the girls still waiting to hear their fate. Now that Holly had been sent home, it was down to Paige and Lauren.

Evan pulled the camera back to focus on Cassidy. He didn't want to watch her reaction when Brad read the last name out loud, but that's what he was paid to do. He sucked it up and pushed his zoom in closer to Cassidy, focusing on her face and the lines of worry creasing her forehead.

"I'm sorry girls, but I have to do this," Brad said, sounding genuinely forlorn. "I think both of you are great girls and I had no reason to put you in this position other than I simply felt like I had more chemistry with some of the other girls."

Sliding the card out of the envelope, he paused before reading the name found inside. "The last girl going home tonight is...Paige."

Tears spilled down Cassidy's cheeks as she stared at Paige. Evan's heart twisted in his chest at the sight of Cassidy crying for her friend. He would have given anything for the ability to comfort her, but he was working and no amount of wanting would make it okay for him to comfort Cassidy.

He was still upset about the kiss at the skydiving school, but her tears instantly dampened his annoyance. He may not be able to look at Brad without wanting to punch him in his Cassidy-kissing face, but he could still look at Cassidy all day, every day. And right now, all he could see was the sadness darkening her eyes.

Paige gave each girl a hug. Some whispered kind words in her ear, others could barely be bothered faking it for the cameras. When Paige got to Cassidy, the two hugged so tight, Evan thought they may suffocate each other, but the sounds of gasps and sobs let him know that they were indeed still breathing, even if it was through a veil of sadness.

"I know there's someone else out there for you," Cassidy whispered so quietly the mic pack almost couldn't pick it up.

"I'll miss you."

"I'll miss you, too. I'll call you as soon as I'm out of this house."

"I know it's hard to see friends leave," Spencer said as Paige walked away, "but the good news is the four of you are still here and the journey continues. For the next challenge, you need to pack a small suitcase with a few essential things."

"I have something to say," Lauren said from Spencer's side.

Spencer looked shocked for a fraction of a second before regaining his calm demeanor. "Of course, Lauren. What is it?"

"I—I'm leaving tonight, too." There was a shocked silence while her words sank in. "I know I made an agreement to stay until I was voted off, but, um, I haven't been feeling well. I saw the medic this morning and he advised me to seek proper testing with my regular doctor. I'm so sorry but I have to go."

Spencer put his arm across her shoulders in an unusual show of support. "I'm sorry, too. We're all sad to see you leave. Please take care of yourself."

As Lauren hugged each of the women goodbye, Spencer turned to face directly into the camera, addressing the viewing audience. "We'll see you again in a few days as we find out what crazy adventure these *three* girls will go on next and who will be one step closer to becoming...The One."

*

Cassidy sat on the interview sofa, her insides still turning and twisting. She knew she looked like hell, too. The makeup person had tried to make her less puffy and red, but pressed powder could do only so much.

The sooner this interview ended the sooner she could go to her room and hide for the rest of the night. It wasn't the end of the world to say goodbye to Paige, but it certainly hadn't been fun, either.

"Can we get started now, Evan?"

"Absolutely," he said sitting down behind the camera. "Let's start with the elimination this week. How do you feel about the girls chosen for the bottom three?"

"I'm really bummed. My good friend Paige was in the bottom three and America didn't give her enough votes to stay." Cassidy twisted a tissue in her hands, swallowing the tears threatening to fall. The last thing she wanted was to be on television with a snotty nose and mascara streaking down her face.

"She's a really awesome girl and I think Brad is a moron for sending her home. Of course, he never was the sharpest knife in the drawer. You know, I had to change the battery in his smoke detector because he couldn't figure out how to get the old battery out."

Evan smirked behind the camera. "Did you get a chance to say goodbye to Paige before she left?"

"Yes. It was really hard to say goodbye. Harder than I thought it would be, but then I hadn't really expected to make such good friends while I was here, either. The night we found out she was in the bottom three again, we spent some time together hanging out. I really didn't expect her to be the one sent home, and I was sad to say goodbye."

"I believe there was some celebrating done as well? With champagne?"

"Not celebrating her leaving, but we did celebrate our friendship. And yes, there may have been a glass or two of champagne involved while we packed up her stuff."

"Only a glass or two? Not, say, a bottle?"

Of course, Evan already knew the answer since he'd seen the drunken mess she'd become after said bottle of champagne, but he had to ask so the viewing audience would know her little secret, too.

"A glass, a bottle. Who's to say? Next question, please." Cassidy giggled, feeling slightly better than she had earlier with the memory of her last night with Paige.

"Why don't we talk about the challenge this week? What did you have to do this time?"

Cassidy took a deep breath before answering, happy to not have to deal with any more questions about Paige. That also meant she'd probably be able to make it through the entire interview without crying, which was a huge relief. She wasn't one of those girls who was a pretty crier. There was nothing pretty about snot, splotchy red cheeks, and puffy pink eyes.

"This week we went to an indoor skydiving facility. We flew in a vertical wind tunnel that simulates the free fall a skydiver experiences. It was so much fun."

"How did everyone do in the tunnel?"

"A couple of girls, like Paige, didn't really get the hang of it and had trouble in the tunnel, but everyone else seemed to do well."

"How did you do in the tunnel?"

"I actually did okay for a change. I know I've sucked at everything else so far, but this time I did great. I loved every minute of my flight."

"And Brad flew with you?" Cassidy heard the tone in his voice change.

"Yep, Brad went on a two minute flight with each of the girls."

"Did you enjoy your flight with him?"

There's that tone again.

"Yeah, I mean I enjoyed the experience overall." Memories of flying filled her thoughts. "Brad was actually great to fly with. He stayed calm in the wind, so he made me feel less nervous than I would have been if I'd had to go by myself."

"Do you think you'll do something like that again?"

"Sure. It was fun and different from anything I've ever done before. I would love to try it again."

Cassidy noticed Evan lean back in the chair as though he was trying to put as much distance as he could between them. It reminded her of the ride back from the challenge. That was another item on her list of things to talk to him about. Soon.

"Tell me about your flight with Brad?"

Cassidy put on the best happy face she could conjure. "When it was our turn, we had to put on these huge goggles. It wasn't the sexiest outfit ever, but I tried not to focus on how stupid I looked." She laughed, hoping to lighten the serious mood suddenly filling the room. "We held hands in the tunnel so we would stay together and not bump into each other. It was like one long belly flop in the air. When our two minutes was up, the instructor pulled us to the side to where we were able to stand."

"Then what happened?"

Nothing.

Cassidy's palms were moist from nervousness. This wasn't the line of questioning she wanted to answer. "Then Brad took the next girl for a flight."

Evan cleared his throat. "So nothing else happened after your flight with Brad and before his flight with the next girl? Nothing at all? You guys didn't speak to each other or—anything?"

Why is he pushing this?

"We felt great after the flight when the adrenaline kicked in. We laughed and hugged and talked about how awesome it was to fly."

There, now let it go.

"And then what happened?"

"Then he—uh," she sighed, feeling defeated. "He kissed me."

"And how was it?"

"Unexpected."

"Was it good?"

"It was..." She twirled a strand of hair, trying to find the right word. "Surprising."

"Did you want Brad to kiss you?" Evan sat forward in his chair.

"I wasn't even thinking about Brad kissing me, so I wouldn't say I wanted him to. I wasn't hoping for it or anticipating it." *Why is he being so hard on me? Move on already.*

"I was excited about my flight and I was so happy to have shared that experience with Brad. We hugged and it felt great. Sort of like hugging a good friend you haven't seen in years—and then he kissed me and I didn't have a chance to think about it because it happened so fast."

"So Brad is a good friend now? You guys have gotten past your differences and are rekindling a friendship—a relationship?"

There was attitude in his voice Cassidy had never heard before. She didn't like it.

"I was trying to explain how I felt after the experience. I wasn't saying Brad and I are best friends or anything, and we certainly aren't in a relationship again. No matter what happens between us, in some ways I'll always feel like he's an old friend. When you have memories with someone—especially romantic memories— it's hard to forget them. But, that doesn't mean we're best buddies or anything. He's still my ex and one spin in the wind tunnel isn't going to make me forget that."

Her temper rose like the steam from the subway vents on a hot July day in the city. *Why is he being such a jerk about everything? I've kissed Brad a million times. It's not a big deal.*

"Are you excited to be staying for the next challenge?"

She took a deep breath, thrilled to be onto a different subject. "I'm definitely excited to still be in the competition. I can't even guess what they'll make us do next, but I'm curious to see what it'll be."

"How do you feel about the private date with Brad? Are you already looking forward to kissing him again without the other girls around?" Evan almost hissed the words.

No, I'm not. Not unless you count the feeling of dread sitting in my stomach like a lump of cold oatmeal at the thought of another sloppy kiss from Brad.

"I don't know what Brad plans to do or not do, so why waste time thinking about it? This whole thing is very strange to me, okay? Can we stop talking about a kiss that may or may not happen?"

"Fine. We're done here."

Chapter Sixteen

"What do you mean, 'we're done here'?" Cassidy walked up to Evan and stood in front of him as if demanding he give her his undivided attention. He slammed his camera onto the table and started logging the footage, ignoring her.

Evan filled out his paperwork as fast as his tense fingers would allow him. It had been a very long day and they'd gotten the last interview timeslot of the night. He was tired, annoyed, and ready to put this day behind him.

"I thought it was pretty self-explanatory." He shuffled papers around the desk angrily, annoyed he had to do this tedious work when she wouldn't leave him alone and let him think. "We're done. There are no more questions to ask."

"You don't usually end the interview so abruptly, that's all."

"I ran out of questions." Evan tried to focus his energy on the papers littering the desk instead of the turmoil eating away at him.

He hadn't wanted to snap at Cassidy and end the interview prematurely, but he couldn't bear to ask her any more questions about Brad. Every time he said that name, a spike of anger ran through his body.

"Why are you so grouchy? You're acting like a jerk." Cassidy touched his arm, but he shrugged her hand off. "What's your problem?" she demanded.

Evan finished his paperwork and set it aside for the production assistants. "I'm not in the mood to be interrogated by you." He picked up his camera and brushed past Cassidy. "Goodnight."

Cassidy's stare burned into his back as he walked out the door. He should be back in the room filming her every move, not doing his own thing, but he didn't care. What he "should" do didn't matter anymore. For weeks, he'd been doing exactly as he should, but tonight he was going to do exactly as he wanted—slack off on his filming responsibilities. He was breaking the rules and he didn't give a damn.

Evan took the stairs two at a time, putting as much distance between himself and Cassidy as he could. He needed space to be able to figure out what the hell was going on with him, because he honestly had no idea why everything concerning Cassidy got to him.

Evan jammed his room key into the lock, shoved the door open and let it slam behind him. He sat on the end of his bed, angrily kicking off his shoes. Peeling off his socks, he threw them in the general direction of the closet, not caring where they landed and curled his toes into the carpet in an attempt to ease the tension.

What I wouldn't give for a cold beer and a long hike in the mountains with Aspen right now. Whenever he was stressed, Aspen and a hike always made everything better.

Cassidy was right. He was being a jerk, but he couldn't help it. He couldn't stand that little weasel Brad.

When he'd seen Brad hug Cassidy, it had been all he could do not to slug him—but when he had to watch Brad kiss her, it was more than he could stand. He'd never wanted to punch someone as much as he had in that moment. If the situation were different, he would have walked up to him and punched the smug smile right off that asshole's face. Instead, he was forced to seethe behind the camera and tighten in the focus.

What am I going to do when they have their private alone time? Try not to rip his lips off, that's what.

Evan slid back on the bed and leaned against the wall, flipping channels with the remote, stopping when he found something with lots of guns and blood splatters.

Excellent.

A quiet knock at his door interrupted the gunshots—the door leading directly to Cassidy's room, which meant it could only be one person. Sighing, he dragged himself from the bed.

He hoped she didn't expect him to follow her down to the pool or anywhere else. He was done filming for the night and if she wanted to go anywhere other than her room, she would have to go alone. Chip could yell at him in the morning, but he wasn't filming anything else tonight.

Evan opened the door and folded his arms across his chest. "What's up?" He tried to make his voice sound neutral.

"What's up with you?" She scowled at him and crossed her arms to mirror his.

"What do you want, Cassidy?"

"I want to know what the hell is wrong with you."

Evan sighed. "If you're upset about the interview, don't be. Chip will be happy with the footage we got. Sorry if I didn't ask a million questions about you and Brad and your budding relationship, but I'm tired and it's been a very long day. Okay?"

"No, Evan, it's not okay. What's wrong with you these last couple of days? I've tried to be patient with you, but your little hissy fit after the interview was the last straw." Cassidy pushed passed Evan into his room.

"Now," she continued, "you're going to explain how one minute you can stare at me like I'm a steak dinner and you're a contestant on day thirty-nine of *Survivor*, and then kiss me like I've never been kissed before, only to turn around and ignore me for the next two days."

"Hissy fit?"

"Yep. Explain."

"I did not have a hissy fit." Evan shook his head and smiled despite his anger. "Men don't have hissy fits."

"You're dodging the question and I deserve an answer."

"No, you deserve an award for kissing two different men in only a matter of hours. That's gotta be some kind of record."

"Hey, that's not fair. You and Brad both kissed me. I never asked him to."

"Well you certainly didn't try to stop him."

"What was I supposed to do, Evan? Slap him and tell him to fuck off?"

Hell, yes.

Evan smirked. "I would love to have seen that."

"Get real. I couldn't do that and you know it." Cassidy sighed. "Do you really think I wanted him to kiss me after the kiss you and I shared?"

"I don't know, Cassidy. You tell me." Evan sat on the bed as Cassidy paced the room.

"Let's stop pretending we don't know what's really going on." She'd stopped walking and was now facing him, hands on her hips, challenging him. She was feistier than he'd ever seen her. He liked it despite being totally annoyed.

Stop liking it.

"You're jealous of my *ex*-boyfriend. You're jealous of that stupid kiss with him." She didn't have an ounce of uncertainty in her voice. Damn it.

"I don't know what you're talking about, Cassidy."

"Oh no?" Cassidy sauntered toward him swinging her hips, her voice low and sexy. "So you didn't mind when he grabbed me and pulled me into his arms and kissed me, hard on the lips?"

He flinched at the memory of Cassidy and Brad kissing. Every agonizing second of that kiss was burned into his brain, and he'd done nothing but compare that kiss to one he'd had with her only hours earlier. Which had she liked more? His anger toward Brad flooded back to him.

"You're right," he admitted bluntly, annoyed that Cassidy knew what he was really thinking—that he couldn't hide his feelings from her. He hadn't exactly been subtle, but he hadn't thought he'd been obvious either.

Evan stood up from the bed, mere inches separating himself and Cassidy. She took a step backward, but he caught her arm, stopping her. Minutes earlier, he'd wanted nothing more than to be far, far away from her, but now he didn't want her to go anywhere.

"I was jealous… No, I *am* jealous, because ever since I kissed you, I haven't been able to think of anything else." *I've never had a kiss like that before.*

Evan swept the back of his hand along Cassidy's cheek and traced the line of her jaw until his hand stopped under her chin. He held her there, his gaze locked on the green eyes staring back at him.

"All this time, I've been fighting to stay away from you, trying to ignore the desperate urge I feel to kiss you." He sighed, fighting for the right words. "That kiss—it was…amazing. Stopping was one of the hardest things I've had to do in a long time."

His thumb stroked her bottom lip. He wanted to kiss her again. *Don't do it. Stop.*

"I hated seeing you kiss Brad. It was as if someone decided to use my chest for batting practice." He tried not to focus on her inviting mouth. "I couldn't believe the same lips I'd just had the most intense pleasure of experiencing, were now smashed up against the surfer boy's undeserving smart-assed mouth."

A small gasp escaped her mouth as her lips parted. The urge to kiss her flared inside him, the desire she sparked in him overwhelming. "I acted like a jerk, and I'm sorry."

He didn't want to feel this way about her. It went against his plans, but he couldn't help it. Cassidy was simply too much to resist.

"I'm sorry, too," Cassidy whispered. "I only ever wanted one man to kiss me that day, and it wasn't the surfer boy. And, there's only one I want to kiss me again."

His mouth hovered above hers. "I'm going to assume you mean me."

Without waiting for her confirmation—without letting his conscience protest—he claimed her mouth. Her lips were as soft and delicious as he remembered. Cassidy's tongue caressed his top lip, exploring and tasting him with gentle licks. The thought of her tongue exploring him anywhere else was almost too much for him to dream about.

Her tongue plunged into his mouth, her eagerness apparent, fueling the fire burning inside him. He wrapped his arm around her, pulling her body tight to his. Her every curve melted against him. His body instantly responded. Sliding his hand down the small of her back, he kneaded the rounded flesh hiding beneath her jeans.

Cassidy groaned in response, running her fingers through his hair and kissing him deeper. Her breath grew heavy and ragged to match his.

Evan's head spun as he told himself to stop. What they were doing was a serious breach of contract, but where they were headed was absolutely forbidden. Not to mention, he was pretty sure once he'd been with her fully, there'd be no way he could stay away from her—no way to avoid getting involved.

Goddamn, Susan was right—he was doing it again. But it was different this time, wasn't it?

Cassidy dropped her hands to his waist and slipped them under the edge of his shirt. Her fingers lingered low on his abdomen, caressing the trail of hair leading to the place he couldn't wait for her to find.

As she ran her hands up his abs, teasing his sensitive flesh with every stroke, he knew there was no going back. He wanted Cassy tonight and she wanted him, too. His body tingled under her touch. Her hands trailed along the ridges of his pecks, her fingers brushing past his nipples sending an electric pulse rushing through him.

Every inch of his body was aroused because of her. He needed her. Soon.

Cassidy pulled his shirt over his head. He smiled as her eyes skimmed his abs and chest with approval before meeting his gaze again, with eyes half-lidded—obviously heavy with desire.

He carefully unbuttoned her shirt, lingering for a moment

after each button to savor the small patch of ivory skin it revealed. When he released the last one, the shirt fell from her arms leaving her standing before him in only a black lace bra and jeans. He didn't know why her mic pack wasn't still wrapped around her waist, but he didn't care. He was just happy it was out of his way—one less thing to take off.

He paused, taking in the beauty of Cassidy's body that he'd only be able to dream about until now. She was stunningly gorgeous and perfectly simple at the same time. She was everything he never knew he wanted or needed. And she was going to be his.

He unfastened her bra, letting it fall to the floor then caressed her ample breast, his fingers dancing across her nipple. She arched her back and gasped as he sucked one beaded peak into his mouth.

Cassidy slipped her fingers inside the waistband of his jeans, tugging them open. Evan growled at her touch as she stroked his hardened length. He felt liked he'd waited an eternity for this moment.

"You're irresistible, Cassy." He lifted her into his arms and tossed her gently onto the bed. He kicked the adjoining door shut, grabbed his "just in case" condoms from his wallet, and shed the rest of his clothes before joining her. He quickly tugged her jeans and panties off, dropping them on the floor.

He kissed his way up her body, starting with the beautiful, delicate ankle she'd twisted days earlier. She giggled as he licked the inside of her thigh, his chin stubble tickling her skin. But when he found the junction of her thighs, her giggles turned to soft moans until she trembled beneath him.

A quiet gasp escaped Cassidy's mouth the moment he thrust into her, their bodies finally joining fully. They moved together, finding the perfect rhythm as she wrapped her legs around his waist and moved her hips in time with his. Her warm heat surrounded him, threatening to send him plunging over the edge, but he held back, hoping the night would never end.

*

Cassidy's eyes fluttered open. The room was dim and quiet, but a steady rhythm beat beneath her ear. The constant rise and fall of the tanned muscle against her cheek told her Evan was still asleep.

She sighed deeply, her thoughts drifting back to their evening together. Outstanding. Amazing. Unbelievable. Those adjectives didn't even come close to describing her night with Evan. The thought of it made her shiver with desire again.

Best sex ever. Twice!

Cassidy traced her fingers along the line of Evan's ribs. She tilted her head to watch him sleeping only to find him staring back at her with a lazy smile. She propped herself on one elbow, moving away from Evan slightly to get a better view of him.

"Don't even think about going anywhere," he mumbled, yawning. "I'm not done with you."

She blushed at the suggestion of repeating what they were already recovering from. The warmth of a smoldering fire sparked to life inside her again. "I'm not going anywhere yet. I just wanted a better view."

"I think I'm the one with the good view."

His gaze traveled down the length of her naked body. Her cheeks warmed to what must have been a bright red and she reached for the blanket to cover herself.

Evan shifted beneath her and in one quick movement she was on her back as he hovered over her. Every part of her body flared to life when he brushed her hair back from her shoulder and left a trail of soft kisses from her collarbone to her belly button.

Oh my God, he's like the Energizer Bunny.

"You," he said between kisses, "are not allowed to hide in the sheets. I've been tortured by you wearing little pink bikinis and sexy dresses for weeks. Now that I get to see you, all of you, I plan on looking. A lot."

"You didn't seem tortured," she said, breathless.

"Only because you couldn't read my mind." He smirked. "Let

me assure you, Cassy, what we did last night was tame compared to what I've been doing to you in my head."

"Evan, stop." She hit him on the shoulder, embarrassed by his words. "I can't even imagine anything more than what we've already done."

"Don't worry. You won't have to imagine for long."

Cassidy held her breath as he kissed her with more affection than she expected. Passion burned in his kiss, but an undertone of something else was present now too—something that lingered in the pit of her stomach even after he pulled away.

She forced her eyes to focus on him, not wanting to get carried away in the moment again before they'd had a chance to talk. She didn't know anything about Evan. This wasn't typical Cassidy behavior, but that's why she'd come here in the first place—to do something unlike her normal life. She hadn't realized that would include doing *someone*, too.

"You know, I don't even really know you and you've already gotten me into your bed."

"I'm pretty sure you're the one who came to my room asking for trouble."

"True. But I was looking for answers, not sexy time."

"Sexy time?" He laughed. "I like that. We should do less talking and a lot more sexy time."

"No, you should tell me about yourself, Evan—great. I don't even know your last name."

"Last names are highly overrated. But it's Burke. Evan Burke."

"Are you related to Bond, James Bond?" She couldn't help but smile.

"We're only related by our amazing ability to seduce unsuspecting women into our beds." He grinned. "It's a superpower, really. We should come with a warning label."

"So where are you from?" She tried not to laugh at his bad joke. She didn't want to encourage him to make more of them, even if he did make her giggle. "What do you do when you're not here filming me? Any other women in your life I'm going to have to worry about hunting me down because of this?"

"I'm from outside of Denver. I have a nice little cabin in the woods. I film all kinds of stuff. This is my first reality show and it may be my last if anyone finds out about what we just did. And yes, there is another woman in my life."

"What?" Cassidy gasped and tried to wriggle her way out from underneath his weight.

Evan held her tight. "Cassy, stop wiggling. It's driving me to distraction. There is another woman. Her name is Aspen and she's a chocolate brown lab who drools. Trust me, she's not going to hunt you down. Unless of course you've got a medium rare steak in your back pocket."

Cassidy stopped wiggling. She could feel his arousal and now she was the one distracted. She shifted, hooking her ankle behind his knee and tilted her hips slightly. Evan groaned and grabbed a handful of sheets beside her.

"I think I may have a superpower, too."

"If only you knew the extent of your powers over me."

"Now, about Aspen." Cassidy stared at him and narrowed her eyes. "It's not funny, toying with my emotions."

"It's not nice that you toy with *me* either." He referred to her leg intimately wrapped around him.

"True, but it is fun," she teased and adjusted her lower body again, getting as close to him as she could.

"You're playing with fire, Cassy. Careful, or it might get too hot for you. Now, any men I need to know about besides douche bag Brad?"

"None. Brad's my ex-boyfriend and I want to keep it that way."

"Oh really?"

"Yes really. What we did tonight should have proven that to you. I'd like nothing more than to be done with this whole show right now, but I'm stuck here until America sends me home."

"Well, then we're just going to have to get you sent home."

"That should be easy enough."

"We need Brad to put you in the bottom three and then America to send you home. Maybe if you're a complete bitch to him it would help?"

"I think that might send up some red flags. I need to act the same toward him. Besides, I don't want to come off as the bitchy girl on the show, that was Zoe's role and I don't want to fill her shoes."

"True. Well, there must be something really annoying you used to do to drive him crazy. What was it?"

"I don't know. We didn't really go into all that when we broke up." A part of her still wondered exactly why he'd broken up with her. It couldn't have all been only about surfing, could it?

"Okay, how about if you really suck at the next challenge without appearing like you're throwing it? That shouldn't be too hard for you," he smirked, "and I'll convince Brad anyone so terrible at the challenges shouldn't be here. Besides, he's already been with you. He should try out someone new."

"I know I suck at the challenges, but you don't have to rub it in. And could you not make it sound like I'm some used up old shoe?"

"I think you're adorable in the challenges, but from now on, you're going to have to work harder to do badly at them. We need Brad to get frustrated with you so he'll put you in the bottom three. Can you do me a favor and *carefully* suck at the challenges? I don't know if I can handle seeing you get injured anymore."

"Aww, is the big, tough cameraman worried about me?" she teased.

"I am. These challenges are no joke. I'm a little pissed Chip's putting you guys in these situations to begin with. And I might not be able to save you every time you have trouble." He rubbed his hand along her side.

She batted it away. "I don't need saving. I'm not some kid you have to protect. I can take care of myself." If there was one thing she was really sick of, it was being treated like she was too fragile to accomplish anything. Brad never thought she was tough enough to try any of the extreme sports he liked, but he didn't get any say in what she did now.

She could compete and no one, not even sexy Evan, was going to stop her.

"I'm sure you can, I just have a thing about dangerous activities."

"I'm not sure horseback riding and cooking pizza count as dangerous." She rolled her eyes.

"Did you get hurt by the horse?"

"Yes, but she was a stupid horse." Cassidy tilted her chin defiantly, a smile playing on her lips.

"I rest my case. Be careful, okay?"

"And what happens if he kisses me again? Will you save me from that, too?"

"Then I'll have to kill him."

"No, you won't. You'll have to ignore whatever goes on with me and Brad. Deal?"

"Do I have a choice?"

"Neither of us have any choices right now." She stroked her hands along the ridges of his washboard stomach. "We're officially stuck between some rock hard abs, very enjoyable abs I might add, and a hard set of signed contracts. You know, I signed contracts saying stuff like what we did is strictly against the rules. I could get sued for breach of contract. You could lose your job or be blacklisted from filming. We took a big risk being together."

"Some risks are worth the reward." He kissed her.

She kissed him back for a moment, fighting to keep her thoughts in order. "If anyone finds out about this, we'll both be in deep shit."

Evan rolled back onto the bed beside her. "I know. You're right, we broke the rules, and I'd do it again in a heartbeat if you'd stop talking for a minute and let me." He trailed his hand between her breasts and across her stomach. She shivered with his touch as a familiar ache grew again. He grabbed her hips, sliding her toward him.

"I hope it doesn't take too long to get booted off the show. I'm really going to miss these hands of yours."

"Let me give you some lasting memories to tide you over until I can get you all to myself again." Evan caressed her breast and she moaned with pleasure.

How was she ever going to pretend Evan was only a cameraman to her, when every time she looked at him she'd be thinking of these moments they'd spent together? Their plan was good, but would it be enough?

Chapter Seventeen

The bus pulled to a stop in front of an enormous chateau nestled into the base of the Rocky Mountains. The dark wooden siding made the structure appear to be part of the mountains instead of something unnatural and manmade. The warm afternoon sun cast long shadows over the immaculately manicured lawns and gardens surrounding the whole complex.

As the girls were guided into the lobby of the main building, Cassidy was awestruck by the huge pillars of wood that seemed to hold up the expansive roof above them. Rustic chandeliers of sculpted bone and horns hung from the ceiling creating a comforting glow of amber light.

But nothing prepared her for what—or *who*—she saw next to Spencer.

Zoe.

"Welcome to the beautiful and luxurious Stony Peaks Chateau." Spencer stood in the middle of the breathtaking lobby. For such a normally big personality, even he seemed small in the massive space.

"As you can see, Zoe is back for another chance at becoming The One. When Lauren had to leave, we needed to fill her spot. We asked Brad who he'd like to have back for another chance and luckily Zoe was able to join us again."

"Lucky us," Cassidy grumbled.

"This is where we'll be staying for the next few days. This is also where we'll have our last elimination ceremony. Only two of you will be finalists, and it's only those two girls who will return to the house. Each of you received a key to a room and in it you'll find the bag we asked you to pack after the last elimination ceremony.

"While we're here, you'll each go on a special private date with Brad. Erica and Cassidy, your dates are tonight. Zoe and Savanna, you'll go on your dates tomorrow night. Erica," Spencer said, turning his attention to her, "Brad will pick you up at your room at six." He turned to Cassidy. "And he'll be at your room at nine. All right, girls. Go find your rooms."

Cassidy and Evan squeezed into the elevator with Zoe and her cameraman. They rode to the fourth floor in silence, watching the numbers as the elevator rose. Finally, the door chimed and slid open in front of them.

Cassidy glanced between her key and the brass plaque on the wall and followed the arrows pointing in the direction of her room. She stopped outside room 415 and stuck the plastic keycard into the lock, twisting the handle. The door didn't budge but the red light beside the lock blinked brightly.

"What do you think you're doing?" Zoe snapped beside her. Cassidy jumped, not realizing Zoe had followed her down the hall from the elevator.

"I'm trying to get into my room. What does it look like?" Cassidy shoved the keycard into the lock again, frustrated.

Why the hell can't I ever open a frickin' door?

"That's my room. Did you forget how to read numbers?"

Cassidy took a deep breath and squared her shoulders. "What's your problem, Zoe? I can read fine. This is my room."

Sneaking a peek at her key, Cassidy checked to see if the number on it matched the one on the door. She sighed with relief when they did. She slipped the key gently into the lock and waited for a light to blink. This time, the lock blinked green instead of red. She pushed the door open. *When will locks stop hating me?*

"There must be a mistake. My key says 415 on it and—" Zoe fell silent.

Just inside the door sat two suitcases. An envelope sat neatly placed on top. Beyond that, a large sprawling room stretched out in both directions and large picture windows offered an amazing view of the mountains.

Cassidy picked up the envelope and read it quietly to herself. "It says the two of us are supposed to share this one suite. Camera crew included because of ongoing filming and lack of additional wall-mounted cameras throughout the hotel."

It's not enough she's back, now I have to share a room with her? Awesome.

Cassidy stole a quick glance at Evan, unsure of whether this was good news or bad. Well, it was bad that they were stuck with Zoe, but it could be good to be stuck with Evan. Of course the temptation of Evan sharing such close quarters with her could be bad, very bad.

Zoe laughed. "Well played, Chip. Well played. I didn't see this twist coming." She wandered into the suite. "Of course, I'm not too crazy about sharing."

"It's only for a couple of days. I'm sure we can manage to live with each other that long."

Zoe put her hands on her hips and faced Cassidy with an expression of amusement. "I would rather sleep in the lobby than bunk with you. But the show must go on, as they say." Her eyes flickered to Evan. "Maybe bunking with your hot cameraman isn't so terrible."

Zoe grabbed her bag and disappeared into one of the bedrooms, slamming the door in her wake.

"I think that room is officially yours," Cassidy said to Zoe's cameraman, pointing to the room beside Zoe's closed door.

Cassidy walked across the living room to the other bedrooms. "I'll just go get myself settled and ready for my date tonight." Evan followed Cassidy into her room and she closed the door behind them leaving Zoe's cameraman standing in the living room alone.

"I can't believe they stuck me and Zoe in the same room," Cassidy whispered, clicking off her mic pack. "They'll be lucky if we both make it out of here alive."

Evan put down his camera and did a quick check through the room for hidden cameras. Despite what the note had said, Cassidy guessed Evan trusted Chip just about as much as she did, which wasn't a lot.

"I think our bigger problem is making sure we don't get caught being too friendly with each other," Evan said. "Zoe's waiting for an excuse to get you thrown out of the competition."

"I want out, but not in a way that will lead to me being sued. It's only a couple of days. We'll be on our best behavior and hopefully I won't make it past the next elimination."

"If you can manage a crappy enough private date with surfer boy, it should be easy for him to eliminate you. Until then, it's going to be tough keeping my hands off of you." Evan wrapped his arms around her and pulled her into a tight embrace. "I hate that you're going on a date with Brad tonight, and I hate even more that I have to be there to witness it."

"I promise I won't enjoy a single second."

"You better not. And you better do something to avoid another kiss with him. He had his chance with you already. His loss is my gain." He traced the outline of her lips then kissed her softly.

"I'll try, but what am I supposed to do if he tries to kiss me? I'm on a dating show, remember? And it's not like we've never kissed before, so I can't use the excuse of not wanting to kiss someone I've just met."

"Don't remind me."

"I need a good reason for not kissing him."

"How about don't brush your teeth and eat something with lots of onion and garlic? Oh and cough and sniffle a lot like you're getting a cold. Snot is not sexy."

"Thanks for the tips. Maybe my dragon breath will be enough to scare him away so I won't have to use the snot tactic. Snot is not good for television ratings."

Cassidy slid her hands up to his broad shoulders and pulled him toward her. Brushing her lips against his, she took a moment to savor the surprise on his face before pressing her lips to his. She longed to be with him again. To feel his naked body pressed against hers. The bed behind her was all too tempting.

Cassidy pulled away from Evan and gave him a slow smile. "Sorry, I couldn't resist."

"Don't ever be sorry, Cassy." Evan held her tight for another few seconds, his hands stroking her back. "Just remember this moment later tonight when the surfer boy tries to put the moves on you."

"I won't be able to think of anything else, trust me." She pulled out of Evan's grip and switched her mic pack back on. Walking across the room, she lifted her suitcase onto the bed and zipped it open. As she started to unpack, Evan picked up his camera and began to film in silence once more.

If only America knew what really happened when the cameras stopped rolling.

*

Cassidy heard a knock at the door and cringed. It was time for her date with Brad and she would rather sit naked on a ski lift in the middle of winter than spend another moment alone with him. But she had to go. It was part of the show and she couldn't bail on dinner.

She grabbed her handbag and opened the door to find Brad grinning. "Hi, beautiful."

"Should we get going?" Cassidy asked, ignoring his term of endearment. The quicker they left, the quicker the date would be over.

"Yeah, I have big plans for us tonight." He arched his eyebrows at her suggestively.

Cassidy's stomach rolled. "Oh, that's great. What exactly do you have planned?"

"I can't tell you, it would ruin the surprise." He took her hand and led her out the door. "I'd rather show you."

They walked hand in hand to the elevator. Brad punched the button for the sixth floor. As the door closed in front of them, he let go of her hand and put his arm around her waist.

Her back stiffened involuntarily at his touch until he pulled her gently to his side. Her body fit into place under his shoulder like she remembered. The soft musky scent of his cologne drifted in the air around him, making her relax.

The scent brought back a flood of memories she'd forced herself to forget when he'd left. Suddenly, she was back in Central Park, with Brad's arm around her like this as they'd wandered through the park on their way to watch the ice skaters twirl on the rink. His body was warm next to her on that crisp, cold day. Her mind skipped forward two weeks later to the day he'd left her standing on the sidewalk alone and heartbroken.

Her heart ached at the memory of a time when they were happy together.

The elevator chimed, bringing her back from the photo album in her head and the doors slid open revealing the entrance to the chateau's most upscale restaurant. The lobby floor was paved with river stone. Fake votive candles bobbed on the surface of small pools of water which had been set directly into the floor and covered with glass, their light forming the pathway into the restaurant. Along one wall, a waterfall trickled from ceiling to floor creating a slight mist in the air. The overall effect was enchanting.

"Good evening, Mr. Murphy," a young girl dressed all in black said. "It's nice to have you join us again tonight. Miss Quinn, it's a pleasure to have you with us. If you'll both please follow me."

Classy. He brought Erica here earlier.

They followed the hostess through the dining room to the outdoor terrace. Cassidy's eyes widened as she took in the scene before her. Immediately in front of them was a small table set for two with pristine white linens, gleaming silver settings, and a small candelabra in the middle bathing the table in a soft circle of light.

Beyond that, a queen sized outdoor sun bed was draped in a canopy of white organza that billowed in the slight breeze as it hung gracefully to the floor. A collection of pillows and a strategically placed blanket created an ideal setting for a romantic encounter.

Millions of pillows on a bed big enough for two, candles, and a freaking amazing view. Hmm, someone's hoping to rekindle some magic tonight.

The view was breathtaking, but Cassidy couldn't bring herself to enjoy it. She wanted to be here with Evan, not Brad.

Brad stood beside her. "Amazing, isn't it?"

"It's gorgeous."

"The view's not the only gorgeous thing here tonight." He draped his arm across her shoulders. "I'd forgotten how beautiful you are."

She shrugged his arm off—the familiarity of his touch was too likely to bring back more memories. "I'm sure there are plenty of beautiful women in California. I can't imagine you would've wasted too much time thinking about the one you left in New York."

"Let's not do this here, Cassidy." Brad shifted away from her. "Why don't we sit and have a little dinner. It's late. You must be starving by now."

She turned to face Brad. "I guess you're probably not hungry if this is your second time here tonight."

"True, I was here earlier with Erica. But, I saved the best for last. Now that she's out of the way, we can relax and see where the night takes us without any time limits."

It's going to take me back to my room in about, oh, two hours.

Cassidy sat at the table and laid the napkin across her lap. "Is there a menu, or is someone going to bring us the house special?"

"I hope you don't mind, but I've taken the liberty of ordering for you." Brad smiled, confidently. He poured himself a glass of red wine before filling hers. "Cheers," he said, raising his drink. "To a wonderful night to come."

To making it out of here without tongue wrestling any more Basset hounds.

Cassidy took a sip of wine. The alcohol instantly warmed her insides. It wasn't the best wine she'd ever had, but it wasn't the worst. She would have preferred white wine tonight instead red, as usual—not that she expected Brad to remember that.

A waiter appeared and set two small plates on the table. Her stomach twisted as she peered at the gray slime in a shell someone called food.

"Oysters on the half shell. I hope you like them." Brad smiled.

"I can't say as I've ever had them." Cassidy picked up an oyster to examine it. It wiggled in the shell, taunting her.

"Well, you forced me to try one of your favorite foods, so I thought it was only fair that you have to try one of my favorites."

"Oysters and pizza are not a fair swap."

Brad put a shell to his lips and tipped it into his mouth. He swallowed it quickly, motioning for her to try one as well. "You know, they say oysters are an aphrodisiac."

Cassidy tipped the wiggling gray contents of her shell into her mouth. As it slid to the back of her mouth, her gag reflex triggered. Quickly, she spit the oyster into her napkin, trying to be discrete.

"Do they also say they're slimy?"

"Not your thing I guess. At least I had the decency to swallow your pizza."

Is he upset that I didn't like what he ordered or that I didn't eat the aphrodisiac? It would take more than that, surfer boy.

Two waiters materialized on either side of the table. The first whisked the oysters from the table and the other placed two new plates in front of them. A few leafy greens and some mixed vegetables lay in an artistic pile in the middle of a large plate. A deep red dressing drizzled in a zigzag and a petite triangle of cheese finished the dish.

"Enjoy your dinner," the waiter said.

Dinner? This isn't dinner. This is the salad that comes after the appetizer and before the dinner.

"Hopefully you'll like your salad a little more than the oysters."

Cassidy ate her salad in silence, enjoying the mix of sweet and savory as the ingredients mingled together in her mouth. *Would it kill them to stick a little chicken on here?* "That was...nice." She wiped her mouth with her napkin.

"Good. I figured why bother with steaks when you girls are

always watching what you eat. It's such a waste when you pick at your meal instead of actually eating it."

Wine. I need to drink more wine. Stupid surfer boy must be used to dating anorexic waifs in California. I like steak. I eat steak.

Cassidy sipped her wine and remembered that this date was only a sham. She wasn't here for Brad anyway so if he was a total idiot, it didn't matter. He would be someone else's idiot soon enough and she'd finally be rid of him for the last time.

Then she could have Evan. Wonderful, kind, super-hot Evan. Evan, whose biceps bulged deliciously while he held the camera. *Yum. He'd make a good snack later...*

"Cassidy? Earth to Cassidy."

Cassidy's attention snapped back to Brad.

"Where did you go on me? I want to know exactly what you're thinking right now."

"Nothing. Just enjoying the view. It's so gorgeous, it's hard to stop looking." Her eyes flickered from the mountains to catch Evan's gaze. A knowing look flashed between them as instantaneous as a spark from a match. Apparently they were both thinking about other things they'd rather be doing right now.

"I think our dessert is ready." Brad reached across the table and refilled her wine glass. "Let's take our drinks and move to the bed where we can be more comfortable."

Brad took her hand and helped her out of her chair as she grabbed her wine glass. He led her to the sun bed and sat down, patting the mattress for her to join him.

Crap. How am I going to get out of this one?

She prepared herself for what she knew was going to be a completely awkward situation, and sat, carefully perching on the edge of the bed.

Brad chuckled. "That can't be comfortable. Come and lie on the pillows with me and really enjoy the view."

Cassidy gingerly climbed onto the bed and lay back against the pillows. Brad stretched out beside her, one arm tucked behind his head, the other holding his wine glass.

"This is the life, huh? Nice wine, a beautiful woman, and a great view. The only thing missing is the ocean and this night would be perfect."

That's uncharacteristically sweet.

"Do you miss the ocean?" she asked. "You must've gotten used to spending a lot of time at the beach again since going back, huh?"

"I miss it more than I expected. But she'll be waiting for me when I'm done here, and I'll be back in the water before I know it, hopefully with a hot new babe beside me on a board of her own."

"Is being a surfer a requirement for a girlfriend? You know that's not something I'm going to do anytime soon."

"No, it's not a requirement, but my next girlfriend has to be willing to at least try. I love the water and I can't imagine being with anyone who feels differently."

"Then why are you keeping me around? You know I'm not getting back in the water again after what happened with the canoe."

She'd been twelve at the time. Her family was vacationing at the Finger Lakes again and had borrowed a couple of canoes from other campers. A water fight broke out. Everyone laughed. Cassidy stood to splash Keira but had flipped the canoe instead. Cassidy remembered hitting her head and then everything going dark. They told her later that her father pulled her out of the lake unconscious. She'd been terrified of water since.

Brad shook his head. "I don't understand why you let that stupid fear run your life. If you're my girl again, are you going to sit with your ass in the sand your whole life watching while I ride the waves?"

"Or maybe I'd have my own life and I wouldn't be stuck sitting around watching you. Did you ever consider your girlfriend might have her own plans which don't revolve around you, or do you plan on finding a puppy to follow you through life?"

The silence was thick between them. She hadn't meant to be

catty, but he made it so easy to dislike him. Why did he always have to say something stupid?

"I'm sorry. I didn't mean to imply you wouldn't have a life of your own. I'm hoping to find a girl who *wants* to ride the waves of life with me. I thought there might still be a chance you wanted to be that girl."

Cassidy sighed. She'd overreacted to Brad and he hadn't meant to be jerk to her. He was trying to find the right person like everyone else. She'd forgotten how sweet he could be.

"I'm sorry, too. I didn't mean to jump on you like that. I guess if you mean waves figuratively speaking, then that's very sweet. But if you're being literal, I'm not sure what to tell you. I'm not ready to ride any waves yet, but I guess maybe for the right guy, I might be willing to get out on the water again. Eventually."

Brad rolled onto his side facing her. He clinked his glass against hers and smiled. "Here's to getting you out on a board one day."

What could she say to that? She'd forgotten his romantic side, but sitting with him now, it was easy to listen to his idealistic hope for the future.

Brad readjusted himself on the pillows and set his wine glass on a table beside the bed. She sipped of her own wine before resting the base of the glass on the bed between them. He stroked his hand up and down her arm, lingering in the soft fold at her elbow like he'd done many times in the past when they'd been cuddling on the couch in her little apartment.

She closed her eyes and could almost remember the feelings his touch used to spark inside her. So many nights they'd stayed in, enjoying each other's company. She'd been so lonely when he'd left for California it was like her tiny apartment had doubled in size. Opening her eyes, Cassidy remembered Evan behind the camera and any thoughts of those old feelings about Brad faded a little.

"Cassidy, I'm sorry I left you the way I did. The truth is, I've missed you. A lot. I've missed us—together."

I've missed you, too. She glanced at Evan again, uneasiness settling in her stomach with the wine.

"I want to start over, Cassidy. I want you back in my life and I know we'll find a way to make it work."

Cassidy's head spun. How many nights had she laid awake wishing to hear him say those words? Finally hearing he regretted at least a tiny bit of his choice made her feel a little more whole again. Maybe she wasn't a person who no one would ever love enough to stay with. Maybe she really could have a future with someone—now the question was, *who?*

Chapter Eighteen

Brad wrapped his hand around the back of her neck, pulling her toward him, their lips inches from touching. His hand tangled in her hair. "Cassidy, I want you. Let's see if those old feelings are still here."

He moved toward Cassidy so quickly she didn't have time to move her glass before he rolled into it, sloshing the wine out of the glass and onto her shirt. She yelped as the dark red liquid seeped into her clothes.

"I'm so sorry." Brad took her glass out of her hand and blotted the front of her shirt with a napkin.

Cassidy leapt off the bed and away from Brad's groping hands. "I don't think that's going to help. I need a clean shirt."

"Sure, let's get you back to your room so you can change and then we can continue our date."

Cassidy tried to hold her shirt away from her skin. It was chilly out on the terrace in wet clothes. But her wet shirt wasn't the only reason for the chill dancing along her spine. She wasn't even sure she wanted to kiss Brad again—especially not in front of Evan.

This date had gotten way too serious way too fast and she wasn't sure she was interested in exploring any old feelings with Brad. She'd spent so long getting over him she didn't want to bring those feelings up again. They were best left in the past, weren't they?

"I don't think so, Brad. I need to take a shower and rinse off. And if I don't soak this shirt right away, it'll be ruined."

He stuffed his hands into his pockets. "Fine. I'll walk you back to your room."

They left the terrace and walked back to the room in silence. Cassidy couldn't think of anything to say that wouldn't lead to Brad thinking she wanted to carry on the date. She hadn't planned on spilling her drink all over herself, but it had worked as a great excuse to end the date early and without a kiss. If her blouse was the only victim in all of this, then it was a small price to pay.

"Good night, Brad. Thanks for the, um, interesting date," she said, stopping in front of her room door.

"How about a quick kiss to end our evening?"

"I'm not sure I'm ready for that yet. Okay?"

"You didn't object last time."

"Last time I didn't have time to object. I'm sorry. I'm just not ready." She opened her door and exaggerated another shiver. "I'm getting a chill from being out in the cold in this wet shirt, which is going to be ruined soon if I don't deal with it. I'll see you at the ceremony, okay?"

She disappeared into the safety of her room without waiting for a reply, sighing with relief that she'd managed to survive the night kiss-free. Now she had to survive living with Zoe without pushing her out the window.

She also had to find a way to keep her hands off Evan when all she wanted to do was explore every inch of his delectable body. That shouldn't be too hard, right?

*

Evan stood by the window silently filming Cassidy reading on the couch as Zoe buzzed around the room, stopping in front of every mirror to check her reflection and straighten her clothes. Cassidy sank into the corner of the couch, as if trying her best to be invisible.

"What are your plans for this evening, Cassidy? Oh right, nothing." Zoe asked while touching up her lip-gloss in the mirror. "You know, since you screwed up your date with Brad, you might want to pack your things."

"Maybe I will. You enjoy your date with Brad. It should be really original since it's his fourth in two days." Cassidy smiled. "How does it feel to be chosen last? Silly me. You're used to being last, aren't you? That's why you keep doing reality shows, isn't it? Because you always lose."

Cassy has claws.

"He saved the best for last, that's all. He wanted to get all the other dates out of the way so he could have a real date with me."

"If I know Brad—and I do *know* Brad—he's had a line for each girl about how special her date is to him. I wonder what line he'll use on you."

"You're just jealous because Brad realized his mistake letting me go, but he never did with you, did he?"

"You're right. I'm totally heartbroken that my ex is still my ex."

They were interrupted by a knock at the door. Zoe fixed a few stray hairs in the mirror before casually answering it.

"Hi, Brad." Zoe's voice sounded sweeter than a child eating cotton candy while floating down Willy Wonka's chocolate river, and equally as nauseating. "Let's get out of here before Cassidy tries to salvage her chance with you."

"She's welcome to join us if she wants another chance. The more the merrier, right?" Brad laughed.

"Wrong." Zoe practically growled, pushing Brad out the door and slamming it behind her.

Silence fell over the room. Cassidy flipped pages of her magazine and yawned. Rubbing her eyes, she stretched like a cat awaking from a deep sleep.

"I can barely keep my eyes open tonight." Cassidy yawned again. She got up from the couch and put her glass in the sink, rolling her shoulders like she was trying to ease the tension in them after a long day. "I know it's early, but I'm going to call it a night. See you tomorrow."

Evan stood where he was and kept filming as Cassidy walked into her room and closed the door.

One corner of his mouth turned upward in a crooked grin as he clicked off the record button on the camera. He lowered it to his side and gently knocked on Cassidy's door before opening it without waiting for her reply.

She lay on the bed, her eyes filled with passion and need. Her mic pack was already off and in a pile on the bedside table.

"Tired enough to go to bed before ten, huh?" he joked, stepping into her room and closing the door tightly behind him.

"Extremely tired. I can barely keep my eyes open long enough to get out of these clothes and into bed."

"I'm sure I can help you with that, Miss Quinn. What kind of a gentleman would I be if I didn't help a lady in distress?"

"Still trying to save me, huh?"

"About that," he started. He didn't want to talk about this now, but he couldn't go on letting Cassidy think he was some overbearing boyfriend, either. "I'm not trying to be overprotective. It's just...I lost my sister-in-law in a rock climbing accident. I can't help but worry whenever I see someone I care about do something dangerous."

"I'm sorry, Evan. I had no idea."

"I don't think you're incapable. Klutzy, yes. Incapable, no."

"Well at least you've finally figured out the difference."

Crawling up the bed, he raised the hem of her shirt to reveal her silky ivory skin beneath it, and caressed the soft line of her hips that peeked out from under the edge of her pants. He gave her side a nip with his teeth.

He fingered the zipper on her jeans, peering down at her trying to take in every detail of her perfectly irresistible body. She was beautiful in front of the camera, but she even better in real life. He wanted nothing more than to have his way with her again, even though that was the last thing they should be doing if they wanted to keep their secret safe.

"Wait. We can't do this," she said as if she'd just read his mind.

"Cassidy, it's fine. No one will find out."

"No, Evan, please. Not like this." Her eyes pleaded with him.

He knew in that instant he would do anything to make her happy. He gave her a quick kiss before settling himself on the bed beside her instead. He tried to think of something other than the sexy woman lying next to him.

"I know we shouldn't do this, Cassy. I just have so much trouble resisting you when I finally get you alone." He sighed deeply. "I guess we could talk instead?"

Evan startled as Cassidy climbed on top of him and straddled his hips, running her hands up his chest. His body ached under her.

What the—?

"Who said anything about talking? Just because I'm a girl doesn't mean I want to spend all my time talking." Cassidy toyed with the buttons of his shirt.

He could see the desire in her eyes. He wasn't sure he understood what was going on, since one minute she told him to stop and the next she was on top of him. But he was willing to go along for the ride.

"I've had to watch you hiding behind that camera for days and the only thing I've been able to think about is what I'd do to you when I finally got you alone. Now that I have you, I want to do things my way."

"Don't let me stop you," he encouraged.

"Don't worry, I won't."

Evan ran his hands up her thighs, stroking them in anticipation. He held his gaze on hers as she fondled the top button of his shirt. He assumed she would tease him by opening each button slowly, so he steadied himself against his overwhelming desire to take control of the situation and speed things up. If she wanted to do things her way, he would do everything in his power to resist his own temptation to ravish her, even if it was torturous for him.

Without warning, Cassidy grabbed the edges of his shirt and ripped them apart. The buttons tore from the threads and scattered across the room making little clinking noises as they hit the floor around the bed.

Holy shit. That's hot.

"I've always wanted to do that." Cassidy giggled before pressing her warm lips to his newly exposed chest.

He sucked in a quick breath as her mouth opened, her tongue gently flickering across his erect nipple. Desire raged inside him as he struggled not to rip off her clothes like she'd done to his shirt.

"Oh God, Cassy. You're driving me crazy," he moaned.

"Good," she mumbled against his chest. "That was part of my plan."

Cassidy's hands traveled down to his waist and quickly unfastened his button. She shifted to the side, putting all her weight onto one knee while still hovering over him. Pulling his remaining clothes off, she discarded them at the end of the bed before running her hands back up his now naked legs. She positioned herself over the top of his thighs, her eyes roaming across his fully naked form. His body ached under her touch as she slowly stroked his length.

"Maybe we should talk a little since I still don't know much about you." She pulled her shirt over her head, throwing it to the side of the bed and out of the way. His took in the blue satin and lace bra hiding her breasts.

"How many brothers and sisters do you have?"

"One brother, but I don't want to think about him right now." Carter was the last thing he needed a reminder of while he broke his own rule and got more involved with Cassidy.

He skimmed his hands back up her thighs and wrapped them around her hips, pulling her further up his body, her jeans rubbing against him in the best possible way. He reached for the button on her pants, but she batted him away.

"No touching. What's his name?"

Evan tried to focus on her question as she reached behind her back with one hand to undo her bra. She wrapped the other arm across her chest holding the bra in place as the straps fell loosely down her arms.

Brother? Name?

"I have no idea. You're killing me, Cassy. I need you."

"How sad. You can't even think of your own brother's name."

She let her bra fall from her chest and tossed it to the side. "I have a sister. Her name is Keira. She also lives in New York City."

Evan's toes curled as he tried to find the strength to play along with her game. She was lucky he had the patience of a kindergarten teacher.

He gripped her hips hard with both hands so he wouldn't be tempted to reach up and touch her breasts. They were possibly the most luscious things he'd ever seen. *Have your fun now, Cassidy. My revenge will be sweet—and slow.* He shook his head to clear the fog of desire preventing his brain from thinking.

"What's your favorite food? What do you like to do when you're not working?"

Evan's body shivered with desire as Cassidy flipped the button open on her jeans and unzipped them, revealing the smallest glimpse of blue satin. His pulse raced as the back of her hand brushed against him. She peered up at him through heavy lashes and bit her bottom lip.

"His name is Carter," he said in a rushed voice. "There's almost nothing I like better than a grilled steak and a cold beer. I like fishing, hiking, and working on my cabin, and if you don't have your way with me soon, I'm going to pass out from lack of blood to my brain."

"You're not enjoying my little 'get to know you' session, are you?" Her body vibrated against his as she laughed, making his ache infinitely worse.

"I want to get to know every little thing about you. But right now, the biggest thing I want to know is how much longer you plan on torturing me."

Cassidy leaned forward, her breasts only a fraction of an inch from touching his chest. She placed her arms on either side of his head, propping herself up so her body wasn't touching his. Her mouth came down on his hard and firm, demanding his full attention.

He responded, tangling his tongue with hers. His hands fondled her breasts, enjoying the fact that she was too busy holding herself up to stop him.

She pulled back from their kiss, her eyes sparkling. He wasn't sure he'd ever seen anything as beautiful in his entire life.

"Just one more question."

"No more questions." He flipped her onto her back, peeling off her remaining clothes, throwing them to the floor and out of reach before she had time to protest. He was done with her games. "I tried your way, but your way takes too damn long."

Evan wrapped his arms around her, pulling her body tight against his own, and rolled onto his back, bringing her with him. She straddled his hips again, pausing for a moment while he put on a condom before sliding into her heat. He moaned with pleasure as her hips rocked to meet his thrusts.

"This was my way," Cassidy whispered, before kissing him again.

Together their breathing grew labored with the steady rhythm of their bodies moving in unison. Their pace quickened and she arched her back, saying his name in a raspy breath. As she trembled around him, he gave in to his own satisfaction.

"Maybe I do like your way," he said between heavy breaths.

"I thought you might."

Evan liked feeling Cassidy pressed against his side with her head resting on his chest. *I'm getting in too deep.*

"You, Cassy, are a bad girl in a Catholic school girl uniform." He sighed again, stroking his hand along the length of her side, enjoying her soft curves and caressing the intimate areas he found.

"Evan, stop," Cassidy said, even though her body clearly didn't want him to listen. "Zoe will be back soon."

"Fine, but next time we do it my way." He kissed her deeply, his body instantly becoming aroused again. "I guarantee it'll involve a few games, and not one of them will be twenty questions."

"I look forward to—" Cassidy's voice trailed off as the sound of muffled laughter interrupted her.

Evan froze. The laugh definitely belonged to Zoe and it didn't sound far away.

Chapter Nineteen

"Shit. Zoe's in the hallway outside the suite." Evan sprang from the bed. He scrambled around the room collecting his clothes and throwing Cassidy's in her general direction.

"Quick. Get dressed before they come in," he ordered, slipping into his pants. He pulled on his shirt and attempted to button it only to realize it no longer had buttons.

"Sorry about that." Cassidy giggled while pulling her shirt over her head. She ran her hands through her rumbled hair.

"Another time, you won't hear a single complaint from me, but right now, I need a new shirt."

Evan grabbed his camera and bolted from the room, his shirt flapping open behind him. Just as he reached his room, the front door opened and heels clicked on the tiled floor.

Instinctively, he lifted his camera to his shoulder, turned and began to film.

"Evan. What are you doing up? Where's Cassidy?"

"I heard something so I got out of bed and started filming. I thought you were Cassidy. I guess she must still be in bed...or something."

He hoped to hell he sounded casual. He clicked off his camera and held it by his side.

Zoe's eyes narrowed, taking in his attire as she walked across the room. He felt naked with his shirt hanging open.

"Sleeping, huh?" She trailed a single finger across his stomach. "I'm sorry I woke you. If you need help getting back to sleep, I'm pretty sure I can think of a few ways to tire you out."

Evan shivered at her touch. It was like ice, and not in a good way. "Thanks, but I think I can manage on my own. Besides, didn't you just come from a date with your dream man?"

"Yeah, but he left me at the door. You could walk me to my room."

"I'm going back to my room since it appears Cassidy's still sleeping and I'm not needed. I'm sure your cameraman can make sure you get to your room safely."

"You know where I am if you change your mind." Zoe lifted the edge of his shirt and fingered the hanging threads where a button used to be. "You're missing a few buttons. Did your shirt give you some trouble tonight?"

Evan held his gaze steady on hers. "Buttons can be complicated."

"True, sometimes I have to use my teeth."

"Thanks for sharing. Goodnight, Zoe." He backed into his room.

"Sweet dreams, Evan. I know mine will be."

Evan closed his bedroom door and collapsed onto the bed.

That was too close. Cassy is off limits from now on. I can't ruin my reputation with work or get more involved with her than I already am.

And what the hell kind of repellent can I buy to keep Zoe away from me?

*

Brad paced in front of Evan and the other crewmembers. "Dudes, I don't know who to pick." He ran his hands through his hair.

"You must have at least one front runner." Chip spoke, the impatience clear in his voice already. In all the years Evan had known Chip, patience had never been one of his strong suits.

"Oh yeah, Zoe. That chick oozes sex appeal. I bet she's a tiger in the sack based on how she kisses."

"Great. So Zoe is in the final two automatically, and the others are in the bottom three. America can fight it out for who gets to stay."

"No, wait. I'm not sure." Brad rubbed his forehead again. "What about Cassidy? I know she's totally playing hard to get with me because I broke up with her. It's driving me crazy. What if America votes her out? Maybe she should be the sure thing and

Zoe should be in the bottom. There's no way America would vote out Zoe again, right?"

The crew remained quiet.

"Come on. Someone must have an opinion." Brad started to border on whiny.

"I'm not sure I'd trust America with Zoe again. They didn't like her the first time she was in the bottom three. Who says they've changed their minds?" Evan didn't want to sway Brad's opinion too much, but the sooner Cassidy was off the show, the better it would be for everyone and putting her up for the vote might just get that accomplished.

"True," Brad replied, obviously still unsure of his decision.

"It's not hard. Just pick one girl you really want at the end and let America figure out the rest for you," another crewmember said.

"I know what I need to do." Brad walked away without any confirmation of who he'd decided to put in the bottom three.

"So who's he going to choose?" Jake asked from beside Evan.

"Not a clue."

"Doesn't really matter in my case. My girl isn't one of the favorites to win, so I think I'm going home tomorrow."

"Erin and the kids will be happy to have you home again."

"Yep, and I'll have enough time and funds to take the family on a quick vacation before school starts." Jake patted him on the back. "Looks like you're sticking around until the end with Cassidy, huh?"

"Seems that way."

"What's with you two, anyway?" Jake dropped his voice. "You seem pretty close these days."

Evan's heart jumped into his throat. "What are you talking about?"

"Seems you're interested in more than good camera angles on this project."

"You're imagining things."

"After all these years of friendship," Jake said, shaking his head,

"I thought you knew you could trust me."

"If you're throwing the friend card around, then I'm going to use it. Be a friend and stop asking questions you know I can't answer." Evan held his breath while he waited for that to sink in.

Jake nodded his head and looked Evan straight in the eye. "You do what you need to." Jake's voice was so quiet Evan had to strain to hear him. "Just don't get caught doing something stupid."

"It's not like that, Jake. You don't know this girl."

"She worth losing your job?"

"I don't—" Evan shrugged. "Maybe." It was the best he could offer his friend. The truth was, Evan didn't know for sure one way or the other. All he knew was at this point, he owed it to himself to find out.

"What about your vow to not get involved with anyone? You finally figured out that's impossible and stupid?"

Evan sighed. Had he decided she was worth that risk? Was not being with Cassidy a better alternative than being with her and maybe getting hurt someday in the future? "Maybe. I don't know, okay?"

"Don't worry. I'll keep this quiet. I'm going to pack. I want to catch a ride home as soon as my girl gets voted off."

"Tell Erin I say hello."

Evan hoped he'd said enough to convince Brad to put Cassidy in the bottom three, but not too much to cast suspicion on his motives. Only time would tell and the elimination ceremony couldn't get here fast enough.

*

Evan was in complete disbelief that Cassidy sat across from him in the interview room again. He'd been sure when Brad had put her in the bottom three, America would vote her out. But for some reason, they hadn't.

"How do you feel about being one of the final girls in the competition?" He started the interview with the provided questions.

"I'm shocked," she said, shaking her head. "I never dreamt I'd make it this far. I thought I'd be the girl who gets sent home the first week."

"Let's talk about your last challenge. This time it was a private date with Brad, correct? Where did he take you?"

"We had dinner outside at the Mountain View Terrace restaurant in the chateau. We shared a nice meal and admired the view of the mountains for a while."

"Sounds romantic." He didn't want Cassidy thinking romantically about Brad.

"Yes, I suppose it was romantic with a table set for the two, and an outdoor bed with about a million pillows so we could relax together and enjoy the stunning view. I'm sure most girls would dream of this as a perfect romantic moment."

But did you?

"Did you take advantage of the romantic setting to get closer to Brad?"

"Um, well..." Cassidy blushed a light pink. "We lay on the bed talking for a while, which was nice. I know Brad really wanted to kiss me, but when he leaned it for it, he bumped my glass of wine and it spilled all over my blouse."

"That's terrible. Were you able to continue on with your date after you'd cleaned up the mess?"

"No." He could tell Cassidy struggled not to giggle. "Unfortunately," she continued, "the wine was going to stain my shirt and I needed to get it cleaned right away so our date ended a little early."

"Did Brad walk you to the door and kiss you goodnight to end your very romantic private date?"

"He did walk me to the door, which was nice and I appreciated it, but after the wine spilled on me, I was cold and really wanted to take a shower and get into some clean clothes. So no, we didn't kiss at the door. I think we left the romance on the terrace with the dessert we didn't eat."

Ah, poor douche bag Brad. Epic date failure.

"Are you hoping you'll get another chance for a kiss during this last challenge?"

Evan wasn't nearly as bothered by these questions as he would have been a week ago. He knew Cassidy's feelings for him were strong and Brad wouldn't get another kiss any time soon. Still, a little part of him couldn't help feeling jealous at the idea of having to watch them together again at the last challenge.

"Since I don't know what the challenge is, it's hard to know what to hope for."

"The competition is down to two girls. How do you feel about Zoe being here with you?"

"I'm happy for Zoe since she really wants to be in the final two, but I wish I had someone more enjoyable to spend my last few days in the house with."

"What do you mean?

"I don't think it's any secret that Zoe and I aren't best friends." Cassidy rolled her eyes. "She's made it very clear she's the only one meant to be with Brad and the only one who deserves to be here. I guess since she's the last woman standing, maybe she's right." Cassidy finished with a shrug like she admitted defeat against Zoe.

"But she's not the last woman here. You're still here. Doesn't that mean you deserve to be here, too?" He cocked his head to the side.

Doesn't she realize she is way more amazing than Zoe will ever be?

"I guess America must think so since they voted for me to stay. Or maybe they want to keep me around so they have someone to laugh at. Everyone loves the underdog, right?"

"So you think Zoe is the running favorite to win?"

Cassidy adjusted herself on the couch, tucking one leg under the other. She looked tired of answering the relentless string of questions.

"I don't know. America doesn't get to vote for who wins, so the choice is all up to Brad. I'm not sure which of us he likes better. I guess the last challenge will probably help him make his decision."

"Are you worried about who he'll choose in the end?" he asked, honestly curious.

"No," Cassidy replied sounding confident. "Zoe and I are two different people. Once he has a chance to spend a more time with each of us, I think he'll realize he likes one person a lot more than the other. We're so different, I think one of us will simply be a better fit in his life."

Better be Zoe.

"Do you think your history with Brad will make a difference in his choice?"

"Of course it will. How could it not? We have memories together. He already knows what it's like to date me, so he'll have to decide if he wants me again or if he wants to try someone new."

"Are you ready to date Brad again if he chooses you?"

"I don't know. I wish I had an answer for you, but I don't."

Evan scanned the sheet of questions. "I guess that's all the questions I have for you today. Enjoy the last challenge and good luck."

"Thanks," she said, smiling one of her amazing Cassidy smiles at him. "I need all the good luck I can get."

I think we both need that.

Chapter Twenty

Cassidy stood in the kitchen comforted by being back in the familiarity of the house she'd called home for the last few weeks. Especially since it meant she finally had a little space from Zoe. Sharing a suite with her at the chateau hadn't been a picnic for anyone.

Cassidy whisked eggs in a bowl and dumped them into a hot skillet, then topped them with cheese and ham. It wasn't healthy, but it reminded her of home and that's exactly what she needed right now.

Everywhere she went there seemed to be a lot of packing going on. Cameras were coming down from ceiling corners, mic packs were being inventoried and placed in boxes, even decorations were being removed from the walls and bubble wrapped.

She'd snuck downstairs when she'd heard Evan go into the shower so she could have a few camera-free moments. The alone time was bliss.

"Whatcha making?" Zoe asked, coming up behind her, also without her cameraman. Seemed they'd both managed to ditch their responsibilities.

So much for bliss. "An omelet." Cassidy rolled her eyes and wished Zoe away.

"Make me one, too."

"How about you make it yourself?"

"I don't know how." Zoe leaned back on the counter to watch Cassidy. "Now if you asked me to make Death by Chocolate Cupcakes, that I could do. An omelet, not so much."

Give her one and she'll go away.

Cassidy sighed and put the finished omelet on the plate and handed it to Zoe. "It's not low-fat and borders on burned. Enjoy." She turned her back and started fixing herself another omelet— one she'd actually get to eat.

Zoe grabbed a coffee and wandered out the back door with her omelet in hand and without so much as a thank you.

Bitch.

The door opened again.

"What now, Zoe? Need me to hand feed you, too?"

"I can feed myself, thanks."

Cassidy turned, spatula in hand. Susan stood with her arms crossed and looking—well, looking pissed. "Hey, Susan. What's up? More helpful tips for me today?"

"I know you think this is all gonna work out between you and Evan after the show ends, but it's not, so you should get over him now and save yourself the heartache later."

Oh boy.

Cassidy attempted to look innocent. "I'm not sure what you think is going on, but Evan's just my cameraman."

"Sure he is." Susan took a few steps closer. "Listen. I've worked with Evan a long time, so I know the signs. He may say you're different, but you're not. You're just like every other girl he screws on production."

Cassidy cringed at her words.

"I wouldn't waste your time on him. You actually have a chance with Brad, don't mess it up by screwing around with Evan."

"Thanks for the advice, but mind your own business and I'll mind mine." Why did people always think they could tell her what to do? She wasn't anyone's pushover.

Susan's face turned scarlet, her eyes narrowing to slits.

Yep, I've pissed her off. Great.

Susan opened the back door again, but paused halfway out. "If I were you, I'd dress up tomorrow unless I wanted to look stupid on TV, but I wouldn't want to stick my nose in your business or anything. Your eggs are burning." She disappeared through the door without another glance.

Cassidy turned back to the skillet to see smoke rising from the pan. She grabbed it and tossed the whole thing into the sink, running water on it. The water hissed and spit as it hit the hot pan.

She suddenly felt like her future with Evan had gone the way of her uneaten omelet—burned and unappealing.

*

Cassidy and Zoe been told the final challenge would be away from the house, so they needed to pack a small bag, as well as get the rest of their belongings ready to ship home.

Cassidy had enjoyed the experience, but she was ready for the show to end. The sooner they were on their way to the final challenge, the sooner the show would be over and she'd be free.

Free from Brad bringing up feelings from the past she didn't want to explore.

Free to be with Evan—if he still wanted her. She had thought he would before, but after talking to Susan, she wasn't so sure anymore.

Cassidy grabbed the black backpack provided for the challenge and began thumbing through the T-shirts folded on her shelf. Of course, since she didn't know what they were doing, packing was a challenge in its own rite.

"Any hints as to what I might pack?"

Evan stared at her silently.

Cassidy sighed. Going back to the silent treatment got harder and harder every time. She couldn't wait to be away from the camera for good. To be normal around Evan, if he stuck around long enough.

"Okay then, I guess I'll pack one of everything and hope for the best. The least they could do is hint at what kind of clothes we might want to bring."

Of course, Susan had hinted, but could she be trusted after the whole Corona incident?

She rummaged through her dresser drawers pulling out clothes and separating them. Some went right into the overnight bag for the challenge, everything else needed to go into her suitcases to ship back to New York.

Her stomach tightened at the thought of going back to the city. With the show almost over, she'd have to face real life again. Her chest ached when she imagined waking up in her cramped little apartment after getting used to the sprawling mansion.

How would she feel about Brad once she was surrounded by memories of him again? Was she really ready to head home with nothing—with no one? No Evan or Brad.

Did she even want to go back to the city? Back to the subway station, lost among the throngs of busy people fighting their way to work. She could almost smell the ripe, hot stench streaming out of the street vents and the stuffiness of the thick air in the subway tunnels.

She stared at Evan who was leaning back against her dresser casually recording her every move. She studied his face, the line of his jaw, and toned muscles of his arms.

Or would she rather stay here with him? Was that even an option? Or maybe she should try somewhere new—somewhere warm, like California.

He peeked his head out from behind the camera and gave her a curious look. She read his lips when he mouthed, "You okay?"

Tears sprang to her eyes. Her head spun with uncertainty. Everything seemed so confusing all of a sudden.

The possibility of not seeing Evan, not being near him, stole her breath away. *What am I doing? I barely even know him and I'm worried about not seeing him every day.*

She ran her fingers under her eyes, wiping away the tears before they started and wouldn't stop. She wouldn't cry about this. Not yet. She didn't even know how she felt about Evan yet, let alone how he felt about her. There was no sense crying over something she didn't even understand.

Cassidy placed the backpack on the top of the dresser. She could finish the rest of her packing later, but right now she needed to relax in a nice warm bubble bath.

She sat on the edge of the tub adjusting the water until it was hot enough to soak the tension out of her weary muscles. She grabbed one of the fancy little bottles of bubble bath and poured the last bit of liquid left from it into the water. Hundreds of bubbles came to life, floating across the surface of the water. The delectable scent of chocolate filled the air.

Cassidy wiped her eyes again to make sure no tears still lingering on the brink before turning to face Evan and the camera. "I'm going to have to ask you to leave so I can take a bath." She tried her best to make her voice sound strong. "I'm sure America doesn't need to see that."

Evan clicked the record button off and set his camera aside on the counter. He took her in his arms before she could protest. His hands found the mic pack hiding in the small of her back, which he expertly removed and shut off, placing it on the counter next to his camera.

Cassidy inhaled deeply, savoring the scent of his cologne as he wrapped her in his arms. He was strong and gentle and incredibly handsome. How could she ever believe memories of Brad could compare to the reality of Evan? But how could Evan ever catch up to the history she already had with Brad?

Evan kissed the side of her neck sending a shiver down her back.

"Evan, be good."

"I'm very good. Haven't I proven that to you enough times yet?"

"That's not what I mean." She hit him playfully on the shoulder, pulling back from him. "I mean you shouldn't be in here with me. You should be out in the bedroom where the cameras can see you're *not* in here with me."

"I'll go in a minute and no one will be any the wiser." He gazed at her, his eyes serious. "But first I want to know what's wrong. You were almost crying a few minutes ago."

"It's nothing," she said. "I'm just feeling a little overwhelmed."

"Cassy, if there's something wrong, please, let me help you."

She tried to put on a happy face. "Really, I'm fine."

And deeply confused.

She wasn't ready to tell Evan she'd been tearing up at the thought of not seeing him every day. He'd probably think she was crazy.

"I'll let you keep your secret, but you know you can talk to me if you need to. You're not in this mess alone." He paused for a moment before sighing and continuing like it pained him to say the words that came next. "If you're starting to have feelings for Brad again, you can tell me. I'll try to understand enough to talk about it."

"It's not that."

It's both of you.

"It makes me very happy to hear that." Evan kissed her and her body melted into his. She wanted more than anything to stay in this moment forever and forget about Brad, the show, and everything else around her.

She kissed him back harder, holding on to the feeling of his lips on hers before pulling away. Would she be able to remember this feeling when she was alone in New York again? When he left her like he had all the other production flings?

"Can I get in the tub before the water goes cold and the bubbles disappear?" she asked, swallowing the lump in her throat. "I won't be long if you want to hang out in your room for a bit. I'll knock on your door when I'm finished."

"I'm going to need a cold shower while I wait. It's torture picturing you in all that hot, soapy water and knowing I can't join you."

Grabbing her butt, he gave it a squeeze before letting her go. "When we finally get finished with this stupid show, I might not let you out of my sight for a long, long time."

"I might hold you too that." She smiled weakly, tears threatening her eyes again. "Now go." Cassidy pushed Evan out of the bathroom and closed the door before he could see her eyes well up with tears again.

She undressed and sank into the tub. Hot water washed over her skin, soothing her. She closed her eyes and leaned back against a towel, only then allowing a couple of tears to trickle down her cheek.

Cassidy didn't understand why she had this strong of a reaction to the thought of leaving Evan—and to the thought of Brad walking away from her again. When Brad told her he hoped she might still be the girl to spend his life with, it was like she'd gotten back a little piece of herself. It felt great to know at least a part of him still regretted how he'd treated her—regretted how he'd left things.

And then there was Evan, the man who made her feel something she'd never experienced before—something new, something deeper than lust or desire. A man who made her forget there was a world going on around them when she was in his arms.

A man she didn't know if she had any future with outside of this house.

Chapter Twenty-One

"Seriously?" Cassidy's voice came out tighter and squeakier than she'd meant it to. "I can't believe this is our last challenge." Everywhere Cassidy looked was nature, nature, and more nature.

Susan was a bigger bitch than Zoe.

Dress clothes my ass. Cassidy shifted her weight on her already sore feet—feet that were trapped in three-inch-high torture devices. *Of all the days for the medic to approve of me wearing heels again, it just had to be today.*

"Okay, Chip. Now you've gone too far even for me." Zoe wore a distinctly sour expression.

We'll actually have something in common. Oh my God, did I really just admit to having something in common with the she-devil? Kill me. Kill me now.

Spencer and Brad appeared before them.

"Welcome back," Spencer said with a TV smile. "You should both be very proud of yourselves. I'm sure Brad picked both of you for good reasons, and I for one, can't wait to see how this will all play out."

Spencer took a moment to scan the area then moved to stand beside a pile of gear. "This is your final challenge and as such, we've decided to put you to the ultimate test. This challenge will test your survival skills, your physical ability, and also your emotional stamina.

"First, you'll grab your gear and use a map to hike to your campsite. Second, you'll have to set up your campsite. This will include pitching tents and starting a fire. I hope you brought some matches." He laughed.

Cassidy didn't.

"Now, I know you didn't stop at the grocery store on your

"

way here, so in with your gear, you'll find everything you need to prepare a gourmet outdoor meal."

Brad laughed and slapped Spencer on the shoulder like they were best buddies. "Wow. It sounds like I'm in for a good time. I can't wait to see how these girls handle living outside for a full twenty-four hours."

"This challenge will give the girls a chance to really show you who they are and what they're made of. I should also add you'll get a private date with each of the girls. This will be your last chance to learn everything you need to know about them to help make your final decision."

"Sounds good," Brad said.

Spencer grabbed a backpack from the pile of gear and placed it on the ground in front of Cassidy. He did the same for Zoe. Along with their sizable backpacks, there were also tents, bags with dishes, food and cooking utensils, as well as sleeping bags, creating a rather intimidating pile of gear.

Are we driving to camp?

Spencer handed Cassidy a paper rolled like a cigar and put a small round object into Zoe's hand. "That's the map and compass to help you find your camp. Grab the rest of your gear and good luck. I think you'll need it."

Spencer didn't linger. Instead, he walked over to the production trailer and disappeared inside.

The challenge had officially started and they were on their own.

Cassidy unrolled the map and held it out to get a better look. A highlighted line indicated the hiking paths they needed to use and a campsite number they needed to reach to find their final destination. It didn't seem quite as complicated as Spencer made it sound.

"Okay, it looks like we need to go north until we find the tree split in two and then we hang a left onto yellow trail five. Which way is north?"

"You're actually going along with this?" Zoe asked.

"What do you mean? This is the challenge."

"You're willing to wander into the wilderness to find some stupid campsite? You know, if we both refuse, they'll have to take us to the campsite some other way."

Cassidy studied the map again. She wasn't thrilled with the idea either, but it didn't seem like that hard of a hike. "I think we'll be okay."

"Come on, Zoe." Brad squeezed between them, putting an arm around each of their shoulders. "You've always been up for a good time before. Don't go changing on me now."

"I, um. I guess I didn't realize you'd be joining us on our hike," Zoe stammered. "Cassidy, read the map already and tell me where to go so I can use the compass."

Oh, I'll tell you where to go.

Zoe stood with her hand on her hip waiting for Cassidy. Never mind that Cassidy had already told her they needed to go north. Now that Zoe knew Brad was involved, a whole new girl came to play.

"I said north. Do you know where north is?"

"Of course I know where north is." Zoe stared at the compass, first spinning in one direction, then the other. "Great, they gave us a broken compass. Now what are we supposed to do?"

Zoe held a simple compass with the four coordinates clearly marked and a needle spinning in the middle. Cassidy had never used a compass before, but how hard could it be, right?

"What part isn't working?" she asked.

"Well, when I spin, the little dial thingy spins, too. The little arrow is pointing to the N over there, but when I turn toward the N, then the arrow points a different way. Are we supposed to follow the N or the arrow?" Zoe handed the compass to Cassidy. "I give up. You figure it out."

Cassidy held the compass flat in her hand. *I couldn't be that hard to figure it out.* She tried to recall all the things she'd ever heard about using a compass, which wasn't much.

"Never eat shredded wheat," she mumbled.

"What are you whispering about?"

"Nothing." Cassidy noticed the arrow in the middle had one red end and it was currently pointing at the E.

That must mean something.

She turned and the red end of the arrow stayed where it was, while the directional letters spun beneath it.

"A compass always points north, right?" She turned a little further until the red end of the arrow pointed directly in front of her and the N was underneath the arrow. "So, this must be north?"

She glanced at Evan hoping for confirmation before they set off on their hike. He gave a quick nod and crooked smile.

"You better be sure about this, Cassidy. If you get us lost in the wild, I will eat you to save myself," Zoe said.

"That's disgusting. No one's eating anyone. Besides, it's a TV show. Are you really stupid enough to think they'd let two contestants, the hunky guy, and a few cameramen all wander off into the woods to get lost and never be heard from again?"

"You still think I'm hunky. I knew it." Brad snickered like she'd admitted wanting to do dirty things with him.

"You—you know what I meant." That sounded pathetic, even to her.

Great. Now he'll think I want to kiss him again. Do I?

"I know *exactly* what you're saying, or not saying since you seem to enjoy playing that way." Brad winked and puckered his lips in a kissing face, teasing her.

"Okay, let's go." Cassidy hoped they'd start moving before she said anything else to accidentally encourage Brad. Cassidy hoisted her backpack onto her shoulders, grabbed another bag of gear, and a toolbox. She laughed as Zoe lifted her backpack and almost fell over under its weight.

Brad looped the rest of the bags onto his shoulders like a pack mule. Beads of sweat broke out on his forehead before he'd taken a single step.

The group headed out on the trail with Cassidy leading the way. She held the compass in front of her to make sure the arrow always pointed at the N. She took careful steps on her wobbly heels over the uneven ground. This wouldn't help Evan not worry about her hurting herself again.

After what seemed like eternity, they finally came to the tree she'd seen on the map. They turned left and followed the trail marked with yellow painted rings on nearby trees and stakes with the number five etched into them spaced every few hundred feet.

A few stakes later, a placard with the number twenty-three painted in bright blue appeared along the trailside.

"This is it." She dropped her gear to the ground and collapsed onto a seat at the picnic table, instantly kicking off her shoes and rubbing her feet. "Thank God it wasn't any further. I'm not sure how much more I could have carried those packs."

"You're telling me." Zoe sauntered into camp, filing her nails. "These shoes were not made for this kind of abuse."

"Finally." Brad staggered into the camp. He dropped Zoe's backpack to the ground as well as all the other things. "You're carrying your own bag on the way back, Zoe."

"No, I'm not." She flopped down on the other side of the picnic bench and lay down across it like she was sun tanning at the beach.

"Can you move over so I can sit, too?" he asked, standing beside the table.

Zoe didn't respond.

Cassidy sighed and slid down the bench to make room for Brad. He sat directly beside her, leaving little space between them. He put his arm around her shoulders and pulled her against him.

"Thanks, babe. You gonna make room for me in your tent, too?"

Cassidy blushed. "I don't know. I'm not so sure that's a good idea. We're on TV, remember? America might jump to the wrong conclusions."

"Or the right ones if you ask nicely. Besides, it'll be great for ratings."

Cassidy glanced at the bags in a heap on the ground. It had to be nearly lunch by how loud her stomach growled and it could easily take all afternoon to figure out how to set up one tent, let alone four tents. "We should get started on those tents soon. I don't want to sleep out with the animals tonight." *And I'm not sharing.*

"Don't worry, I'll protect you," Brad said.

"Great. Um, thanks."

Cassidy unzipped a tent bag and pulled out a sheet of instructions, studying it. She knelt in the dirt carefully tucking her skirt under her legs so she wouldn't accidentally give America a peek at anything too interesting while she attempted to erect the tent. She had zero experience pitching a tent since every camping trip with her parents involved a cabin, a bed, and indoor plumbing.

"Hey, Zoe. Do you want to work together to pitch our tents?" Cassidy hoped for an extra set of hands, but wasn't sure she wanted them to be attached to Brad.

"No, I don't plan on pitching a tent."

"Okay, so you're sleeping with the bugs tonight? Because you're not sharing my tent."

"I wasn't planning on sharing with you." Zoe arched her eyebrows at Brad.

Brad grinned at Zoe and turned to face Cassidy. "Oh, this just got a lot more interesting. Are you going to let her stake her claim on me like that?"

Crap. What's the right response?

"I said I was setting up a tent to sleep in. I never once said I'd be sleeping alone."

Oh, good one.

"My, my, my. The gloves come off," Brad teased. "No need to fight over me, ladies. There's plenty of Brad for everyone to enjoy."

There wasn't that much, if I remember correctly.

Cassidy pulled hollow poles attached with some kind of stretchy string out of the bag and compared them to the set of instructions on the ground. *Where are you when I need you, Keira? I bet you'll laugh like crazy when you see this on TV.*

It took Cassidy a few minutes to lay the tent out on the ground with long crisscrossing poles on top and clipped to the fabric. Now, she had to raise all four sides at once to make it dome-shaped like the picture showed. Grabbing the poles, she glanced at Evan for encouragement. His head nodded slightly, and he offered her a crooked smile. They were almost in position when one slipped out of her hand and fell back onto the tent, bringing the other pole and Cassidy with it. A muffled chuckle came for the direction of Evan's camera. She straightened her skirt, determined to prove to herself and everyone else that she could pitch a stupid tent.

A while later, Cassidy stood with sweat streaming down her face and a wide grin stretching across her face. She gazed at the tent she'd erected. It was a little misshapen, but it was up. Hopefully it was secure.

She grabbed a bottle of water from one of the bags they'd carried. She chugged half the bottle in only a few gulps, then tilted her head back and poured the rest of the water onto her face, cooling her off and washing away the sticky sweat and dirt. It meant she'd have to steal a couple of minutes away in her tent to retouch her makeup, but at least she'd be clean.

"That's reminds me of a shower we took once," Brad said.

Cassidy's mind skipped back to the showers they'd taken on mornings after Brad had spent the night at her apartment. She always ended up late for work those mornings. The memory made her smile—until she glanced up to find Evan staring at her. *Oops.*

Cassidy rummaged through a bag until she found a stash of granola bars. She chose one covered in chocolate—exactly what she needed to recharge. She took a seat at the picnic table to eat and rest while she watched Brad help Zoe with her tent.

A few minutes later, Zoe joined her at the picnic table while Brad tossed sleeping bags and pillows into each of the tents. Zoe had done a good job at playing damsel in distress, which meant Brad had basically erected her entire tent himself.

"I think we're all set for tonight." He sat at the table. "Now, I don't want you girls fighting over me too much. You're both welcome to share my tent."

"So what's next on the list for this fun challenge?" Cassidy didn't want to say anything that would either incriminate her or encourage him.

"I hope it's a pedicure and massage. I need it after all this manual labor." Zoe checked her still-perfect nails. "When's catering getting here? I'm starving." Zoe peered into the trees like she might suddenly see a Starbucks.

"I don't think there's any catering."

Zoe's eyes clouded over in panic. "What do you mean no catering? What are we supposed to eat? Leaves? Berries?"

I bet Keira would know how to make a meal out of that. God, I miss that veggie-loving freak.

Zoe grabbed Brad's bottle of water out of his hands and shook it at him. "Tell me there's Perrier in that bag. I don't drink pond water." She threw the bottle on the ground with a flourish.

"I don't think there was," he said in a soothing voice. "But don't worry. It'll be okay. This stuff is good, too, and we're only here for a day." He put his hand on her knee, gently rubbing it.

Zoe's icy demeanor melted at his touch. "Fine. I guess I can drink this. I've had to do plenty of other crap for shows. Now I need to freshen up in the ladies room. Where do you think that's hiding?"

Cassidy and Brad glanced at each other, terrified. The only bathroom available was most likely an outhouse.

"Um, I'm pretty sure we passed a port-a-potty on the trail a few yards back." Brad didn't look Zoe in the eyes as he spoke.

Cassidy thought Zoe might faint. It wasn't Cassidy's ideal situation either, but she tried to make the best of it. It was camping, after all. What could you expect?

Zoe took a few deep breaths while her body visibly shook. When she'd finally steadied her temper, she sulked off in the direction they'd originally come.

"Well, she took that better than I expected." Brad laughed.

"God help the poor production person who has to answer to her." Cassidy shrugged. "Some people aren't meant for roughing it."

"I sure hope she pulls herself together soon or she might actually lose her mind when she finds out what we're doing this afternoon."

Cassidy stared at Brad with nervous anticipation. "Why? What are they making us do this afternoon?"

"Well it wouldn't be much of a surprise if I told you. Let's just say I'm not the only good catch around these parts."

Oh no. He did not just imply that we're going to be fishing, did he? I don't like fish. I don't touch fish. I don't eat fish. I don't touch the bait that catches said fish. I need to change out of these ridiculous clothes.

Evan grinned at her from behind his camera as though he found the idea of her fishing incredibly amusing. She didn't find it amusing at all.

Chapter Twenty-Two

Cassidy stood on the riverbank in jeans, a T-shirt, and sandals. The clear water rushed downstream over boulders and fallen trees strewn along the river's edge. Just beneath the surface, shadows moved with the current.

Cassidy didn't like to eat fish and had absolutely no desire to catch one. The only fish she could tolerate were the kind that were served battered and fried to a nice golden brown with a side of tasty tartar sauce. She could imagine Chip enjoying a good laugh when he'd come up with this idea.

It wasn't enough they had to camp outside, build their own shelter, and use a portable toilet. Nope. They also had to catch their dinner. To prove what, she wasn't sure.

Beside her, Zoe scowled at the plastic containers of bait. Once again, they shared the same feeling. Weird.

"Okay, Brad. What do I do first?" Cassidy asked.

"I think we take one of these things here, and stick it on the hook." Brad scrunched up his eyes like he was trying to solve a complicated physics problem in his head.

"Wait. You've never fished, either?"

"Nope. Not even once."

"Ugh, then why in hell are they making us do this? I thought this was something you loved. At least if it was one of your hobbies or something I could understand. But if you don't even go fishing, then this is simply to make us look bad on national television."

"It's fun." He laughed. "We can be fishing virgins together."

Brad handed her a rod, then took a worm from the bait jar and handed it to her.

"Careful. Don't push too hard, you don't want to skewer your finger. Ouch." He cried out and stuck his finger in his mouth. "Damn it, that hurt. My finger tastes like bait."

Cassidy laughed at Brad's clumsiness and slid her worm onto the hook. She heard quiet laughter from behind her and turned to see Evan trying very hard not to laugh at Brad. He failed miserably. She held up her hook with the worm on it and smiled at the camera.

"I did it." Cassidy wished she could talk to Evan instead of to the camera. "What now?"

"Now I think you cast it into the water," Brad said.

Cassidy glanced between the rod and the water. She'd seen fishing on TV a few times, but there wasn't much fishing talk in New York. She sighed feeling foolish for not knowing how to cast the line, but she honestly didn't. On TV, it looked like you wave your arm and the line sails out in a beautiful arch and lands gently in the water.

Easy as catching a cab on Fifth Avenue, right?

She held the rod in one hand with the hook dangling out to the side. She bent her arm back and then threw it forward like she was throwing a baseball. The hook swung forward, landing in the mud along the shore.

"I guess I didn't do that hard enough." She'd spoken out loud, but no one except Evan seemed to be listening.

And laughing, she noted.

She bent her arm back again and threw the rod forward as hard as she could, trying to make it to the water. The rod slipped out of her hand with the force of her throw, landing in the water with a splash.

Cassidy heard a distinctive snort from Evan's direction, but was too embarrassed to find out if he was laughing at her or with her. *Stupid fishing pole. Stupid fish.*

She perched on the edge of the river and reached forward as much as she could to try and grab her fishing rod without actually stepping into the water. She touched the end of it right as it started to float down river. She wrapped her hand around the rod and pulled it toward herself as she stood. She was halfway up when the rod pulled back against her hand and she lost her balance, falling face first into the cold river with a rather large splash.

"For the love of all things holy! Again, I make a fool of myself. Can someone help me out of here?"

Brad came to the edge of the water and pulled her to her feet. "You didn't have to make such a splash to get my attention. Are you okay?"

"I'm fine. Wet and humiliated on TV again, but fine." Her wet shirt clung to every contour, making her feel like she was standing there naked. She tried to pull the shirt away from her body, but as soon as she released it, it suctioned right back against her like a second skin.

Awesome. Let's give the people a show, Cassidy.

She scanned the surrounding area for a private place to change. Thank goodness she'd planned ahead and figured with her track record, something like this was bound to happen and had brought extra clothes. Otherwise, it would have been a long, cold, revealing afternoon of fishing.

"I need to get out of these wet clothes."

Brad winked at her with a lopsided grin spreading across his face. "I can help you with that. It's not like I haven't seen it before. In fact, I've been seeing a lot of you in my dreams lately."

"Thanks for sharing, Brad, but I'll just go find a big bush to hide behind."

Cassidy wandered into the woods away from the stream with her extra clothes in hand. Evan followed behind her with a huge smile on his face.

"What are you smiling at? Do you think you're going to see me naked? Think again." She wandered behind a tall bush before taking off her top and putting on a clean, dry T-shirt.

"Or maybe you're laughing at my clumsiness again. That's it, isn't it?" She pulled on a fresh pair of jeans. "You're laughing because this is another challenge I suck at. I'm trying my best."

Evan pushed his lips together into a tight line but she could see he still fought not to laugh. Every few seconds a snort escaped and his face turned a brighter shade of red from lack of oxygen.

She stormed back around the bush, gripping her wet clothes in a fist and breezed past him. "I'm going to try again and this time I'm going to catch a stupid fish and prove you wrong. Got that?" She turned to face the camera head-on. "Did you hear me, America, I'm going to catch a fish."

"You know you're not supposed to talk to the camera, right? That's like reality show 101," Zoe said.

"Oh, shut up, Zoe."

Stomping back to the edge of the river, she picked up her fishing rod. She checked to make sure the worm was still secure on the hook. Then she reached back her arm, held tight to her rod and threw it toward the river. The line sailed through the air with a zing and plunked into the water ten feet away.

"Nice one, Cassidy."

"Wow." Zoe voice dripped with venom. "She threw a hook in the water. Let's see her catch an actual fish without needing another change of clothes."

"At least I'm trying."

Zoe grabbed her rod and came to stand beside Cassidy. "Brad." Zoe fluttered her eyelashes. "Can you help me?"

"Sure." Brad moved to aide Zoe again.

Brad fed the worm onto the hook for Zoe then showed her how to hold the rod. He stood behind her and put his arms around her waist, placing one hand over hers to help guide the rod. Together they flicked the rod forward and back a few times, shifting their weight with each movement. Finally, they threw the rod forward and sent the line sailing into the river.

By the expression on Brad's face, they'd also had a nice bump and grind session and Cassidy was pretty sure he was ready to use his rod to cast a line of his own. A twinge of something—jealousy maybe—ran through Cassidy. She still wasn't sure she wanted to ever get involved with Brad again, but that didn't mean she was okay watching him get frisky with Zoe.

I don't think the fish in the river are the only little swimmers ready to make their way upstream. I can't believe they act like that on national television.

Cassidy's fishing rod jerked in her hand as something tugged on the end of the line. "I've got something."

Brad let go of Zoe and rushed to her side. "Reel it in."

Slowly reeling in the line, she could feel the fish on the hook swimming back and forth as it tried to get away. The rod bent toward the water as she pulled on it, trying to reel the fish in. Just as her arms were starting to tire, the fish broke through the surface of the water.

She lowered the fish to the ground and grabbed it. Its cold, scaly skin slipped through her fingers as she tried to get the hook out. She slid the hook out the way it had gone in and held up the fish in both hands.

"I did it. I caught a fish. I can't believe it." Cassidy held the large fish, trying to find somewhere to put it now that the excitement had worn off. "Um, what do I do with it now?"

Evan tapped the bucket beside him with his foot and winked.

"Oh, right. The bucket makes sense." She dumped the fish into the bucket, rinsed her hands in the river, and wiped them on her jeans.

"I guess since we have dinner, thanks to my girl Cassidy, we can call it quits with fishing and head back to camp."

"Thank God. I really wasn't in the mood to teach you how to fish," Zoe said dropping her pole to the ground.

"You don't know how to fish. Brad just showed you."

Zoe winked. "I went fishing every Sunday with my dad after church. I was just having fun with Brad's fishing pole."

"Gross. I thought Brad was the one with the sleazy moves, but you're just as bad."

"Aren't you a sneaky girl," Brad said snuggling up to Zoe again. "What else do you need me to teach you that you already know?"

Zoe whispered into Brad's ear. Brad's smile widened. Cassidy felt nauseous.

She spun on her heel heading in the direction of camp. She'd impressed herself by pitching a tent and catching a fish. Maybe camping wasn't so bad after all.

Zoe, on the other hand, was just as awful as ever.

*

Evan sat at the picnic table with his elbows resting on the tabletop while supporting the weight of his camera. His shoulders and back ached and he could hear his pulse pounding in his ears.

Today had to be the longest day he'd suffered through in a long time. He and Zoe's cameraman had had to capture every moment of this challenge, which meant they had little time for breaks.

Across the campfire, Cassidy sat with a plate on her lap. After they'd come back to camp with her catch, they'd had to fillet it and cook it over the fire. To his surprise, Cassidy had done great. She hadn't been skittish about touching the fish or prepping it. In fact, it seemed like she'd really enjoyed getting her hands dirty.

Zoe, on the other hand, was currently surviving on diet soda and granola bars. She might know how to catch a fish, but she apparently didn't eat it. But she did know how to flirt with Brad.

Cassidy's eyes flickered up to meet Evan's gaze. He could feel the heat between them and it had nothing to do with the campfire. He longed to be alone with her again—to learn more about her and her life back in New York.

He had about a million questions and no way to ask. The only chance he ever had to find out anything about Cassidy was when they were alone, which was rare, or when Brad decided to ask her a question about her personal life, which was rarer still. He had no choice but to bide his time and be patient. They would be alone soon enough and then he'd get a chance to find out everything and anything he'd ever wanted to know about her.

When they were finally alone again, it would be uninterrupted and unrestricted. His pulse quickened at the thought of where that would inevitably lead.

For the first time he could remember since his sister-in-law's accident, he didn't feel afraid at the possibility of getting closer to someone. As long as that someone was Cassy.

He cocked an eyebrow at Cassidy and stifled a laugh as she turned a bright shade of pink. He enjoyed being able to make her blush and he hoped that would never change. Pink was a good color on her.

"Cassidy." Brad's voice interrupted their private moment, bringing Evan out of his thoughts and back into the present. "Would you join me on a sunset walk?"

"Sure. That sounds nice."

Does it?

"Zoe, you'll be all right here alone for a little while?"

"I'll be fine. But don't leave me for too long or I might have to hunt you down and bring you back." Her laughter rang out, sounding a little too *Fatal Attraction* for Evan's taste.

"Don't worry. We'll be gone an hour or so and then I'll be all yours." He rubbed Zoe's hand before circling around the fire and taking Cassidy's.

"Let's go before the sun sets and we're left to find our way in the dark." Brad grinned. "On second thought, that sounds like more fun."

Cassidy walked with him out of the campsite as Evan walked backward a few steps in front of them, close enough to hear what they said but far enough ahead to not get in their way. It was tricky to film and walk backward, but the footage was better.

Evan tried not to focus on the fact that they were holding hands for fear that might lead to him punching the surfer boy in his pretty face and the whole world finding out about his feelings for Cassidy. Instead, he focused on angles, catching the right light, and walking without falling over anything.

"You did great in the challenges today. You really surprised me. I had no idea you could be so outdoorsy."

Cassidy laughed. "Thanks, I surprised myself. I had no idea it was so much fun to rough it in the wilderness. Is this kind of stuff normal for you in California? Because you certainly didn't do anything like this in New York."

"The fire yes, everything else, not really. We usually have big bonfires on the beach after a day of surfing."

"That sounds like fun."

Brad nodded. "It is. And you know, I think you'd really like it, too. We cook, drink beers, and watch the stars twinkle over the ocean. It's heaven."

The trail came to an end at a scenic outlook. There was a picnic blanket set up overlooking a view of the sun setting behind the mountains with a few cushions strewn around to sit on. Alongside the blanket was a bottle of champagne on ice and an assortment of little desserts.

It was romantic and exactly the kind of place Evan would take Cassidy if he ever got the chance. Instead, he was forced to film her enjoying it with surfer boy. His annoyance built inside at the frustration of the situation he'd gotten himself into, annoyed he'd let himself develop feelings for someone.

"Why don't we sit? This sunset is too beautiful to miss," Brad said.

As they got settled, Evan took his place leaning against the safety rail separating the viewing area from the cliff. He was off to the side of them so he wouldn't block their view, but was still able to get a good shot of the two of them together.

Brad popped the cork on the champagne and poured them each a glass. "To us. To finding the person you want to ride the waves with for the rest of your life." He clinked his glass against hers.

Dude. Totally lame.

"Since the last time we tried to eat dessert and enjoy the view didn't work out so well, I hoped we could try again. A second chance to get things right." He picked up a chocolate covered strawberry and held it toward Cassidy. "Maybe it's a third chance by now. I've sort of lost count."

Cassidy reach out to grab it, but Brad gently pushed her hand away. "Uh, uh. This time we're going to do things right." He held the strawberry to her mouth so she could take a bite.

"Really, it's okay. I can feed myself." She tried to protest as he shoved half the berry into her mouth. With an expression of reluctance, she took a bite.

Brad popped the rest of the strawberry into his own mouth, wiped his hands on the blanket and reached for another.

Cassidy held up her hands. "I'm good. Thanks. That was great. Very yummy."

"Are you still searching for a guy like me, Cassidy?"

Or do you want a guy like me?

"I don't even know what kind of guy you are anymore. I thought I knew who you were, then you left me."

"I know I did, and I'm sorry." He twirled a strawberry in his fingers. "Maybe you can tell me what you're hoping for and I can tell you if that's me."

"Okay. I'm hoping for someone who's strong, not necessarily physically, but you know, mentally and emotionally. I'd like someone who has goals and dreams. Someone who wants a family someday. Someone who's funny and makes me laugh." Cassidy's face turned wistful and dreamlike. "Most of all, I want someone who loves me for me, just the way I am."

Damn, that's me. Whether I want it to be or not, that's me.

Brad took her hands—his face serious yet kind. "I'm strong. I go out into fifteen-foot waves and surf some of the most dangerous waters. I have goals and dreams, too. One of them is to have a beautiful girl like you on the beach waiting for me each day." He cupped Cassidy's jaw in his palm and stroked her cheek with his thumb.

Okay, surfer boy. Back off.

"I like you for you, Cassidy. I always have. I was stupid to ever let you go. All I need to know is if you still want me, too."

Before Cassidy could answer him, Brad's lips were on hers. He pulled her closer and Evan watched in horror as their mouths parted and tongues emerged—not just Brad's, Cassidy's, too.

What is she doing? She said she wouldn't kiss him. That's not even a kiss. It's a tonsil hockey tournament.

Cassidy put her hand on Brad's chest, but Evan couldn't tell if it was to pull him closer or push him away. What Evan did know was that the kiss went on far longer than it should have.

What the hell is this shit?

Finally, they decided to come back up for air. Brad had a big goofy smile on his face. Evan's blood turned to lava.

How could she do this to me? We had a deal.

"God, I've missed your kisses, Cassidy." Brad sighed, leaning back on the blanket.

"Thanks," she blushed a deep shade of red, "for saying you like me for me. It's nice to hear after months of thinking I wasn't good enough for you. Why did you choose surfing over being with me?" Cassidy sank back on the blanket beside Brad so they were both staring up to the stars.

Oh great, now you're going to lie down with surfer boy. Just invite the guy to stay the night already.

"At the time, I chose surfing because I missed it so much, but I'm not so sure I made the right choice." Brad rolled onto his side and put his arm across Cassidy, essentially trapping her on the blanket. "Come to California with me. We could have a perfect life together if you'd only find a way to get over your stupid fear of the water. We could have everything we've ever wanted."

Brad kissed her again, hard on the mouth. His body shifted onto her, obviously pinning her to the blanket.

Evan watched as Cassidy started to struggle underneath of Brad. Her hands pounding his shoulders and he could hear her mumbled protests.

I'm going to kick the shit out of this asshole once and for all.

Evan lunged for Brad just as he cried out in pain. Brad rolled off of Cassidy and back onto his side of the blanket, grabbing his groin, groaning.

Evan reached out a hand to Cassidy, but she shook her head and waved him to stay where he was.

"What the hell was that for, bitch?" Brad gulped in big breaths of air.

"It's not a stupid fear, you jackass. And if you really liked me for me—like you claimed you did two minutes ago—you wouldn't insist on trying to change me. I'm sorry my stupid fear of water doesn't fit into your perfect little world. Oh, and how about for forcing yourself on me? Just because you've had the privilege of kissing me before, doesn't mean I want you pinning me to a blanket in the dark, in the middle of the wilderness. Think with your brain for a change."

Cassidy kneeled near Brad's face. "If you ever call me a bitch again, that little ouchie you feel right now is going to feel like a mosquito bite compared to what you'll feel next time. I'm a New Yorker. We don't put up with garbage like that."

Evan followed Cassidy as she strode back toward the campsite. He turned on his camera light so she could see where she was walking.

"Cassidy, wait," Brad called. "I'm sorry. I thought you wanted me to kiss you again."

The scenic outlook hadn't been far up the trail so they made it back to the campsite quickly. That also meant Brad wouldn't be far behind them. Evan hoped for a few more minutes walking on the trail since he still hadn't figured out what the hell just happened back there. He needed more time to sort things out.

He wasn't sure who he should be mad at more, Brad for forcing himself on Cassidy, or Cassidy for letting Brad kiss her in the first place. She was supposed to avoid kissing him, not encourage him.

"Didn't you forget someone?" Zoe stumbled out of her tent in a sequin top, skinny jeans, and what had to be three-inch stilettos.

Apparently she thought there was a possibility of going clubbing later.

"Yeah, he was a little sore after our hike, so he stayed behind to rest." Cassidy snapped. "Nice outfit. Great choice for hiking."

"Wow, sounds like you had another winner of a date. What are you at now, zero for three?"

"I don't know. I guess it depends if you count the challenges plus the fact he's my ex-boyfriend. That could put me at zero for like…a thousand." She grabbed the paper plates from dinner and tossed them into the garbage bag.

Zoe put her hand on her hip. "You really did have an awful date, didn't you? I guess you're not the kind of girl guys like Brad want to date, huh?"

Cassidy balled her hands into fists at her side. "I did not have an awful date and for your information, Brad does want to date me. He kissed me, not once, but twice tonight. Okay? Oh, and did I mention he asked me to come back to California with him? So why don't you do something useful for a change and shut up until it's your turn to play second-fiddle again?"

Cassidy stormed into her tent leaving Zoe with her mouth hanging open like a suffocating guppy.

"Cassidy! Where are you?" Brad hobbled into the camp. He limped to the door of her tent, breezing past Zoe without a glance. "Come out and talk to me."

"There's nothing to talk about. Go have fun with Zoe."

Zoe sauntered over to Brad with her best bedroom eyes firmly locked on his. She stood in front of him, blocking his way to Cassidy's tent and put a hand on either side of his face, forcing him to look her directly in the eyes.

"Why get upset about her when you can have me and be happy?" Zoe practically purred. "Just say the word and I can make you forget all your troubles."

"I know, but we had a misunderstanding. I wanted to clear it up before my date with you, Zoe, if Cassidy would just give me a chance to explain."

He tried to move around Zoe to get to Cassidy's tent, but Zoe quickly diverted his attention again by kissing him. A small groan escaped his mouth.

If I have to watch this joker kiss another girl...

"Let's get out of here." Brad broke away from her kiss, his eyes glazed over with lust. "I'm sure we can find a nicer place to continue this."

"Sounds good."

Brad gave one last glance back to Cassidy's tent before he slipped his arm around Zoe's waist. "Your loss again, Cassidy," he called over his shoulder as he strolled out of the campsite with Zoe, leaving a quiet tension in their wake.

Evan sighed. He turned his camera off and set it on the picnic table. His shoulders ached. Even with the weight of the camera gone, he still felt weighed down. He had to talk to Cassidy now while everyone else was away from camp. It might be the only chance they got to try to sort this out.

Cassidy stepped out of her tent. "Are they gone?"

"Yeah, lover boy has gone off on his date."

"Don't call him that."

Cassidy sat down opposite Evan at the picnic table and threw her mic pack to the side before putting her hand on his. He folded his arms across his chest. "What the hell happened back there, Cassidy? How could you do that to me?"

"Evan, you can't be serious. You know I didn't want to kiss him."

"I'm not so sure anymore. You didn't even try to push him away. Hell, you were thanking him afterward for saying a few nice things about you. What the hell?"

"I did push him away, or did you forget I put my knee in his very sensitive place?"

"No, I saw that, and I'm glad you did. I was on my way to save you, despite your earlier actions."

"Again, Evan? We're really going to do this again? Jealousy is really ugly on you."

"Brad is really ugly on you."

"You're so frustrating," Cassidy yelled, getting up from the table and pacing around the fire. "I'm doing exactly what I'm supposed to do. I'm playing along with the show. I don't know what you expect from me."

"Really? 'Cause I was pretty sure we agreed you'd do everything you could not to kiss that punk and the first chance you get, you're swapping spit together. Just tell me the truth. Do you still have feelings for him?"

"Evan, how many times do I have to tell you it's not like that? I had to kiss him or it would blow our cover."

"You didn't answer my question. Do you still have feelings for him?" His pulse pounded in his ears.

Cassidy wiped a tear trickling down her cheek. "I don't know, okay?"

Evan didn't think his blood pressure could get any higher. "You shouldn't still *maybe* have feelings for him if you're getting into bed with me."

Cassidy looked at him with tears streaming down her cheeks, but he didn't care. The hurt, the betrayal in his heart because of her made those tears almost invisible.

She sniffled and wiped her nose with a corner of her sleeve. "I don't think so, but I can't help it if I have some unresolved issues about our breakup. I promise you I didn't want to kiss him again."

"Well, you didn't have to like it so much."

"I didn't like it. I would think a smart guy like you could see through what I was doing and not be so petty and jealous."

Evan fumed. He could feel his anger and frustration pushing past levels he wasn't accustomed to dealing with. He'd never been so messed up emotionally and he had no idea what the hell he was supposed to do about it. How had he ever believed a girl would be worth this effort, this annoyance—this pain?

"I thought a smart girl like you would've been able to see a better way out of a situation other than kissing a guy you *think* you don't like. That leaves me with one thought. You wanted to kiss him. You wanted a chance to feel those old feelings for him again. You wanted another chance to test the water with him before you jump in and leave me on the shore at the big finale."

Cassidy's face fell. "We had a plan and I tried my best to follow through with it so we wouldn't get caught. You have to believe I didn't want to kiss him. Brad is my past, regardless of what old feelings there may or may not still be between us." She took a step toward him and he took a step back. "You are my future. Okay? Please, believe me. I did that for us."

Tears ran down her cheeks as she stared at him with pleading eyes, but all he could see was her lips on Brad's.

"Thanks for taking that bullet for us, Cassidy. That makes me feel so much better about you kissing another man—to help me out."

Images of Cassidy and Brad swirled through his thoughts. He could still hear the smacking of their lips as their mouths parted, letting their tongues explore what they'd been missing all this time. He shook his head trying to force the moments from his memory—trying to force the ache from his chest.

"I want to believe you, but after what I witnessed tonight, I can't. I can't sit by and watch this anymore. After tonight, our working commitment to each other is fulfilled. I'm going to say you turned in early after your exciting date so I'm done filming. I'm going to bed. Alone."

Like I will the rest of my life. He picked up his camera and headed toward the tent designated for the film crew and equipment.

"Evan, stop. You knew Brad was my ex and there would always be more between us then there was with the other contestants. You knew I had to finish this show without breaking contracts, so don't get all high and mighty on me now. You're just as much to blame for this mess as I am."

Evan stopped walking and turned around to face Cassidy. Pain and betrayal pounding in his chest. "How would you feel if I'd given in to one of Zoe's advances? I've certainly had plenty of opportunities."

Anger and jealousy flashed across Cassidy's face but she

remained silent. There was nothing she could say and he knew it.

"This—it's different. You didn't sign a contract saying you'd be on a show to date her."

"I didn't know a contract was so important to you." Evan shook his head feeling defeated. This wasn't what he'd signed up for. This wasn't what either of them had signed up for. "I know you didn't come here expecting to fall in love with your ex-boyfriend again—or to have some fling with me." Evan sighed, feeling the pain of his next words before he even said them. "But I can't share you, Cassidy."

Fire sparked in Cassidy's eyes before she spoke again, "Susan was right to warn me about you, wasn't she? I was just another checkmark on your production to-do list. And using my obligation to the show against me is just your way of conveniently ending things."

His jaw clenched at the mention of Susan's name. How dare she meddle in his life? Again. "Susan should have kept her mouth shut for once. She doesn't know anything about me or my history with other girls."

"Really? Because she certainly seemed to know a lot about you."

Regardless of what Susan had said, Cassidy made her own choices—including the choice to kiss Brad tonight. "You were nothing like the others. They were silly little flings. You were..." Evan shrugged. "It doesn't matter anymore. You don't even know who you want, and I'm not about to wait around while you figure it out."

"Don't do this, Evan. I only have feelings for you—just you. Brad broke my heart a long time ago. Don't you go breaking it too, Evan Burke!"

Evan wanted more than anything to wrap his arms around her and tell her everything would be okay. But it wasn't okay. Not when all he could see was Brad and her together.

Everything he'd always feared about falling in love had come true. He'd lost the love of his life—it just happened sooner than he feared it would. Lesson learned.

"I'll see you at the finale, Cassidy."

Chapter Twenty-Three

Cassidy gazed into the full-length mirror. A deadpan expression was the best she could summon, what with the gapping void where her heart used to be. It was either that or crying and she desperately wanted to make it through the finale without tears.

After the fight, she'd spent the night alone in her tent, trying not to cry loud enough to draw attention to herself. The last thing she'd wanted was to explain the reason for the mascara streaks running down her cheeks.

She wasn't sure if Evan heard her crying that night or not. If he had, he hadn't cared enough to comfort her. But then why would he? He was the reason she'd been crying in the first place. He was the one who didn't want to be with her anymore. He left her—just like Brad had.

Susan had been right. Evan left her as soon as his production commitment was over. She was an idiot for not seeing it coming sooner. The kiss with Brad was probably the perfect excuse to leave her. She'd fallen right into his trap.

Cassidy had only seen Evan for a few hours the following day while they'd packed the tents and hiked back to where they'd started. He hadn't said a word to her. He hadn't winked, cocked an eyebrow in her direction, or even clenched his jaw. If there was ever a real-life description of a stone cold expression, it could be found by looking at Evan.

When he'd shut off his camera for the last time back at the production trailers, he turned and walked away without a goodbye. He may as well have stuck a knife in her chest and cut out her broken heart. She'd managed to hold back her tears until she'd been dropped off at the isolation hotel to wait overnight for the finale. Then she'd spent the night hiding in bed with a box of tissues and chocolate chip cookies from room service.

So far today, she'd managed to keep it together, but she wasn't sure what would happen when she finally saw Evan again. As far as she knew, he was still scheduled to film the finale. If he was out in the studio, there was a distinct possibility she'd make a huge spectacle of herself by becoming a sobbing mess on the interview couch.

Even if they weren't together anymore, she still needed to make it through the finale with their relationship, or lack of relationship, hidden. She didn't want to risk getting on Chip's bad side and end up meeting the show's lawyers.

Cassidy straightened her dark blue dress against her body and fought back tears. Squaring her shoulders and raising her chin, she tried to appear more put together than she felt. Instead, she ended up looking like a constipated drill sergeant.

She already knew Brad would choose Zoe—the sounds of kissing coming from their shared tent was all the evidence she needed. How could he possibly choose her after everything they'd been through? After she kneed him in the groin? That wasn't exactly a turn-on for most men.

She didn't love Brad, anyway.

The pain stabbing her chest with every stilted breath and memory of Evan was her irrefutable proof.

If she could get through this last ceremony, she'd be free. Free to go back to New York and put this whole messy affair behind her. She could get back into her work, spend time with Keira and her friends, and somehow find a way to forget Evan and the life she'd never have with him. Maybe at some point, her heart would stop hurting. Maybe someday she'd figure out why every man she loved ended up leaving her.

"Are you done staring at yourself yet?" Zoe said, trying to see into the full-length mirror. "I don't think that look's going to get any better."

Cassidy stepped aside and let Zoe primp in the mirror by herself.

"Why're you so quiet today? Have you finally realized there's no way anyone, especially a great guy like Brad, would ever choose you?"

"I don't have the energy for this today, Zoe. It's stressful enough going on live TV without getting flak from you. Aren't you nervous?"

"Nope. I have an awesome guy who's going to tell me he wants to be with me. Now, if I were you, I'd worry about acting like a fool in front of America. Thank God I'm not you."

"Thanks. That really helped."

Cassidy stood in front of the smaller mirror hanging over the vanity and put a few finishing touches on her makeup. Zoe was right. She was going to make a fool of herself today when Brad rejected her, but it was still better than being chosen by him. That wasn't a curse she'd wish on anyone. Well, except Zoe. Those two were made for each other.

Zoe paused while reapplying her lip-gloss. "Feeling all alone without your cameraman following you around?"

Cassidy eyes narrowed. It was as if Zoe knew that was the one comment that would hurt Cassidy the most. "What's with you?" Cassidy waved the mascara wand at her like a weapon, her chest heaving as she tried to hide the hitch in her breath.

"I guess some of us are better suited for life in the spotlight."

"Why did you come on another reality show anyway? Did you lose the first one so badly you needed a chance to redeem yourself? Or are you so insecure you have to come on television to feel superior?"

Zoe stiffened as she glared at Cassidy through the mirror. Her chin quivered once before going rigid again. "Not all of us are lucky enough to have had a Brad in real life."

What? No way did bombshell Zoe have trouble dating.

Cassidy laughed. "Nice try, but I'm not falling for your act. That's a good one, though. I'm sure America will eat that up."

Cassidy shook her head. She was too tired for this.

Zoe got a very strange look in her eyes. One Cassidy hadn't seen before. It made her uneasy. "Yep, you figured me out. I'm all a big act." Zoe grinned but something about it didn't look as convincing as it should.

If only Cassidy wasn't so emotionally exhausted already, maybe she'd have the desire to push Zoe's buttons and find out what she was getting at. If only she cared enough to bother.

"Whatever." Cassidy flopped onto the couch. "If you want to live your life thinking you're better than everyone else, that's fine. After today, leave me out of it."

Zoe put her hand to her heart and stuck out her bottom lip. "Oh, that makes my heart hurt. What ever will I do if Cassidy doesn't like me anymore?"

"Oh, come on now, Zoe. You know I never liked you to begin with."

"It's time to come to the stage," Chip said, sauntering into the room. "Save the drama for the cameras."

Chip guided them through the confusing backstage hallways until they were stage side, but still out of sight. The din of the live studio audience became white noise to Cassidy. The stage itself was flooded with bright overhead lights and all around the perimeter, cameramen faced toward the cluster of couches and chairs cluttering center stage.

Cassidy's chest tightened. She tried to see the faces behind the cameras, but the lights were too bright to see past. Everything beyond them was cast in shadows.

Are you one of those shadows, Evan?

"This way," Chip said, leading them on stage. A cheer rang up from the audience as they stepped into the light.

Cassidy heard people chanting her name as well as Zoe's. It's a good thing the final choice wasn't up to America or, by the sounds of the cheers, it would be a deadlock tie.

"Smile to your fans. They've been waiting hours to finally see you."

Cassidy waved, feeling self-conscious that someone would actually wait hours to see her. She settled herself on the couch beside Zoe and faced out to the audience.

Behind her, the other contestants sat in chairs. From the

middle of the row came a wave and a smiling face Cassidy had missed more than she realized. Waving back at Paige, she wished she could give her a big hug.

Spencer walked across the stage, taking a moment in the center to smile and wave at the audience. He positively glowed, basking in the warmth of the lights and the cheers of the audience. Finally, after many over-appreciative bows and waves, he took his place on the empty couch set off to Cassidy's right side.

"Are you ready to start?" He spoke softly so only they could hear him.

Cassidy nodded. She was more than ready to get this over with.

Spencer waved his hand and the room grew quiet.

Is he a magician, too? How the hell did he get all those people to shut up?

Beside the camera directly in front of the stage, Chip held up an open hand, palm side toward Spencer. He pulsed his hand, each time counting down one finger until he got to one. At that, he pointed at Spencer, who started speaking on cue as if controlled by some external source.

Man, this guy is good. Is he the world's largest ventriloquist dummy?

"Welcome to the final ceremony of *The One*." He waited for the applause to settle before speaking again. "We're here today to find out who will finally be chosen as The One. I know we're anxiously awaiting his decision, but before we get to that, we'd like to spend a little time chatting with some of the ladies Brad *didn't* choose."

Spencer turned his body slightly so he faced more toward the back of the room to where the row of other contestants sat. They all seemed eager to have their chance to speak.

"Let's start with you Savanna and Erica. You were both here almost to the end. How did it feel to make it so far and then not get into the final two?"

Erica laughed. "Well, it didn't feel good. It was hard making it almost all the way to the end just to get voted out at the last minute. I would happily have stayed and done any challenge they'd asked of me, if it meant I could've had another chance with Brad."

A chorus of sympathetic sighs spread through the audience.

"So it's safe to assume you're heartbroken?" A softness filled Spencer's voice.

Erica blushed. "Well, I was at first. But then I went home and I had a chance to think, and I realized we weren't meant to be. So I'm not heartbroken anymore. In fact, I'm ready to date if anyone out there is interested."

"That's great. We're all glad to hear that." Spencer turned to Savanna. "And what about you? How are you doing since leaving the show?"

Savanna flipped her long hair over her shoulder. "Oh, me? I'm fine, sugar. I have plenty of gentlemen wanting to be my friend lately, so obviously Brad wasn't the only one for me." She giggled and gave a demure wave to the nearest camera.

"Do you miss being in the house with all the other women?"

Savanna glanced around at the women sitting on the stage. "Well, now I wouldn't say I missed them. Y'all are great girls, but I like the quiet of my house."

"We had a pretty big scare when Lauren was forced to leave the show for medical reasons," Spencer said. "Lauren is here with us today and looking as beautiful as ever. How are you feeling?"

Lauren smiled. "I'm happy to report that all testing came back fine. I think I wasn't cut out for the stress and drama involved in a show like this."

"We're so happy to hear you're okay. Now, about the drama, we did see our fair share of that in the house. What did you think about the drama between the girls, Paige?"

Paige startled at her name and faltered for a moment before answering. "I think most of the drama was pretty trivial. It's hard to share a space with this many girls even when it's a huge mansion. And a little extra drama happened between a couple of girls."

"Which girls were those?"

Paige faced flushed a deep pink. "The two finalists, Cassidy and Zoe."

Spencer nodded his head for a moment before turning to face the two in question. "What do you think of that? Were you two the reason for the drama in the house?"

"Let's just say not everything was sunshine and roses between myself and Zoe," Cassidy said.

Zoe rolled her eyes. "It would be impossible for anyone to live with a girl like Cassidy."

"Sounds interesting. Care to elaborate a little for us?"

Zoe plastered on her most paparazzi-worthy smile. "I'd be happy to. You see, some people are meant to be leaders," she pointed at herself, "and some are meant to be led." She pointed at Cassidy. "And the two are not meant to share the same space."

Oh, for the love of all things chocolate.

Cassidy turned to Spencer. "What Zoe's trying to say is that she's a giant bitch—can I say that on live TV? She's a spoiled, self-indulgent brat who's never figured out she isn't nearly as awesome as she thinks she is."

Zoe's face turned a few shades of red before she finally opened her mouth to respond, but Spencer spoke first. "Let's hope the censor was paying attention. I didn't realize there was this much animosity between you. Anything you'd like to say?" He turned to Zoe.

"Cassidy tends to have these little outbursts with me. I'm not sure why. I think it's because she feels intimidated by my successes, here and in real life."

"Yep, that's it, I'm intimidated by the wannabe singer who had to come on a reality show—again—so she could feel good about herself. You figured me out."

Careful now, C. Calm down. This isn't you.

She sighed. "You know. I think Zoe's probably a great person in real life. It's just, being in the same house with a bunch of girls for a few weeks is enough to drive even the nicest people to their limits."

"All right, before this gets messy, maybe we should bring out our main man and get his thoughts on everything. Let's hear it for Brad Murphy."

Spencer stood from the couch and greeted Brad with a warm handshake while the fans in the audience cheered like they were at the Super Bowl. Brad almost seemed embarrassed by the adoration of the audience as he took his seat beside Spencer.

Zoe straightened her back and waved when Brad smiled hello to them. Cassidy couldn't bring herself to do more than nod.

"So, Brad, you've been listening backstage. What's your take on the tension between your two final ladies?"

Brad laughed. "I think it's pretty obvious, don't you? It's hard for these girls to get along because they're both after the same guy. If you and I were fighting for the same girl, Spencer, I wouldn't like you very much either."

"Good point. Do you think your previous relationship with Cassidy has anything to do with it as well?"

"The fact Cassidy and I dated a few months ago definitely added some tension between the girls. It added tension between us, too. Neither Cassidy nor I expected to see each other here and we really had to deal with everything in our past while also taping the show. It certainly added some excitement."

"What was this process like for you?"

"Wow. Dude, it was totally awesome. I'm mean, what's not to like about ten girls all wanting to get with you? It's every man's dream."

Spencer turned on his serious face. "Now, I know it wasn't all fun and games. You also had some really tough decisions to make each week. Are there any girls you wish were sitting here instead of your finalists?"

"Dude. You ask such loaded questions. I'd have to say no. I'm happy with Cassidy and Zoe being the final two girls. But that's not to say there weren't other girls I was sad to see leave. It was challenging to get to know each of the girls in such a short amount of time. I definitely wish I could have spent more time getting to know each one of them, but I'm confident that in the end, I still would have ended up with the same finalists."

"Let's take a moment to recap some of our favorite moments between you, Cassidy, and Zoe."

An enormous screen hanging on the wall blinked to life. Images of Cassidy flashed across the screen while a bad instrumental version of Bryan Adams's "(Everything I Do) I Do It For You" played over the speakers.

Oh fun, there I am falling off my horse. Oh, and getting stepped on by that stupid horse. Falling into the river, also a highlight. Thank you production people for portraying me so gracefully. I'm the blooper reel.

After an agonizing few minutes, the screen grew dark and the last image of Zoe and Brad snuggling on a picnic blanket faded away. The music was replaced by another chorus of cheers from the audience.

"It must be fun to see those moments again, huh?" Spencer spoke to no one specifically. "I know the audience and the ladies across from me are growing tired of the suspense. So, let's not keep them waiting anymore. Brad, I hope you're ready, because it's time to tell us who you've picked to be The One."

Brad sat forward on the edge of the couch. Cassidy could make out tiny beads of sweat coming to the surface of his forehead.

Here we go—the big rejection.

"Zoe," Brad started. "I think you're an awesome girl. You're always up for having a good time and you live life by taking control and getting what you want. I love those things about you. You don't seem afraid of anything and you're willing to take big risks to get big rewards. And you're incredibly hot. Any guy would be lucky to have you as his girl."

Zoe beamed. Cassidy thought Zoe might jump across to the other couch and do dirty things to Brad right now if it wasn't for the live studio audience keeping her libido in check.

"Cassidy, you have an amazing personality."

Great, I'm getting the "it's not you it's me" speech from him again, and on live TV this time.

"You're more reserved and laid back than Zoe. You're willing to try some new things, but you still have your little hang-ups holding you back. You're sarcastic, opinionated, and passionate. You constantly challenge me. I haven't always made the best choices when it comes to you and me, but I'm trying to learn from my mistakes. You're definitely not the easy choice—but you're my choice. Cassidy, you're The One."

Chapter Twenty-Four

Wait, what?

"You've always been the one for me and I was stupid to let you go. I can't wait to see where this takes us." Brad stared at her with dream-filled eyes.

Cassidy's heart galloped in her chest making her feel faint. This wasn't supposed to happen. This wasn't the choice he was supposed to make. Guys don't date the girl who knees them in the groin, who doesn't share their interests, and who constantly gives them a hard time.

Beside her on the couch, Zoe shook. Cassidy wasn't sure if it was from anger or sadness, but her heart suddenly went out to Zoe who obviously had feelings for Brad. Before Cassidy had the chance to worry about Zoe's reaction, Brad hauled Cassidy to her feet and wrapped his arms around her in a tight hug.

Spencer clapped. "Cassidy, tell us what you're feeling?"

"I'm, um, shocked. I didn't think he was going to choose me." Cassidy could hardly manage to string words together into a proper sentence.

"Brad, why don't you make it official with a kiss? I'm sure everyone is dying to see your happy ending."

Brad stared deeply into her eyes. He looked so happy. How could he not tell she didn't feel the same?

Please don't. What if Evan's filming this? I can't.

Brad put his hand under her chin and forced her to look at him. His lips edged closer and closer to hers.

"Wait!" a voice called from off stage.

Brad dropped his hand and turned to see who'd called out. Cassidy stepped to his side so she could see who she could thank for saving her from yet another kiss she didn't want.

Chip stood facing them. By the expression on his face, it was clear something major was about to happen, but Cassidy didn't have the faintest idea what. "Brad, I'm afraid there's something you need to see that may make you reconsider your future with Cassidy." The audience fell silent. Chip eyed Cassidy. "Is there anything you'd like to tell us? Anything you need to get off your chest?"

Um, this is probably bad, right? But it couldn't be.

"No, I don't think so." Her voice was a whisper in the huge room.

Chip motioned for them to turn their attention to the big screen again. "Roll the tape!"

Cassidy's heart stopped beating as images came to life on the screen. This could possibly be the second worst moment of her life, the first being when Evan walked away from her at the campsite. Both made her feel like she was under water again, fighting to find the surface before the darkness encompassed her.

Video clips of Cassidy and Evan's romance played for the whole world to see. Cassidy sank back onto the couch staring at the screen in horror as tears filled her eyes and streamed down her cheeks like black rivers of ink.

There were quick clips of smiles, winks, and nods that happened between them while Evan filmed. Looks they'd thought no one else had seen, but clearly someone had. These clips were from another camera that had captured both of their faces.

Other clips were of Cassidy, looking at the camera with an expression only meant for Evan's eyes. The messages she sent him in those moments filled with flirtation.

Cassidy struggled to swallow as more tears fell down her cheeks and dotted the front of her dress like fallen rain. She wiped them away with the back of her hand, not daring to take her eyes off the screen for even a second.

Evan.

Cassidy gasped as a video from inside Evan's room played.

She'd never thought there'd be cameras in his room like there was in hers. He was staff. Didn't he get privacy at least?

Her breath started coming in ragged gulps as she watched their first time together being played for everyone. Images of Evan kissing her and tossing her gently on the bed sent her back into that moment. She could feel the heat from every touch of his hands lingering on her body. She licked her lips at the memory of his mouth on hers.

Thankfully, the video had been edited for primetime television and not Cinemax. She'd have to thank Chip later for blurring out the bits of her body peeking out from under the blankets—the humiliation could have been so much worse.

Her heart ached watching their private moments again. She still reeled from his rejection and now she had to relive the pain over again in the most public forum she could fathom. Watching the moment she'd given her heart to Evan made the pain a thousand times worse. Knowing he'd turned around and broken her heart weeks later, felt like a gunshot to her chest.

Clip after clip played. How long had someone known about them? She couldn't believe they were able to create such an extensive video from numerous sources in such a short amount of time.

Cassidy put her head in her hands and closed her eyes. It was too painful. She couldn't bear to watch anymore.

But now she didn't need to see it. Someone had found audio clips. *Where did they even get these clips?* She'd purposefully left her mic pack in her bedroom before confronting Evan that night.

And then she realized—if they had cameras in his room, they also had microphones attached to them, too, just like the cameras in her room. *Damn it.* She'd been so careless in the moment. Why hadn't she thought to check for cameras?

"You're jealous of my *ex*-boyfriend. You're jealous of that stupid kiss with him!" She heard herself say the words.

"I was jealous getting... No. I *am* jealous, because ever since I kissed you, I haven't been able to think of anything else." Evan's voice echoed through the studio.

Gasps from the audience chorused around the room. Murmurs and mumblings of disappointment and outrage grew louder as the audio continued, eventually drowning out the sound of Evan's voice. The voice of the man she knew in her heart that she loved, but would never have. The man who'd taken her heart and left an empty shell.

A darkness closed in on Cassidy—anger built deep inside at the humiliation of her torrid affair with Evan shown to the world. She was angry with Evan, too—angry he'd left her, angry that in the end he'd been no better than Brad. He'd treated her like any other fling.

"Stop." She yelled as loud as she could manage.

The sounds of kissing continued. She peeked up from her hands to see a glimpse of her and Evan together in her bathroom. One of the overhead bedroom cameras in her room had been able to catch the smallest hints of movement as the audio picked up their heavy breathing.

My mic pack. I'd already turned it on. Shit.

They hadn't planned that kiss, since it had been their first. It had been completely spontaneous, passionate, and unexpected. She'd never thought to take off her mic pack. Of course there would be audio.

Their first kiss, shared with everyone. No one should get to witness these moments she'd lost forever. Anger, hurt, and embarrassment raged in her chest.

She stood from the couch. "Stop! Enough already. We get it, Chip. Everyone here gets it, okay?" She flailed her arm toward the audience. "I'm pretty sure the audience has the idea, so you can cut the video anytime."

Chip turned his back to the screen and waved a hand. The screen flickered once then went black. His glare pierced through her, but she stood her ground. He'd humiliated her enough and she wasn't going to back down now without a fight. She still had her dignity, or what was left of it.

"So now you have something to say. Now that everyone knows what you've done, you're ready to talk."

"Stop, Chip. There's nothing more to talk about."

"What the hell's going on with you and that camera guy?" Brad demanded.

"Nothing." Her voice quivered, betraying her.

"It certainly looked like more than nothing, so don't give me that bullshit. You owe me an explanation."

"There's nothing going on with me and Evan. There was something between us for a while but there isn't anymore. We're done." She managed to choke out a few final words as more tears fell. "There is no more *us*, so there's nothing left to say."

She wiped the tears away, angry with herself for letting everyone see how upset she was over losing Evan. She wanted to be strong right now, but her emotions crashed through her defensive walls. How would she ever get back into her regular life after this? What kind of life would ever feel normal without Evan?

"How could you do this? You're disgusting," Brad seethed.

"You're no prize either, Brad," Cassidy snapped. "One minute you told me you loved me, then the next you left me on the sidewalk like yesterday's paper."

"Oh, I get it now. This was all a big ploy to get back at me for dumping you."

"It's not like that. This didn't have anything to do with you. I don't know what happened. Evan and I ... we didn't mean to hurt anyone."

Cassidy glanced around for any sign of understanding. She didn't expect anyone to say what they had done was okay, but she hoped maybe someone would realize none of this had been planned to hurt people. Furrowed brows and shaking heads stared back at her.

"I don't even know how you found out about us." Cassidy spoke more to herself than anyone else. "We were so careful while we filmed the show."

"I guess you didn't try hard enough, huh?" Zoe placed a couple of white shirt buttons in Cassidy's hand. "Souvenirs of your indiscretion. I gave them to Susan for safekeeping."

Realization cut through the fog of her emotions. The night she'd spent with Evan at the chateau, she'd ripped his shirt and hadn't thought to pick up the buttons. Zoe had known since the chateau. Zoe had told Susan and *Susan* had gone to Chip.

Susan really had tried to sabotage her the whole time, hadn't she? If she could find her right now, Cassidy would tell her where to stick her fake warnings and concern. But since Susan wasn't around, Zoe would have to do.

"You bitch. You did this to me?" Cassidy felt on the verge of losing it. "I can't believe you would stoop this low to try to ensure you were the one who ended up with Brad."

"I don't think I was the one stooping, do you?"

"Don't you insinuate for one second that Evan is beneath you. He's a good man. He doesn't deserve to be degraded by a stuck-up diva like you."

Cassidy glared at Zoe. "You can have Brad. He's all yours. I'm still in shock he even picked me after everything that's happened between us. Maybe he drank too much ocean water surfing or something, since I can't find a logical reason for him to pick me. But guess what, Zoe? You'll always be his second choice."

Zoe smirked with a look of pure arrogance. "And what are you, Cassidy? You're nothing. You have nothing. You've lost everything because you're a slut. God, you're pathetic."

"Oh my God. I can't believe I felt bad for you a few minutes ago."

"Zoe's right. Kissing me while sleeping with some sleazy cameraman on the side. You should be ashamed of yourself," Brad added.

"Enough. Don't say another word." Evan stepped out from behind a camera. "You've both said too much already. Cassidy's been through enough."

Cassidy gasped. *Evan, oh God, Evan. You heard all of that. You came back.*

"Get out of here before I make you sorry for what you've done." Brad puffed up his chest.

"Back off, surfer boy, before I give you something to whine about. I haven't forgotten how you forced yourself on Cassidy. You've had your say, now it's my turn to talk."

Cassidy held her breath as Evan moved to her side and took her hand before turning to address the audience. His hand was warm and soft wrapped around hers. His thumb drew a circle on the back of her hand, reminding her of when they spoke at the door joining their rooms her first night in the house—the night that started everything.

"What Cassidy and I did was wrong, but we meant no disrespect to the show, the contestants, or the viewers watching each week."

"You're a fraud, Cassidy, and you'll pay for betraying everyone," Chip stated. "Your deception misled the viewers to choose you when they should have voted you out. You ruined someone else's chances of being here and ruined Brad's chance at finding the one he's meant to be with. Don't think your actions will go unpunished."

Cheers went up around the room. Cassidy heard some rather rude statements of agreement, making it clear she was indeed the villain.

"Cassidy didn't do anything wrong." Evan held up his hand at the mumble of voices trying to dispute his statement. "Let me speak before you judge us."

Evan glanced at Cassidy, then back to where the other contestants sat in total shock. Each one of them in a state of stunned confusion—mouths hanging open, gaping at the roadside attraction that was her life.

Paige mouthed the question, "You and Evan?" when Cassidy met her gaze.

Cassidy nodded. She had a lot of explaining to do. A wave of relief passed through her as realized she'd finally be able tell Paige about everything. Soon she could talk to Keira again.

"If we deceived anyone because of what we did, it was accidental. We never meant to take someone else's chance at happiness away. The fact is, Brad was the one who chose who to put in the bottom three each week, not us. He felt something for Cassidy he didn't feel for the other women, and that's why she's sitting here as one of the final two today."

Chip shook his head. "But she did trick America into thinking they were voting for someone who actually wanted to be here to find love."

"America watched the show to see two people fall in love. Cassidy did come here hoping to find someone special, perhaps even find the person who might be the one for her. She can't help it if that person turned out to be her cameraman instead of the bachelor."

Cassidy stared into the deep blue eyes she'd seen in her dreams. The same eyes she feared she'd never get to see in real life again. Hope stared back at her.

Oh Evan, I've missed those eyes, these hands, that gorgeous mouth.

"Cassidy came here to find the love of her life, and that's what she's going to leave with." Evan put his hand on the side of her neck and stroked his thumb in familiar circles along her jaw. She melted into the warmth of his touch.

"I came here to do a job, get a paycheck, and leave. Instead, I found the half of my heart I never knew I was missing. Since the moment I looked into these green eyes of yours, I've known I could get lost in them for eternity."

Evan's gaze penetrated her with such intensity that she knew she'd never love anyone but him. He'd stolen her heart the minute his lips claimed hers with their first kiss.

"Cassy, I love you, and I have since the moment I saw you standing by the piano that first day at the house. These last few days without you in my life have been miserable." Evan paused, looking into her eyes. "I just have one question. Do you still have feelings for him?"

She shook her head without hesitation. "No. I only have feelings for one man and it's not Brad."

Evan smiled. "I've been trying to avoid falling in love because I thought I might end up hurt if something ever happened to you, but I never realized I was hurting myself more by trying to stay away from you. Loving you is worth the risk of whatever the future brings—without you, I have no future to worry about."

Cassidy tried to remain calm. More than anything she wanted to wrap her arms around his neck and never let go, but she couldn't. Not yet.

"I have one question for you too, Evan."

"Anything."

Cassidy fought to hold her voice steady. "Will you ever leave me again like you did that night in the campsite? Turn on me? Turn from me?" Her body trembled as she waited for his answer.

He sighed, his forehead furrowing. "If I could take back one moment, it would be walking away from you. I'll never hurt you again, no matter how jealous I am. I promise."

"Evan, I love you." Cassidy's voice broke over the tears she couldn't stop from falling—tears of happiness. "I'm so sorry for everything. You were right, I should have done things differently, and then maybe we wouldn't be in this mess to begin with. I've missed you so much. I can't imagine a future without you in it."

Cassidy stared at him, not knowing what else to say. *He loves me.*

"Kiss her," a voice shouted from the audience. More voices joined in, calling for them to kiss and make up.

That was all the encouragement Cassidy needed.

She grabbed Evan by the front of his shirt and pulled herself to him, kissing him for the first time with her whole heart, without reservations or guilt or confusion.

As their lips met, she knew Evan was right about everything. She had come hoping for love, and she'd found it in the most unlikely place. Being in love with Evan was more wonderful than she could ever have imagined.

This is where her heart belonged—alongside his, forever.

Evan pulled back and placed his hand over hers on his chest. She could feel his heart beating beneath his shirt, pounding in time with hers. "Careful with those buttons. I didn't think to bring an extra shirt with me today."

She laughed. "Don't start with me, Evan Burke. I've learned my lesson about leaving evidence behind."

"You know, I meant what I said before, about not letting you go once I got you alone."

"And I meant it when I said I was going to hold you to that statement. Now, shut up and kiss me."

Cassidy sank into Evan's arms and kissed him like there wasn't a national viewing audience watching. She was sure they'd be the talk of every water cooler in the country the next morning, so why not give people something juicy to talk about?

This might not have been the ending everyone expected, but sometimes the best endings are the ones you don't see coming.

Epilogue

Paige ran her hand over the glossy cover of the tabloid magazine she'd picked up at the grocery store earlier. She couldn't resist. Seeing Cassidy and Evan's faces on the cover was still too surreal. And seeing how their love affair had captured the hearts of people everywhere was inspiring.

And heartbreaking.

Of course Paige was happy for them. Cassidy deserved to have a man in her life like Evan, especially after everything that happened with Brad and the show. But didn't Paige deserve a man in her life, too?

She tossed the magazine onto the coffee table beside one of the many vases of flowers currently filling every flat surface in her living room and kitchen. It seemed every man in a fifty-mile radius had taken it upon himself to help her get over her national television rejection. And all of them had sent bouquets, each with a note attached proclaiming to be the one guy who could make all her dreams come true.

If only it were that easy.

Her friends were no better. They kept reading the cards and picking out which guys they thought she should go out with. She'd played along for the first few weeks, but the novelty had worn off quickly. Now random blind dates didn't sound so fun. Although, sitting at home—alone—for another Friday night didn't sound too great, either.

Paige peeled herself off the couch at the sound of her cell phone ringing from inside her purse where she'd left it on the kitchen counter. Probably her mother calling to say hello since she knew Paige would be home and not out on some hot date. Because she sucked. And she was just too afraid of being rejected again.

If these guys had seen her on the show, were they really pursuing her because they wanted to get to know the real her? Or did they just want to see what it was about her that hadn't been good enough for Brad?

"Hello?" she said, finally digging her phone out of her bag.

"Paige, sweetheart, how are you?"

"Chip? What's up?" Paige tried but failed to keep the suspicion out of her voice. Sure, Chip had been nothing but nice to her, but she'd seen what he'd done to Cassidy at the finale. Not to mention the lawyers he'd sent after her for breach of contract. If he was calling, it couldn't be good.

"I wanted to touch base with you and see how you're getting along now that you're back to your regular life."

"Things are a little weird, but I'm doing okay."

"Great. I'm glad to hear that." Chip cleared his voice. "So listen. I have a business proposition for you. Turns out that even though you went home in the middle of the show, you stole people's hearts. I've heard you have men coming out of the woodwork for a chance to be with you. So that got me thinking—"

"Thinking about what?" she interrupted. Chip plotting wasn't good. Everyone who had any connection to him knew that.

"About having you on another show, of course."

"I appreciate you thinking of me, but there's no way I can go back on another dating show. I can't handle that kind of public rejection again."

"Well, good news then. It's not a dating show I had in mind, but something much more exciting. It's an adventure show."

"Okay. And you think I'd be good for an adventure show why exactly?" She wasn't the adventuring type. She was more the stay home, relaxing in the backyard where it was safe kind of girl. How could Chip possibly think she'd be good for an adventure show?

Chip chuckled. "I wouldn't, exactly. But Cassidy said she'd

only do it if you were her partner."

"Oh." Now it made sense. *Chip wants Cassidy, not me.*

As if he could read her mind, Chip spoke again. "It's not like that. There were polls going on throughout the show and you always rated very high with viewers."

"Sure, as the person they'd most like to see go home, right?"

"Wrong. As the person they thought should have stayed. As America's favorite sweetheart. Have you really not been to the website or forums?"

"I try to avoid them."

"If you had been to the forums, then you'd already know America loves you almost as much as they love Cassidy and Evan as a couple. So when I was planning this new show and thinking about possible crossover contestants, I instantly thought of you and Cassidy. I know you two would make an awesome team and America would love watching you. Wouldn't you like another chance to show all the guys out there how awesome you are and how stupid Brad is for letting you go?"

Well, when you put it that way. "I guess. What exactly do I have to do?"

"Let's not worry about all those little details now. I need to go back to Cassidy with a solid yes from you and then we'll get things rolling. Sound good?"

Paige flopped back onto the couch. Was she really going to sign on for another show because Cassidy wanted her to? Did she have a good reason not to have an all-expenses-paid trip with her best friend? "Sounds like I don't really know what I'm saying yes to."

"Great! So you're saying yes. I'll get back to you in a few days with more details, proposed filming schedule, and location."

"Chip, wait," Paige said, cutting in before he got off the phone. She couldn't really say yes without knowing all those details up front. That would be ridiculous.

"I'll be in touch soon."

Paige stared at the phone as it flickered off. This wasn't good. She just agreed to some kind of adventurous reality show with Cassidy. She was neither ready to be on TV again nor an adventurer.

This should be interesting.

About the Author

Heather Thurmeier was born and raised in the Canadian prairies, but now she lives in upstate New York with her own personal romance hero (aka her husband) and their two little princesses. When she's not busy taking care of the kids and an adventurous puppy named Indy, Heather's hard at work on her next romance novel. She loves to hear from her readers.

Heart, humor, and a happily ever after.

Website: *http://www.heatherthurmeier.com*
Email: *heatherthurmeier@gmail.com*
Twitter: *https://twitter.com//hthurmeier*
Facebook: *www.facebook.com/HeatherThurmeierAuthor*

In the mood for more Crimson Romance? Check out *Caution: Filling Is Hot* by Tara Mills at *CrimsonRomance.com*.